Also by Hesper Anderson

South Mountain Road:
A Daughter's Journey of Discovery

MacDougal Street Ghosts

Hesper Anderson

Simon & Schuster
New York London Toronto Sydney

SIMON & SCHUSTER
Rockefeller Center
1230 Avenue of the Americas
New York, NY 10020

Book design by Ellen R. Sasahara

Manufactured in the United States of America

1 3 5 7 9 10 8 6 4 2

Library of Congress Cataloging-in-Publication Data
Anderson, Hesper.
MacDougal Street ghosts / Hesper Anderson.
p. cm.
1. Divorced women—Fiction. 2. Divorced mothers—Fiction.
3. Self-realization—Fiction. 4. Greenwich Village (New York, N.Y.)—Fiction.
5. California—Fiction. I. Title.
PS3551.N3647M33 2005
813'.6—dc22 2005044074
ISBN-13: 978-1-4165-8633-3
ISBN-10: 1-4165-8633-4

For my brother Alan

MacDougal Street Ghosts

Chapter One

Moving is hard when you don't want to leave. I had wanted to leave. I'd wanted to leave for at least five years, but I'd forgotten that by mid-March, my chosen moving date, the San Fernando Valley is in bloom. In the backyard of my house on Alta Vista in Studio City the jasmine is sweet, the buds on the camellias are opening, and the gnarled plum tree that shades half the garden is crowded with pink-white blossoms.

In my study, a converted garage that overlooks all this, I'm making boxes and packing stacks of screen and television scripts that I've written over the past twenty years. Some were sold, some not, some filmed, some not. I take a couple of framed writing awards down from the wall and stick them in with the scripts. I place uneven strips of tape across each upended box, turning it over and filling it—taping, turning, filling. I'm tired and sad, part of me wanting to glue myself to these familiar walls, part of me feeling twinges of excitement. I'm going home to the woods. Not the Eastern woods that I grew up in that were dotted with wild dogwood, and trees that never reached the sky, but the woods of Northern California where the pines and redwoods rise above the clouds.

I'm scared too. New places frighten me because I seem to be missing a sense of direction. In 1969 when I moved my children from New York to Los Angeles, I was lost for the first three years. You could find me at freeway exits, crying and huddled in our puttering VW Bug, the one with the back seat missing, completely turned around. I lost a job I needed badly at that time because I couldn't find MGM, which took up about six square blocks of Culver City—hard not to find. I gradually figured out that the hills were south of me, the ocean west, and as a novice writer I learned the routes to the various studios. Now I know this valley and these canyons like the back of my hand, and I'm moving to a new valley, new hills, where I'll be lost all over again. The whole idea makes me break out in a sweat, so I put the scripts down, take deep breaths, and tell myself there's nothing to be afraid of anymore. And there isn't. That was then when everything was new.

"There's nothing to be afraid of anymore," I keep repeating as I stretch, and look around the chaos of moving for something else to do, something to take my mind off the old fears. I decide to tackle the storage closet that I've been avoiding. Lots of books, old toy baskets—I've told my grown children to go through their stuff or it's going out, but they know I don't mean it—all of Danny's Doctor Dolittle and Oz books that he's saving for the children he doesn't have yet. A box of old crayon drawings, crude cartoons and pictures for my wall that say "I love you, Mom" and "Mom, the best is yet to come," encouragement from scared kids.

But we're okay now. We're better than okay, and there's nothing to be afraid of anymore. I keep whispering the words, like a prayer that will make it so, as I pull more boxes out of the closet. Some are labeled, some not, and they clearly haven't been touched since I moved into this house twelve years ago. It was the first house that I was able to buy after putting three children through college at the same time, and I savored the sense of ownership even though the children were on their own by then. They enjoyed coming home to it for holidays, but still I'd wished I'd been able to give them a home when they were young. "Oh, cut it out," I say aloud, shutting off the old guilts as they intrude like unwanted friends at the door. "I did great," I say, as I wipe dust balls and a dead spider off an unmarked box. "Didn't I, Sandy?" At the sound of his name Sandy thumps his tail on the tile floor and looks up at me with warm hazel eyes. He's a mix, God knows what-all in there, but he's got a retriever's loving gaze, which I find comforting at moments like this.

I open the box and see about ten video cassettes, all labeled "Danny's Super 8's." Years ago, I'd transferred all of Danny's old movies to video, and given them to him for Christmas. He must have stored them here, along with his old books and stuffed animals, and we'd forgotten all about them. I take them out of the box and dust them off, part of me tempted to look at them right away, part of me thinking that if I'm trying to leave old fears and guilts behind, that would be a stupid thing to do.

"Come on, Sand, let's go," I say as I dump the tapes back in the box and head for the house and the VCR. We leave the study, walk through the yard, still smelling of jasmine, plum and lemon blossoms, and enter the French doors that lead into the living room. It's quiet, filled with golden afternoon sunlight, and once again I have no idea why I'm leaving. The sunlight in the East was never like this, and I don't know what it will be like in Northern California. But the house is already sold, the new house waiting; it's too late to change my mind. Besides, I'm finally retiring from the business of writing for hire, and thinking again about the novel I'd imagined writing twenty-five years ago. A small house in the northern woods seems like the perfect place to do it.

I stick a tape into the VCR. None of the tapes are labeled—no dates, no places—just pieces of our lives jumbled together out of order. I sit in the rocking chair, close to the screen, and lean forward, staring at a beach that's bleached by time. Where is this? When? Irwin runs into the frame—tanned, young, horn-rimmed sunglasses. He dives for a beach ball, catches it, and throws it back. The camera jerks to Jake, about seven, so adorable that I want to reach out and bring him back to me, just as he was. He catches the ball, laughing, and tosses it to Emma, who's brown, blond and giggly, and grabs it with both small arms. It's Amagansett, the summer of '67 I realize—the summer before '68 when everything erupted in the outside world, and in our lives.

The camera shifts to me, applauding at the water's edge, also looking young and tanned, even happy, though I don't remember much happiness that summer. Then there's a shot of Danny on a raft, trying to catch a wave, and then riding it in, grinning up from the foam. Then Irwin is picking up Emma, carrying her, and they both wave, blinking into the sun.

The screen turns to snow at that moment, crossed by

jumpy, vertical lines, and then a small stucco house appears. There's a ragged lawn in front, a path leading to a narrow, cement porch, and darkened windows. Oh, my God, this is the Whitsett house in Van Nuys. It's '70 or early '71, which was, without question, the worst year of my life. It was probably the worst year of the kids' lives too, but no one would think so as their images bounce onto the screen. First there are trick shots of Jake, making his shoes disappear, then a set-up scene of Emma and Jake arguing, hands on their hips, both so young and sweet that I smile and wipe away sudden tears. Then Danny and a friend—Jake must have been shooting this—are playing good-guy/bad-guy, chasing each other across the low roof. Now I appear, getting out of the VW Bug in the driveway, grinning, doing a little dance step up the path to the house. "I remember," I whisper. "It was the day I paid off that sonofabitch Meekel." The screen again turns to snow, and I stop the tape and close my eyes, rocking quietly in the chair, seeing it all.

Night after night I lay awake, planning the murder of the IRS man. The little bastard must have confiscated hundreds, thousands of bank accounts. He had taken mine that had two hundred dollars in it, and he'd taken my son Jake's that had seventeen dollars and fifty cents. If I stalked the IRS man carefully why would anyone suspect me? I knew what he looked like—hairline mustache, fishy eyes. I knew his last name, Meekel, and I knew where his office was on Hollywood Boulevard. All I had to do was follow him home on a moonless night, shoot him before he got to his front door, and disappear. Getting ahold of a gun would be a problem, but it was possible.

The Cramers, friends of my parents from long ago, lived in Palm Springs, and I drove my children there every three months or so, our VW Bug with the back seat missing, struggling up the long, desert hills for a needed weekend. I knew that Ben Cramer kept a gun in his study, beneath some papers in the top drawer of his filing cabinet. It wouldn't be hard to steal it; he probably wouldn't miss it for a while, but that's where I got stuck, lying awake in the little house on Whitsett. I couldn't figure out how to get rid of the gun.

I'd go through the whole plan at three in the morning, only disturbed by an occasional siren screaming down the avenue, and again at dawn, while the children still slept, and the mourning doves began their mournful calls. I'd see Ben's studio, his wall-to-wall files, his penciled illustrations on his drawing table, and I'd find his loaded gun, put it in my straw beach bag, and take it home. I'd follow the IRS man to his house, put a bullet in his head, drive home in the VW Bug, first praying that it wouldn't stall outside his house, and then what do I do with the gun? If I put it back in Ben's file it could be traced to him. If I went to Santa Monica and threw it off the pier it could wash back up on the beach. If I threw it in a trash can it could be found and traced. If I buried it in the backyard our dog might dig it up the way she'd dug up the baby squirrel that my son Daniel had buried in a shoe box.

Danny, twelve at the time and lonely, missing his father, his home, his old school, had poured milk and love into a baby squirrel—maybe too much of both. He tried desperately to save the animal, keeping him warm on tissue paper in a shoe box, feeding him from a bottle, but the squirrel died and Danny buried him in the shoe box beneath the pepper tree with a note between his paws, saying how much he loved him. Months later our young Labrador dug up the tiny, gray bones, and Danny cried again and buried the squirrel again. I cried with him, silently, watching through the window.

Our black Labrador, Blanca, was bigger now and buried and dug up whatever she could find in our dirt-packed backyard. She would surely dig up the gun that I would use to blow Mr. Meekel's brains out. So, in my angry, circular fantasies, I couldn't get rid of the gun. Even if I'd figured it out, I probably wouldn't have killed him. I say probably. I hated him more than I've ever hated anyone. It wasn't the idea of taking his life that bothered me. It was the idea of jail. I had a horror of being locked up, of being trapped, and here I was, lying awake on a rented sofa bed in the den of a small, ugly, rented house, so deeply trapped that I couldn't see the sky.

I knew that I had done it, thrown myself down this hole, been an emotional idiot craving love, or something. I still didn't know what the something was because I hadn't found it. I was down there in the dark, surrounded by my children, who counted on me. I counted on them too. I knew that I shouldn't, but they were the only family I had.

The night dream of killing the IRS man was preferable to the fear of the next day, or the feelings of remorse that made me sweat and twist in the rented sofa bed. Anger was better than fear or pain. It was higher up on the tone scale. The Scientologists had said that. They were a scary bunch, with some strange ideas, but they'd been right about that. Anger was definitely better than fear, remorse or pain.

I relished my night fantasies, prolonged the image of Mr. Meekel's spattered brains, because the first sunlight brought fear. We were hiding our money, the children and I, in a shoe box (another shoe box) in my closet. We had a few five-dollar bills and some singles and that was it, with no idea of how or when there would be any more. I'd bounced a five-dollar check at Ringside Market on the corner of Whitsett and Van Nuys Boulevard. That's how I'd found out that the IRS had confiscated our bank accounts. Jake was eleven and the seventeen dollars and fifty cents was money that he'd saved, a dime and a quarter at a time, out of his allowance. That and my two hundred were applied to the three thousand I still owed from 1968, my one affluent year.

To explain the debt I have to go back to '68 and a brief financial accounting. The emotional accounting is complicated and will take longer. I had exploded out of a thirteen-year marriage. If I hadn't left, or pushed Irwin out, none of this would have happened. But I had, and it did. When Irwin and I separated we went to Irwin's lawyer and worked out a separation agreement. Irwin was then the vice president of an advertising agency, earning a lot by '68 standards, and we agreed that I would receive close to twenty thousand a year for my children and me. What I hadn't understood, because I knew nothing about such things, was that the money was declared alimony so that Irwin could deduct it, and income to me, which meant that I owed taxes on it. In 1969, after Irwin married Kathleen, quit his job, and showed no income, I owed the IRS seven thousand dollars for that year.

Everyone told me later that I'd been stupid to let Irwin's lawyer work out our separation agreement, but Irwin was still my best friend. I wasn't in love with him, but I loved him and trusted him. I'd believed him when he'd said, "I'll always take care of you and the kids." He'd said it so many times during our marriage, and even after we'd separated, that I'd whisper the words to myself in the dark in the sofa bed, with a kind of disbelief. I had hurt him badly—I knew that—but the children, whom he'd seemed to love so much, hadn't done anything to him. I wasn't angry with Irwin, just confounded. My anger was directed at Kathleen, who controlled Irwin and the money. It was Kathleen's money, after all; Irwin no longer had any. Any checks that managed to make it from Cape May, New Jersey, to Whitsett Avenue were signed Kathleen Riley Epstein.

The last time I saw Irwin was at a meeting with our lawyer in New York when Irwin said that he had to cut our payments down to about a third of what they had been. I said that that was impossible—we wouldn't be able to stay in the city—what was I supposed to do? Irwin shifted in his chair and his eyes were half closed, a look that I recognized. Jake's face would get the same look. Whenever they were uncomfortable, or in unwanted photographs, their eyelids would droop over their beautiful, nearsighted, brown eyes. Irwin squirmed, suggested that I get a job, which I'd already done, and basically said that he had no idea. I turned to the lawyer, keeping desperation in check, asking what I could do, and he explained patiently that no court could order a father to pay child support if he owned nothing and had no job.

"Jesus Christ! You've got to be kidding," I stammered before managing to pull myself together enough to make sure, in writing, that whatever came to us was declared child support, not alimony. Of course, I still owed the IRS seven thousand dollars. I knew that I wouldn't be able to keep the children in the Little Red School House, which they loved, or stay in the city. It took me a while to decide what to do.

I'd visited Los Angeles with my parents when I was young and I remembered how beautiful the canyons were, and the winding drive down Sunset, and the first glimpse of the Pacific. I didn't want to leave New York and the Connecticut countryside where I'd grown up, but I'd heard that it was cheaper to live in Los Angeles and that the public schools were good. I thought I should be able to get some kind of job. Also, I'd sold a couple of short stories, and had a New York agent, who said I might be able to get writing work. Anything valuable, like the silver my mother had left me, her fur coat and a few antiques, I'd sold before we left New York. Most of it went to the IRS; the rest of it flew us from one coast to the other. I'd kept a few treasures—the carved dresser that I'd had as a girl, a golden Oriental rug, my mother's bed and dressing table, a few precious books. I'd put them in storage and hadn't been able to send for them.

After our bank accounts were confiscated the levies began to arrive in the mail, official-looking documents that said that any income or salaries due to me would automatically go to the IRS until the three thousand still owed to them was paid. They were all signed by Mr. Meekel. There was a levy on any salary I might earn, and on any royalties I might receive from my father's songs, which usually didn't amount to much. There was a levy on any work that I might do for Quantis Productions, a company that consisted of two has-been producers who had helped get me through 1970 by hiring me to write a script for next to nothing. When Quantis went bust I answered some ads for real jobs—receptionist jobs, part-time secretarial—but I found that I was hopelessly unqualified. I was a thirty-four-year-old English major with no résumé and no skills. I could barely type. The early stories that I'd done I'd written in longhand and taken to a typist. The small monthly checks that came from Cape May were also levied by Mr. Meekel.

The children were worried about me, and scared, and each expressed it differently. Emma, a gentle nine-year-old then, sat on the front step, waiting for the school bus and prayed silently. Jake tried to make practical suggestions while fixing himself a peanut butter sandwich. Danny decided that he didn't feel well and should stay in bed. I managed to get myself up, take a shower, get all three on the bus, and stick my batch of levies in an envelope. I drove over Coldwater Canyon, luminous in the morning light, and smiled when I reached the spot where the trees got straight. The children had said that you can tell when you enter Beverly Hills because the trees get straight, and they were right. The trees were ragged and haphazard until the Beverly Hills sign, and then they were suddenly tall and stately.

I took my levies to my accountant, Edwin Self, a strange little fellow whom I'd gone to about my tax problem. He had arranged a payment plan with the IRS, a hundred a month until it was paid off, a plan that I had adhered to, and that the little creep Meekel had decided to ignore. Mr. Self, looking up at me with beanlike eyes, told me that I needed to bring in all my receipts to prove that I was feeding and clothing three children so that he could prove to Mr. Meekel that the money Irwin owed was child support, not alimony.

"But it is child support—he's wrong!" I said. "I made sure when we changed the agreement before I left New York that it be declared child support."

"The IRS can be slow to catch up with these things," he answered. "I'll call them. But it would still be a good idea to bring me those receipts."

Determined to keep some sort of forward motion going, I went home, gathered receipts, and then tried to figure out how we could eat until all this got straightened out. I had no credit because Irwin had canceled all of our joint credit cards, and I certainly couldn't get credit on my own. The only thing I thought I could do was to keep running up the milk bill. The milkman delivered once a week—milk, butter, cottage cheese—and I didn't have to pay him until the end of the month. Sometimes he'd let it go for two months. So I figured we could live on cold cereal and whatever I could get the milkman to deliver.

In bed later, with a pile of receipts beside me, and some cash still hidden in the closet, I began to think about being safe, about what it had been like, how it had felt. I remembered my room when I was a little girl, the ivy wallpaper in the moonlight, the tall white birch outside my window, the sound of Eastern rain on Eastern trees, the warmth of my quilt as I drifted off to sleep. I was afraid of ghosts then, and witches, but it was such a different kind of fear. It wasn't the fear of living, the fear of each coming day.

It felt safe when I was married too—too safe. But if I'd known about this kind of fear I never would have left. And if I'd known what the children would go through, I certainly wouldn't have left. I'd wrestled endlessly with that, sitting quietly while they were in school—could I get through five more years of this, ten more years? Could I manage to stay until they were grown up? I tried so hard to stay married because they loved their father so much and he loved them. He was the stability in their lives. They loved me too and I loved them, but no one could accuse me of being stable. I was the emotionally fragile one, or so we all thought. Then why leave them, in desperate circumstances, with just me?

The only answer I could come to was Kathleen. Irwin had turned to her three months after we had separated and she had taken him over. I said once, jokingly, that Irwin had become a walk-in. In science fiction when a soul leaves a living body and another soul comes in that's a walk-in. I was joking, but I simply couldn't imagine how the man that I'd known had turned into the present-day Irwin.

"I'll always take care of you and the kids," Irwin had said. "Yeah, right, shit," I muttered to the ceiling. Then, suddenly angry with myself, I sat up and reached for a cigarette. I lit it with a snap of the match, wondering why I had ever expected such a thing. Why should a woman have the right to be taken care of, and a man not? Of course, it was how most of us were brought up, I answered myself. In the fifties when we were in college a young woman was supposed to be married right after graduation, or before. If not, you were in danger of becoming an old maid. Very few wanted careers; most wanted the perfect husband and perfect babies we saw on the covers of the women's magazines. That's certainly what I wanted; I'd never pictured anything else. And along with that came the idea that the husbands would work, and the wives and children be taken care of. It wasn't fair, I decided, not to the husbands and not to the wives, some of whom would later seem like old children, unable to take care of themselves.

I was twenty and Irwin twenty-two when we were married. I had lost a lot, wanted someone to cling to, and a family of my own. Irwin wanted to be a writer, was scorned by his family of businessmen, and needed me and mine to believe in him. My father had supported both of us until he'd died suddenly of a heart attack only four years after Irwin and I had married. We had two babies by then, a toddler, Danny, and an infant, Jake, and my father had left everything to his new wife. It wasn't that much—a lovely house on Long Island Sound, a car and some royalties—but it left us stranded, and Irwin was faced with having to go to work. He'd wanted to be a journalist, and he was freelancing, selling an occasional piece, but it wasn't enough to live on.

We were both devastated when my father died. I'd been very close to him, and I couldn't imagine this world without him. We were sitting on the edge of our bed, in the small West End Avenue apartment, trying to calm a screaming little Jake, when the call came. I'd answered the phone, handing the baby to Irwin, and heard my older brother, Ted, say as gently as possible that our father had died. He'd been standing in the kitchen, making coffee, and simply fallen to the floor. I didn't cry right away—I was too shocked—but Irwin did. It was the first time I'd seen him cry. He put the baby down, covered his wet face with his hands, and said over and over again, "Now he'll never know." I knew what he meant, that my father would never see him become successful.

Then Irwin did a strange thing—he stopped trying completely. He decided to forget about writing, and all his dreams of success, and become a businessman. He found a job in advertising, was good at it, good with people, and in what seemed a very short time became an account executive. As he kept rising in the agency, I kept telling him that he didn't have to give up writing. He could write in the evenings and on weekends as my father had before he had a few hit songs, as so many artists had that I'd known, but Irwin just shrugged and said, "Maybe sometime." It became clear that he was angry. He had, somehow, not bargained for this—this job of supporting a family. I felt that, as much as he loved us, he was quietly angry from the day he had to go to work. I tried again and again to tell him that the job was just temporary, that if he just kept writing and sending stuff out he could still make it, but he shrugged this off and his desk remained untouched and his typewriter stayed covered.

Years later, early one morning, Irwin brought morning coffee up to me in bed, and in his natty three-piece-suit, and with undisguised irony said, "Well, I'm off to my temporary job as senior vice president of Waller, Burns and Cormic." I laughed, a sad laugh, but Irwin could usually make me laugh. I wondered if he could make me laugh now. The old Irwin could have; I didn't know about the walk-in.

The other strange thing about all this was that once Irwin married Kathleen and quit his job, he started writing again. I guess it's not strange; he got what he'd wanted in the first place. He didn't have to worry anymore about supporting a family or making a living. But what about his children? I kept coming back to that.

When I could no longer pay the orthodontist, and couldn't take the boys to get their braces adjusted, I'd asked Irwin, over the phone, if he could help with their braces but he'd said, "If they were with me I'd pay for it. With you, forget it." That was when I'd begun to understand how possessive his love was. It made sense in terms of me; I'd left him, but it didn't make sense in terms of the children who he'd loved so much. Especially Danny, who had entered Irwin's heart the moment he was born.

Danny had been the most beautiful of the three babies, with gray-blue eyes and long black lashes. The rest of us had brown eyes, but the two grandmothers had had blue, and my mother, who'd died years before, had had the long dark lashes. I don't think that's why Irwin loved Danny the most, but he did—it was obvious. After the other two were born, all eighteen months apart, Irwin took Danny everywhere with him and left Jake and Emma to me. When we went to Amagansett for the summer Irwin drove with Danny and put Emma, Jake and me on the train. When we went to see the Christmas tree in Rockefeller Center, Irwin went ahead with Danny, and I followed with Jake and Emma.

Irwin's favoritism didn't bother me while we were together. If Irwin loved Danny the most, and Danny loved his father the most, that was okay with me because Danny was by far the most active, and when they were little I was understandably exhausted. Jake, at six months, could concentrate for a couple of hours on a simple puzzle; Emma could just sit in her carriage or baby chair and smile at the world. And their temperaments didn't change that much as they grew. Danny, a natural athlete, was always moving; Jake, a natural scholar, was studious and determined; and Emma was bright and loving and increasingly beautiful. So in a strange way—the kind of thing that happens in families without anyone knowing it—Danny became more Irwin's child, and Jake and Emma became more mine.

It worked, kind of balanced itself out, until Irwin and I separated, and it still worked until Kathleen took over. During the spring and the early part of that first summer apart Irwin and I remained good friends. He rented a car for us to drive to the converted barn we'd rented, drew a map for me because I'd never done the trip alone before, and blew kisses to all of us as he stood on the sidewalk and watched us go. Once we were back in the city, the children back in school, and Irwin and Kathleen living together, Kathleen decided that the children's visits were too difficult, and they became less and less frequent.

Danny was the most hurt, of course. I knew that he would be. When I'd agonized for hours about whether I could stick it out for five more years, ten more years, it was mainly Danny that I was concerned about. And I was right. In the boys' room, in the house on Whitsett, Danny slept in the top bunk, hurt and unhappy, and furious with me for taking him away from his father. I told him that he could probably go and live with his father and Kathleen if he really wanted to, but he'd shrug and say miserably that he wanted to stay with us. I don't know if he did, or if he was afraid that Irwin and Kathleen might say no if he asked them.

Chapter Two

I stop rocking and open my eyes. The screen in front of me is still white, the afternoon sun still coming through the window of my empty living room. I push play and see the Whitsett house again. Nine-year-old Emma and her friend Jenny are putting on a play with dolls and stuffed animals. They're sitting on the front steps, gesturing, giving voice to Jenny's Barbie and Emma's Snoopy. The film is silent, of course, but as the reel ends I hear Emma's young voice in the Whitsett house as if she were here with me this minute. I close my eyes again, listening to her voice as she'd cried out in the night:

"Mommy, Mommy, I can't breathe!" And I can feel her small, thin body as she'd jumped onto my bed and into my arms.

"What, honey?" I'd asked, waking quickly.

"I can't breathe," she'd said again, her voice strangled.

"Sure, you can," I'd said, sitting up and holding her, stroking her long hair. "Just calm down, baby, just calm down."

"I think I've got asthma," she'd managed to say between gasps.

"No, you don't," I'd answered quietly. "Jenny has asthma. You don't have asthma."

"How do you know?" Emma had asked after a minute, her breaths evening out.

"Because I know," I'd answered, and that seemed to be enough. After another minute Emma smiled and climbed under my covers.

"Can I sleep in here?" she'd asked.

"Sure," I'd said, and snuggled down beside her, an arm around her shoulder.

We were almost asleep before she'd murmured, "This is fun, kinda like the earthquake, or when the rape guy was here."

"Oh, that was lots of fun," I'd said, almost laughing.

The earthquake was the so-called Big One. It was frightening and damaging for the areas hardest hit, but in Van Nuys it was just a couple of jolts that sent some dishes crashing to the floor. It was about 6:30 A.M., on a school day, and Danny was in the kitchen fixing his breakfast. I had been asleep in the den, and was knocked awake by the house moving and by Danny leaping on my bed. Emma was screaming, and Danny and I struggled to our feet and ran toward the children's rooms. We found Jake in the hall, silently putting on his bathrobe and sneakers, prepared for anything, and a still screaming Emma, whom I picked up and carried to my bed. The boys followed and the four of us stayed in my bed all morning, listening to news reports on Danny's transistor radio and riding out the aftershocks. It *was* kind of fun. School was canceled; we ate milk and cookies in bed and shrieked with every little rumble as if we were on a roller coaster.

The "rape guy" was not fun at all. I'll amend that: the experience was exhilarating in a weird kind of way, a frightening adrenaline rush. And it let me know that I didn't really want to die. I'd wanted to die a few times—or thought I did—ever since we'd landed in Los Angeles. Actually, I'd thought about it, on and off, ever since my mother had died of an overdose when I was eighteen. It had never occurred to me until then. But during those first months on Whitsett living seemed to be so much harder than dying. Rejection or loss could send me to bed, crying and shaking from deep within, and thinking I wanted to die. Or maybe I just wanted the pain to stop. A long coma, a long, sweet sleep, just until things were better, was more what I had in mind.

The crying fits usually lasted for about a day, and after a while I began to call them "anguish attacks." They were like a migraine. On the first day I would feel it coming on, and try to push it away. But by the second day the sobs would take over. I'd try to get the children out of the house to visit friends after school so that they'd miss the worst of it. It would let up on the third day, and I'd start to breathe normally again, bathe my swollen eyes, apologize to my children and to anyone who had received suicidal calls from me the day before. The trick was to get through it, and I'd found that calling those who cared about me—my beloved brother, the Cramers—would sustain me. I'd say, in effect, "I feel like dying; please talk me out of it."

During one of my attacks, in the Whitsett house, the children hovered, not wanting to leave, and heard me crying on the phone. A few minutes later Jake came in, sat beside me and said quietly, "Mom, if you really did want to die, if that's what you really wanted, it's okay. But I want to ask you something; if you did die, would you try hard, in whatever way you could, to be with us?" That did it. That stopped me as no other words ever had, and I felt so grateful for his love, for his generous heart. Of course, I went from there to guilt. If I'd loved my mother that much could I have saved her? If I'd listened to her despair after my father had left, and she'd said that she wanted to die, would she still be alive? I'd go over and over it, lighting one cigarette after another, just as my mother had, wondering if I had inherited all this: my crying fits, my love of smoke, the dread of rejection, the pull toward death.

I prayed that my mother wasn't suffering in some in-between world, a purgatory that I didn't believe in anyway. I wanted to believe that my father and others that I'd loved who had died were happy on some beautiful plane, and checked in on us from time to time. There was a wicker chair in my den-bedroom that often squeaked during the night as if some large person were settling into it. I liked to think that it was my father, coming to help, making sure that we were all right.

Then there was the business with the Ouija board. I'm not sure if it was ours or belonged to one of the children's friends, but Danny, Jake and Emma told me excitedly that every time they tried it it spelled out the same thing. It said, one letter at a time, "I love you, ACH." Those were my mother's initials and stood for Anna Cohen Hyde. All her silverware and linens had been monogrammed ACH. I didn't have any of her things at that point, and I don't think the children even knew what her initials were. At least they didn't know until I freaked out at this message that came to us again and again. Was my mother trying to reach me from that place between life and death and maybe life again? And then it occurred to me that if I died I might not really die. I might have to watch my children cry from the other side of an impenetrable, one-way mirror, and not be able to reach them or comfort them. That was the most terrifying thought of all.

The "rape guy" did it too. I thought wryly, at moments, that I should have thanked him for bringing out a strength in me that I'd had no idea was there. It had been about one in the morning on a blistering August night during our first summer in the San Fernando Valley. Temperatures over a hundred combined with dry, Santa Ana winds, and we sweated and twisted in our soaked sheets. The little house on Whitsett had no air conditioning, and I'd left the windows open and the door that led into the den. I'd closed the screen door but probably not locked it. After years of living in New York City, Van Nuys seemed so safe and suburban to me that I'd forgotten to be careful.

I'd awakened in the sofa bed with the sense that someone was in the room. It was a dense, black night with no moonlight, and when I sat up I dimly made out a shape on the other side of the bed near the screen door. I'd called out, thinking at first that it was one of the children. And then slowly the hunched shape stood up. For a second I thought it was a nightmare, then realized that it *was*—a very large black man gazed at me from across the bed. I don't know what got into me, but I sat up as straight as possible, shoulders squared, and said firmly and evenly, "You get the hell out of here!" For what seemed a long time, the man loomed toward me, then back, then toward me, then back again. On the last lean back he opened the screen door, bolted outside, across the dry, dirt lawn, and disappeared into the alley.

That was when I fell apart. I screamed for the children, grabbed the phone and called the police. The children ran sleepily to my bed and the police arrived soon after. After getting a description, which couldn't tell them much, they told me that there had been three robbery-rapes in the vicinity in the last few weeks, and I had scared the guy away. They were grinning when they said that—all five foot two of me had scared the guy away. I was as astounded as they were.

The police left after making sure that we were all right and the house secure, and I asked Emma to sleep in the den with me. That was the fun part for her, but after her eyes closed I went into the kitchen, got a knife and finally slept, clutching it under my pillow. That's when we got Blanca, our black Labrador puppy. The police had suggested a dog and we'd looked at ads in the local paper, answered one, and found an uncontrollable, adolescent puppy, tied to a tree outside someone's house. Of course we took her, incongruous name and all, and she became our dog and the new love of Danny's life.

It's Jake's young voice that I hear in my mind this time. It's as clear as a long-forgotten voice in a dream. I don't bother to open my eyes; I know by the orange glow beneath my lids that the sun is setting outside the living room windows, the light changing from gold to red-orange. I sit still in the rocker and savor the clarity of the moment that's replaying in my mind.

"Mom," Jake said quietly beside my sofa bed in the Whitsett house, "I've gotta go. Mr. Davies is picking me up in a couple minutes." I smelled coffee and saw early, gray light in the room as I opened my eyes. Jake had made my coffee and was holding a cup out to me.

"Thanks, sweetie. What time is it?" I asked, still half asleep, as I sat up and took the cup.

"Seven. We're going to that math contest all the way out in Agoura."

"Oh, that's right, I forgot," I said, and sipped the coffee and lit the day's first cigarette. "Have you got lunch?"

"Mr. Davies is treating."

"That's really nice."

"I've got something for you to sign," Jake said, holding out a printed form and a pen.

"What's it for?"

"You know those mothers who stand out in the street with stop signs before school? Well, I signed you up. You just have to sign—"

"You *what?*" I said, spitting out smoke and coffee. Jake kept a straight face for another couple of seconds before breaking into laughter.

"Just kidding," he said. "It's just to excuse me from morning classes today." He was still laughing and I started to laugh with him.

"You little—little creep," I said, signing the form, still laughing. A horn honked outside and Jake took the form, kissed my cheek, and hurried toward the door.

"Good luck, hon! Have fun!"

"I will. Love you," Jake called back.

The front door closed as I said, "Love you too," and laughed again to myself. It felt so good to laugh, for a change.

The phone is ringing, and Sandy is barking, and I laugh again as I open my eyes. I let the machine pick up, and follow Sandy outside into the twilight. The night-blooming jasmine and the sweet scent of the lemon blossoms get stronger as I cross the yard and lean against the plum tree. As I breathe it all in I remember the same piquant smell from the trees on Whitsett Avenue. I'd walked outside after getting the good news from Edwin Self that Mr. Meekel and the powers-that-be at the IRS had accepted my pile of receipts as proof that I was indeed supporting three children. That meant that there was no longer a lien on the money that Irwin was supposed to send.

I'd breathed in the spring air, just as I do now—it's a myth that Los Angeles doesn't have a spring—and breathed out the relief that I'd felt. I'd looked up thankfully at the dizzying blue of the sky, and turned back to the Whitsett house. In the den, without hesitation, I'd picked up the phone and dialed Irwin and Kathleen's number. Irwin answered, which surprised me; it was usually Kathleen or a housekeeper.

"Hi," I said. "It's Callie."

"Yes," Irwin said guardedly.

"I just heard from the accountant who just heard from the IRS," I burbled, "and they said they'd made a mistake, and you can start sending child support again right away."

There was a pause before Irwin said, "I don't have to send you a penny."

There was another pause, a shocked pause, before I said, "But it's not for me, it's for the kids—they're yours too."

"I don't have to send you a penny," Irwin said again, in the same flat tone. That was the last time we'd spoken, the last time I'd heard his voice in all these years.

Without even trying to calm myself down, I'd called the brave, or stupid, young lawyer in Cape May, who had said he'd look into my case.

"I don't think he can do that," I'd cried when the young lawyer answered his phone. "Can he do that?"

"Until you take him to court he can do pretty much whatever he wants," the lawyer answered.

"Well, when can I take him to court?"

"It'd take at least a year or two," he said, "but I'll start working on it."

"Thanks," I'd managed to say.

In the backyard Blanca ran in circles around the pepper tree while I sat on the cement step and tried to figure out if I had any options. I thought about Welfare, and decided that if we were really starving, I supposed I could do that. But we weren't really starving—there was still the milkman. I almost laughed out loud when I wondered if the IRS could confiscate Welfare payments. Then I realized that if I could borrow the money to pay off the IRS, the royalties would be freed up, and the liens lifted on any potential income. I knew that I couldn't ask my brother or my stepmother, but the Cramers had been so supportive through all this. Maybe I could ask them, and I began dreaming of what it would be like to be free of Mr. Meekel without actually shooting him. I'd be free of him and the liens and the threatening letters, and I could put whatever money I had in a bank instead of a shoe box.

Blanca knocked her head on the pepper tree, jumping wildly at a teasing squirrel. She yelped, bringing me back to the moment, and as I checked her head, which looked fine, I felt a surge of remorse. It had been a longing for freedom that had brought me here, that had sent our lives into turmoil. But I also felt determined to get us out of this mess.

I sat by the phone in the den for about half an hour, breathing deeply and saying a prayer before dialing Ben Cramer's number in Palm Springs. Ben had been my father's good friend, had known me as a child, and was as fond of my children as he was of me.

"You'll get through this, Cal," Ben said gently, after saying he'd be glad to send whatever I still owed the IRS.

"You really think so?" I asked, after thanking him profusely.

"It's your destiny, baby," he said, and we both laughed. "No, really," he added. "You're going to make it, and those kids are going to make it, and we'll be so proud." I went from laughter to tears and back to laughter as I thanked him again, hung up the phone, and fell back on the bed. I laughed some more with the children when they got home from school, and we all tried to picture that bastard Meekel's face as it would look when I walked into his office and handed him his damn money. I slept that night as I hadn't in weeks, waited the next few days for the check to come, and tried to figure out what to do next.

It *was* fun to pay off Meekel. I'd gone to the Hollywood office that he shared with several other IRS creeps, found his desk, and presented my cashier's check, down to the penny, interest included. His fishy eyes barely made contact; his thin mustache twitched over something like a smile, and he half rose from his seat.

"Don't bother to get up," I'd said. "I'm running late. But please make sure all the liens are lifted, okay?"

"I'm sorry about the alimony, I mean child support," he started to say, but I interrupted, walking away from him.

"Forget it. I'm not getting any anyway."

"I'll take care of this, Mrs. Epstein," he said, holding up the check, but I was out the door.

Chapter Three

It's dark, a crescent moon rising over the plum tree, by the time I bring Sandy back into the Alta Vista house. I stumble over packed and half-packed boxes, turn on the lights, listen to the answering machine—nothing urgent—and give Sandy his dinner. I carry a sandwich and a glass of wine into the living room, eager to get back to the videos, eager to see what part of our lives will jump off the screen at me this time. I put another video in, push play, and settle back in the rocking chair.

On the screen the children, bundled in scarves, mittens, ski pants and jackets, are racing from the corner of Bleecker Street down MacDougal toward our doorway. Their noses are red, their eyes watery from the cold, and they laugh as they slide across patches of ice on the sidewalk. Shoveled, crusted snow, sprinkled with soot, forms ridges between sidewalk and street, and leans against the struggling trees in their squares of dirt. The children are bouncy and happy as they enter the heated hallway of our divided house.

The camera follows them inside—Irwin must have been taking this—as they pass the mailboxes on the left, open the inside door, and then our door that leads into our living room, and then outside into the garden. The change is magical. In the midst of New York City, in the center of Greenwich Village, a block away from the Hip Bagel, Figaro's, Joe's Restaurant and the Mafia undertaker, there's an island of trees, benches and gardens that's called the MacDougal Gardens. Jerkily, on the screen, the children run out our back door, enter their own private park, and head for an unfinished snowman. Once again the screen turns to snow, a different kind of snow, and I see it all in my mind.

We were part of the MacDougal Gardens, usually just called "the garden" by those of us who lived there. It was an enclosed park, only one long block, an island of greenery that could only be reached through the houses that bordered it. There were sixteen houses in all, eight that ran along MacDougal between Bleecker and Houston, and eight that ran along Sullivan Street. They were townhouses that had been built in the mid-eighteen hundreds. A few were still intact, but most had been broken up into duplexes, or single-floor apartments.

Four years before, Irwin and I had moved into a rented duplex on MacDougal, the two lower floors of a four-story house that consisted of a large living room and kitchen downstairs, and a spiral staircase that led to the three small bedrooms upstairs. We also had a narrow garden that bordered on the communal garden where all the children, ours and the neighbors', could play freely and safely outside. The garden children tended to run in a small pack from house to house. We'd be invaded by their clamor and then left, in sudden silence, with muddy footprints and spilled juice. The grade-school children all went to the Little Red School House, a block and a half away on Bleecker Street, and became friends or enemies, as the case may be, and so we gradually met our neighbors, who were also parents, and more gradually met the older inhabitants of the MacDougal Gardens.

It took longer to meet the ghosts, or to hear about them, but they were there all along, long before we arrived, long before we were born. Thinking about it now, in the quiet of my Alta Vista living room, it was the garden ghosts who had started all this, who had propelled us, the children and me, from there to here. But, the stage had been set. My longing for freedom had begun years before I met the ghosts, and Sam, who lived across the garden from us.

The longing had begun once the exhaustion had ended. With three babies and no help I'd been too tired to feel anything. Then Irwin had started to make money; we got a cleaning lady, then a mother's helper, as she was called, then all three children were in school. For the first time in years I had a couple of hours a day to myself. The longing began slowly, during those couple of hours. I missed my father, whom I hadn't had time to mourn. I missed the home we'd had. I missed my mother who had died of her own losses, and I missed Kirk, my first love. I knew that I didn't miss *him,* per se. I missed the minutes of joy before seeing him, the joy of just being with him, and the quiet happiness that followed. With Irwin there were no minutes, or even seconds, of joy. Irwin was safe and sane—a rebound love that I'd curled into like a cocoon.

The first time that I really knew how I felt was when I

watched John F. Kennedy's funeral on the television in the boys' room. It was the only set we had, and I sat on a little chair, surrounded by blocks and miniature cars, and smelled the mice in their cage, and watched Jackie Kennedy put on a performance for the world. I'd leaned forward, taking in her black veil, her sensible shoes, her beautiful children, and whispered to the set, "You're free, you lucky bitch," and then felt terrible about my thoughts. I realized that I wanted my freedom so badly I was envying a grieving widow.

I tried so hard to stay married, but my longing for freedom only gained momentum with each passing day and year. During 1967 I went to five different psychoanalysts, saying to each in turn, "I just don't want to be married. If this is the rest of my life, I can't stand it." They all said essentially the same thing: "It's a phase, you're in your early thirties, you've been married twelve years, you'll settle down." One of them, a bland fellow, in a bland, teak office, actually said, "One of these days you'll wake up and find that you're once again madly in love with your husband." Since I'd told him, clearly, I thought, that I'd never been in love with my husband, I'd simply shaken my head and walked out. Another—old, bearded and Freudian—who specialized in creative types, said that I should stay married, stay home, and find fulfillment in writing my fantasies of passion and freedom. I tried; it worked to an extent, and I would get lost in my pages, reliving old feelings that I'd packed away like dried flowers in old books. But then Irwin would feel the need to interrupt, to bring people home for dinner at the last minute, to need me for something, and all my longings would return.

One psychiatrist seemed to hear me. Dr. Jane Pricket, a

round and down-to-earth woman in her fifties, lasted longer than the others. I saw her three times a week, well into 1968. She sympathized with how trapped I felt, how bored I was, how I dreamed of freedom and, above all, passion. Of course, I had to be free before I could find the love of my life, and all the passion that I imagined went with it. I couldn't find it while married to my best friend. Or so I thought.

I trusted Dr. Pricket enough to tell her the fantasy that I was so ashamed of, the secret and guilty daydream that I indulged in quite often . . . Irwin had died suddenly, no pain or anything, and we were at his funeral. It wasn't as good as Jack Kennedy's, but in my mind it came close. I was beautiful in a black veil, holding the hands of my beautiful children. There was a riderless horse and a solemn drumbeat. By the time my sons saluted the casket I was in tears. By the end of the fantasy I was always in tears.

Dr. Pricket laughed out loud, which made me feel much better, and suggested that I read two recent books: *The Sexual Response of the Human Female* and Betty Friedan's *The Feminine Mystique*. I bought both books at the Eighth Street Bookshop, walked home to MacDougal Street, and dove into them. I found *The Feminine Mystique* fascinating, and comforting, but it didn't seem to provide any answers. Many women, Betty Friedan said, felt as empty and dissatisfied as I did. We had everything; we had attained all the fifties dreams, but we were miserable. But why? Her answer was that we were daughters, we were wives, we were mothers, but we had no identities of our own. Each of us needed our own identity. I thought hard about this, but I didn't buy it. I searched my soul, but couldn't come up with a desire for identity. I wanted freedom, I wanted a grand love, but an identity? It made sense years later, but not then.

Then, after a session, I'd cracked myself up thinking about a day at the beach the summer before when I'd decided that making it as a writer wouldn't do a thing for me. We'd rented a house for two months at Amagansett, near the ocean beach that was wide and glorious—high, curling waves breaking on clean sand, spotted with shells and driftwood. The problem was that we could rarely go to the ocean beach. Unless it was very calm, the children couldn't swim there. So nearly every day we packed up rafts, sandwiches, thermoses, umbrellas, blankets, toys, balls, hats, dry clothes, and drove three miles across the island to the bay beach, sheltered and hot as hell, where the children could swim, and take their rafts out without fear of riptides and six-foot waves.

The bay beach also had swarms of biting flies. They were horrible, noisy and ferocious, and nothing deterred them. As I sat there one day, spraying myself, slapping myself, watching my children splash each other from their rafts, I began to dream about writing a best-seller or a hit play. So far I'd written a few short stories, and was thinking about a novel, not one word of it on paper as yet, but I jumped ahead in my mind to a Pulitzer Prize for fiction. That would surely give me an identity of my own. I was enjoying my fantasy when suddenly a child cried, or a fly bit me, and I came back to reality and looked around me on this sticky-hot beach, and saw Neil Simon and his two daughters a few towels down from us. Further on there was Murray Schisgal and his family, and then Philip Roth with some beauty and her kids. And it struck me that, even if I did become successful as a writer, my life wouldn't change at all. I'd still be sitting here on this same damned, fly-infested beach.

The Sexual Response of the Human Female fascinated me because it had some answers. I got excited just reading it. It was explicit. It described things to do that we had never done. Irwin and I had been young and hadn't known much about sex when we'd married. On top of that Irwin was the kind of person who always wanted to do things the same way. He did Canadian Air Force exercises every morning from seven to seven-thirty. At seven-thirty, on cue, he went to the bathroom; at eight he went into the shower. He liked to go to the same restaurants, to drive the same roads, to rent the same summer place, to have the same Sunday brunch. So I found myself experimenting on myself during the day when everyone was gone. With the bathroom door locked and *The Sexual Response of the Human Female* propped up beside me, I discovered the most delightful feelings.

When I told Irwin, joyously, about what I had discovered he lost interest in me sexually for the first time since we'd been married. Nothing else had ever turned him off—not my pregnancies, not illness, nothing—and his interest never fully returned. As much as I practiced, I couldn't do all this stuff in the book by myself, and I became increasingly frustrated and angry. Dr. Pricket said that I should have an affair.

"I can't," I said. "I know me. I'm such a stupid romantic. I'd have to really love someone, and if I did I'd want to only be with that person, and then what about my husband who I love so much—in a different way, of course—but I do love him? And how could I lie to him, how could I sleep with two people at the same time? No, I couldn't do it."

"You'd be surprised," Dr. Pricket said matter-of-factly. "And don't you think Irwin looks at other women? Don't you think he has fantasies?"

"Oh, God, I wish he did," I answered mournfully. "I wish he'd have an affair."

"Then you'd feel better about what you want?"

"I don't know what I want!"

"But you want something or someone?"

"I want to be crazy about someone again," I said quietly. "Like when I was a kid. I want to feel that fluttering in the stomach when someone touches you. I want to feel— Oh, like last summer at the beach when I watched our friend Dave and his new girlfriend dance together for the first time. You could practically feel the electricity in their fingers. I want that first time with someone."

"But you say you didn't have that with Irwin."

"No, I didn't. I'd given all that up. I'd been so hurt when Kirk dumped me, I didn't ever want that again. This was sane and content I told everybody—my marriage to Irwin—he was my best friend."

"Tell me about Kirk," Pricket said.

"I have already," I answered, irritated. "Just a boy I was crazy about for years."

"But older?"

"Four years. Not that much older. Not a Daddy thing, if that's what you're thinking." Pricket shrugged, and I went on. "I was just crazy about him, and then he finally noticed me and kissed me and wanted me."

"He was your first?"

"Yes, of course. Then he took off, and Daddy left, and Mommy was dying." I was crying by then.

"Then Irwin came along," Pricket interrupted, "and saved you?" I nodded. "Your best friend."

"Yes."

"That's supposed to be good."

"Yeah, right."

"You don't think so?"

"Sure, for some people." I was still crying, and mumbled, "I've tried so hard."

"Well, why don't you go home and think about it. Think about what you want."

"Sure, okay." But I didn't go home; I went to the diet doctor, my appointment after Pricket. My friend Ruthie Marcum, who was also a neighbor on MacDougal Street, had introduced me to our very own "Dr. Feelgood." We didn't know it at the time, but he dispensed weekly amphetamines in the guise of diet pills. Neither of us needed to lose weight, but we'd go, get weighed, get our pills and feel a much needed lift. I never told Irwin, Pricket or anyone about it. Ruthie, and her husband, Josh, also smoked a lot of pot, which I didn't want to try. I didn't want to come down; all I wanted was to be up. The half-hour surge of good spirits after a pill felt wonderful.

Ruthie and I were on a No. 5 bus on our way back to the Village when Ruthie first told me about her affair. I tried to keep the shock off my face, but must not have succeeded. Ruthie grinned, a dimpled smile and mischievous brown eyes.

"You look scandalized," she said.

"No, I—I'm just surprised. I thought—"

"You thought we were as perfect as you guys?"

"You're kidding?"

"You mean you're not perfect?"

"Oh, stop it, Ruthie. Just tell me. Who is it? Do I know him?"

Ruthie nodded, sighed and turned her face toward the street. The bus was creeping down lower Fifth Avenue, heading for Washington Square where the leaves were starting to turn yellow and orange.

"It's Kevin," Ruthie said, still turned away.

"Kevin? Josh's assistant Kevin? But he's so—"

"Yes, so young, I know," Ruthie said, turning back to me. "He's eight years younger than I. But Josh is twenty years older than I am, and we both—Kevin and me—we both love Josh. We wouldn't hurt him for the world." The bus stopped at that moment with a burst of exhaust, and we both got off and began walking across the square. Ruthie's face was drawn, and the shadows under her eyes had darkened.

"What are you going to do?" I asked, after a silence.

"Nothing," Ruthie answered. "And for God's sake don't say anything. Don't let on."

"I'm not a good liar," I said.

"Well, give it a try," Ruthie snapped, and we didn't say another word as we passed the milling students around the fountain, the chess players, the drunks out cold on the benches. We passed the Hip Bagel, Joe's across the street, the undertaker, and turned down MacDougal. My front door was first, and I kissed Ruthie's cheek, took out my keys and opened our door.

One of the messages on my answering machine is from Ruthie. She's in Los Angeles for a few days, knows I'm in the midst of moving, but could we get together? I call the hotel number she's left, ask for her room, and she picks up the phone. Her voice hasn't changed—still low and throaty—but I know that she's visibly aged, her hair steel gray, her skin thickened by too many summers at the beach. We've remained friends, though not close, getting together when she visits Los Angeles, or I visit New York where she still lives. After barely saying hello, I find myself telling her about the videos.

"I found this old box of films from the garden and Amagansett and when we got here, and I'm supposed to be packing—I've got a million things to do—and I keep sitting here and watching them, and seeing my life flash in front of my eyes."

"You're not dying, just moving," Ruthie says in her flat, pragmatic voice, and of course I laugh, and we set a tentative time to get together while she's in town. I laugh again as I hang up, return to the living room, and start another video.

It's spring in the garden. Daffodils and tulips are blooming, covered with a sprinkling of city soot. I lean closer to the screen. "Oh, my God, it's Sam," I whisper. He also looks young, his black eyes reflecting the spring sunlight. He smiles and waves at the camera with both arms, and then the screen goes dark, full of wavy lines. I stop and rewind so that I can get another look at Sam's face and beautiful brown arms. Then I see something else, a small shadow by the swings that's there for an instant and then gone. I rewind again and watch closely. The shadow is there, and then it's not. Maybe, Sam, we've finally got proof of a garden ghost. We thought we'd seen them, but were never sure.

Chapter Four

I heard about the garden ghosts from Diana Lawrence. She had inherited the Van Eck house, one of the oldest on Sullivan Street, from her grandparents. Her daughter, Maryellen, and Emma were best friends, and Diana and I developed a casual friendship. Diana and I were sitting on a shaded bench one Indian summer afternoon, watching the girls play, when Diana first mentioned the ghosts.

"What ghosts? Who?"

"You look scared," Diana said, laughing. "Don't worry. They all seem to be friendly. They're just homesick."

"For what?"

"For the garden. The story goes that sometimes, at midnight or just before dawn, you can see them, just their shadows, sitting on the benches."

"Just sitting here?"

Diana nodded. "Just like we are, chatting, enjoying the garden. Because they miss it, you see, in heaven, or wherever they are."

"Have you seen them?" I asked, increasingly intrigued.

"I've thought so sometimes, but I'm not sure. Probably just wishful thinking. But the Tompkinses swear they have—Hal and Laurette *and* their kids—"

"But they're part of that strange religion, aren't they, that believes in reincarnation and all that?"

"Yeah, but Laurette's from the garden way back, and she's got her feet on the ground. And Susie MacAdams has seen them, and Iris Dakin says she talks to them."

"But she's about a hundred."

"About. Oh, and Sam Messenger says he sees them. He gets home from the theater around midnight, and he says he sees them on the benches—top hats, full skirts, flappers, all different periods, all people that lived and died here and loved the garden like we do."

"Really," I said softly, thinking about it, looking around at the backs of the houses, some painted yellow or blue, some red-brick, all with their small, private gardens, and windows that looked down upon the benches where the ghosts would sit at midnight. I stopped at the Messenger house, on the Sullivan side, across from ours, and tried to picture Sam Messenger out here alone with the ghosts. It was difficult because Sam was so full of life; it was hard to imagine him being quiet. I'd only met Sam and his wife, Shirley, a couple of times, but I'd seen him on stage many times before we'd moved to the garden. He was tall and dark with a sharp nose, a barrel chest and wonderful arms. Arms were important to me, and I smiled to myself as I remembered Sam's arms, the sleeves rolled up as he sang "Sue me, sue me, what'll you do me," in the revival of *Guys and Dolls*.

I began to look for the ghosts. I'd stay up, reading in the living room, or pretending to read, after Irwin went to bed upstairs. It was simpler than going to bed when Irwin did, then trying to sneak downstairs at midnight. He would invariably wake up, sit bolt upright and say, "Whassamatter?" I could also sleep later in the morning. After his shower Irwin would make coffee, get the kids up, fix them cereal and toast, and then wake me with a cup of coffee in bed. Staying up late was a way of being alone for a rare hour or two. It was a way to avoid sex, which had become problematic, and it became a time to dream. I'd watch for the ghosts, and fantasize about their lives. Suppose two garden ghosts fell in love here and kept coming back to recapture their first moments together. Suppose a ghost fell in love with a living person—would he/she just moon around the garden, not able to reach the beloved? Suppose a child had died here, would he/she keep coming back to play in the sandbox, swing on the swings, and search for his mother? I answered my own questions, making up stories, putting the ghosts in their proper costumes and time periods.

During my first few nights of ghost-watching the moon was waxing, becoming a bit more full each night. From my darkened living room hidden corners of the garden brightened, and the few tall trees cast long shadows. It was easy to imagine that I'd seen something—a dark shape that might have been a person on a bench, a white pinafore on a swing, a figure running and then disappearing. Then, as the moon began to wane, I *did* see something—something so white that it glistened in the moonlight. Scared, breathing quickly, I got up from the sofa in front of the window, opened the garden door, and stepped outside. I stayed in our small, private garden, hopefully invisible behind a hedge, and watched the glistening thing come toward me.

It was a shirt, a starched white shirt, rolled up to the elbows, showing the gorgeous, brown arms of Sam Messenger. I stayed perfectly still, just watching him as he walked the garden's circular path. I didn't move, or blink, as he sat for a minute on a bench at our end of the garden. He looked up at the stars, seemed to be whispering, maybe making a wish, and then rose slowly and walked back the way he'd come. I waited until I saw him enter his garden, and heard his back door close before I reentered our house.

After that night I wasn't just watching for ghosts. Actually the ghosts had become less interesting than the man with the beautiful arms. My secret, locked-door fantasies changed. They had a face that had dark eyes and a sharp nose, a muscular body with a barrel chest and perfectly tanned arms and legs.

"So why don't you speak to him?" Dr. Pricket asked. "There you are, the two of you, looking for ghosts at midnight—why don't you just walk up to him and say, 'Seen any ghosts tonight?' That's guaranteed to start a conversation."

"I will. I'm thinking about it," I said. "But maybe he wants to be alone. Maybe he doesn't want to talk to anybody."

"So find out," Pricket said.

"I will—*okay?*" I said, feeling that I was being pushed. But that night I dressed casually and carefully. I wore a tank top, my best jeans, a sweatshirt tied suggestively around my hips, and I even put on some makeup, something I didn't ordinarily do unless I was really dressed up.

Sam Messenger appeared at the stroke of twelve. The chimes were striking as he opened his garden gate and began walking the circular path. I watched him for a minute before opening my door. I strolled to the bench nearest us, as if I didn't know he was there, and looked up at the clouded-over night sky. It looked as if it might rain, even storm, and it occurred to me that we both might run in opposite directions and never meet. But the rain held off, and Sam looked startled as he saw a real live person sitting on a bench.

"Hi," I said. "I'm not a ghost."

"I didn't think so," Sam answered. "You live over there, right?" and he gestured toward our house. "We met at the Christmas shindig, and at school a couple times. My Annie's in love with one of your sons."

"She is?" I asked, genuinely surprised. "No one's told me. It must be Danny—they're in the same class."

"Boys don't talk about these things," Sam said with a grin. "Yeah, she said Danny, that's right."

"That's sweet," I answered. "We should get them together sometime—after school, I mean—at the park or something."

"Sure. Mind if I sit down?"

"No, of course not."

"Though they probably play here after school anyway," Sam said as he sat beside me on the bench.

"I don't know. The boys tend to play with the boys and the girls with the girls."

"How boring," Sam said, with another ingratiating grin. I laughed and there was a silence. I was very aware of Sam beside me, but I had no idea if he was aware of me. After a minute he looked up at the clouded sky, and stretched both arms across the back of the bench. "Looks like rain," he said.

"Yeah, it does," I answered, trying not to react as one of those amazing arms brushed the back of my neck.

"Oh, sorry."

"That's okay." Another silence. He didn't move his arm.

"So what do you know about the ghosts?" Sam asked.

"Nothing really. Diana Lawrence was telling me about them. She said people have been seeing them for years, and she said you've seen one or two of them or—" I shrugged and gestured, accidentally touching his knee. "Oh, sorry."

"That's okay. Yeah, I fell in love with the whole idea—people here from a hundred years ago—and I started looking for them after the show."

"It was great," I said. "We saw it. You were great."

"Thanks. It's a stretch, I can't sing worth a damn but . . ." He shrugged, and his arm dropped a bit lower. "Anyway, the house is like a tomb by the time I get home, Shirley and the kids out cold, so I started coming out here."

"Communing with the ghosts?"

"I don't know about communing, but sincerely hoping to see them."

"And?"

"I don't know, frankly. Sometimes I'm sure I've seen something, and then I wake up the next morning and think I'm crazy, I must've made it up."

"Who did you see? I'll amend that—who did you *think* you saw?"

"A boy and a girl," he said quietly. "But just shadows, you know, and the times I've seen them, or thought I did, they're saying goodbye to each other."

"That's so sad."

"Yeah, it is." He turned to me, very dark eyes just staring at me before he asked, "So do you want to ghost-hunt with me? Gaze into the shadows with me while all these sane people are sleeping?" He gestured toward the darkened garden windows, and I laughed as I said that I'd love to when I could. "I don't know your name," he said suddenly.

"Callie Epstein."

"How do you do, Callie?" he said as he rose and shook my hand. "Sam Messenger here."

"Yes, I know."

I didn't know what to do with myself for the next day or two. My skin burned, and I thought of Sam Messenger during every spare minute. There was an assembly at school the next day, and I watched Danny play the recorder, and scanned the audience for Sam or Shirley. Their Annie, blond and round like Shirley, was attempting the violin (not a good choice) and her parents didn't show up. I watched the garden that night, but no living being entered it. The next day, a Friday, I was out in our small garden, hosing New York soot off the fall flowers I'd planted when Shirley appeared at our gate. While Annie had the beginnings of her ample body, Shirley was round in a robust but pleasing way. She had lots of blond, curly hair, lots of freckles, and innocent blue eyes.

"Hi," she called out, smiling. "Callie?"

"Yeah, hi," I said, and turned off the hose.

"Don't you hate it when everything gets covered with this damn soot?"

I nodded, wondering what she wanted. She'd never gone out of her way to be friendly before.

"Come on in," I said, heading for the low, garden gate.

"Oh, I can't. I have to take Sammy supper before the show. Poor baby can't stand to eat alone." I nodded again as if I knew what she meant. "But that's why I'm here—I didn't have your number—and Sam suggested we all get together on Sunday. It's his one day to spend with the girls. He's off Monday too but they're in school, and he said because Annie and Danny are such good friends maybe we could all take a picnic to Central Park or something?"

"Sure," I said, hesitating, confused. "But I'll have to see what the kids are doing, and check with Irwin."

"That's fine. Let me know, okay? It's KLondike 5-2410."

"We're in the book," I answered quietly. She turned and waved, and I watched her walk back across the garden, repeating the phone number in my head. So it was Sam's idea that we all get together. That seemed odd. I'd thought that Sam and I had shared a kind of secret—do you want to ghost-hunt with me, gaze into the shadows with me? as if it were just between the two of us. I must have been wrong I decided as I walked back inside and headed for the phone. I wrote Shirley's number down on the pad in the kitchen, and called Irwin at work. He sounded somewhat surprised by the invitation, but also eager. I knew that he would want to do it—Irwin liked being friends with successful people.

I went out into the garden again that night. The trees rustled, dropping golden leaves, and the stars were bright. If it weren't for the sounds coming from the street, Figaro's and the Hip Bagel, you could almost think you were in the country. I was looking for the Big Dipper when I heard the Messengers' gate open and close. I watched Sam go all the way around the garden, as if he had no idea I was there, before he made his way to our end and the bench near our house.

"Well, hello," he said, with fake surprise.

"Hello to you," I answered smiling, and gestured for him to join me. He sat beside me, again spreading his arms on the back of the bench. I must have stiffened because he patted my shoulder and gave me a searching stare.

"You okay?" he asked.

"Sure, fine," I said, all of me rising to the bit of skin where his hand lingered. He began to talk about the ghosts we might see on such a brightly lit night, but I wasn't really listening. I was intensely aware of his hand, and wanted to run to Pricket and tell her that this was what I was talking about—those first touches, the possibilities of them, the dreams they engendered. It was dreams that I was missing in this seemingly endless marriage, or the possibility of a dream, even if it never happened. I was dying to tell her as Sam went on talking. He talked about his family, originally the Malinovskys from Odessa, and about his children, Annie and Sandra, and about his first wife, Mona, who had married a well-known director I'd never heard of.

He asked about me, and I told him about my father, who had been a songwriter with a few hits, but nobody really knew his name. Sam interrupted—*he* knew and he began to sing "Angel Face," a sweet song from a forgettable forties movie. He was singing it for me, my father's song, and I shivered, and tears came to my eyes. Sam wrapped his whole arm around my shoulder as he sang, and it was as if Nathan Detroit had jumped down off the stage and was singing a beloved song just for me. It was intoxicating, and I felt loss and joy all at the same time.

We thought we'd seen a ghost that night in the garden when Sam had sung to me, and I'd fallen in love with him, or with my image of him. We'd been reluctant to separate, to go back to our dark houses, when a dim light appeared at the other end of the garden. The light, like a large puff of smoke, was curling toward the swings.

"Look at that! Do you see that?" I'd whispered.

"Maybe it's the kid," Sam said in a normal tone, peering at the light that was suddenly gone.

"You scared it away," I said.

"I thought it was supposed to be the other way around," Sam answered. He took my hand and shook it, his face serious. "The garden ghost-hunters have just spotted their first ectoplasm together," he said and then stood, pulling me to my feet. He held my hand for a moment longer before letting it go and turning away. "Time to hit the hay."

"I guess so," I said. "See you soon." Sam nodded, then turned back.

"Yeah, we're getting together at the park or something," Sam said, as if it hadn't been his idea.

"Yes," I answered, confused again, and watched him walk back along the path to his gate. I remained confused and excited through the next day, which was a Saturday. The plan I'd made with Shirley was that all the Epsteins were to meet at the Messengers' at noon on Sunday. If the weather held we'd bring picnics and take cabs up to the park entrance near the zoo, and find a spot near the carousel. On Saturday afternoon I went to the small market at the corner of Bleecker, and was getting ham and cheese for sandwiches when I ran into Laurette Tompkins, who I remembered had told Diana that she and her husband, Hal, had seen the garden ghosts. I barely knew Laurette, but I reintroduced myself, and said that I'd really like to talk to her. She invited me to stop by on my way home.

All I knew about Laurette was that her garden house had been restored by her grandparents at the turn of the century, and that she and her husband belonged to some strange new religion. As soon as I entered her house I realized that the religion I'd heard about was called Scientology. There were posters and pamphlets everywhere. The strange thing was that there were clearly valuable paintings amidst the posters, pamphlets and office supplies. Laurette saw me eyeing a Matisse and then a Degas.

"I inherited those along with the house. Would you like coffee?"

"Yes," I answered. "How wonderful—I mean to live with these paintings."

"I suppose it is," Laurette said, and pushed stacks of papers to one side of the round oak table. "Sorry about the mess. We've rented an office, but we're not in it yet. Have a seat."

"What kind of office?" I asked as I sat at the cleared part of the table.

"A Scientology office," Laurette answered, as if I should have known. "We're starting our own branch."

"Oh," I said, and couldn't think of anything else to say until Laurette joined me at the table with two cups of reheated coffee.

"So, what did you want to talk to me about?"

"The ghosts," I said. "I thought I saw one the other night—"

"Who did it look like?" Laurette asked.

"I don't know. It kind of looked like a puff of smoke," I said with a nervous laugh. "Heading for the swings, then it was gone."

"Oh, that was Lucy," Laurette said matter-of-factly.

"Lucy?"

"Lucy Van Eck. She was about seven when she died. She loves to play on the swings, but she's very shy."

"You've seen her?"

"Many times. She's used to me now, and doesn't just disappear anymore. More coffee?"

"No thanks." As I shook my head I looked away, out toward the garden. I didn't want Laurette to sense what I was thinking—that this matronly, no-nonsense woman was very possibly out of her mind. "I should be getting home," I said, rising quickly. "But I'd love to hear more sometime."

I walked home through the garden, scanning the Messenger house on the other side. I was dying to tell Sam about my conversation with Laurette. I really wanted to laugh with someone. I couldn't laugh with Irwin because he wasn't in on the joke; the garden ghosts were between Sam and me. The Messenger house showed no signs of life, and I remembered that it was matinee day. Sam had two shows to do and stayed in his dressing room in between. I wondered if Shirley was going to take him supper, and for the first time I envied her. She could see him anytime she wanted to and, of course, I couldn't.

Chapter Five

There'd been a scene in our MacDougal Street house on the morning that we were supposed to go with the Messengers to Central Park. Jake stubbornly insisted that he wasn't going with us because he'd made a date with Joey McAdams, who lived at the other end of the garden, and besides he had nothing in common with Sandra, the younger Messenger daughter. She wasn't interested in jigsaw puzzles, baseball cards or the Pittsburgh Pirates, his passions of the moment. Emma screamed that there would be no one her age to play with, and if Jake wasn't going she wasn't going either. Danny was the only one happy with the plan because he had a secret crush on Annie Messenger, who had a not-so-secret crush on him. We finally settled it; Jake could go play at Joey's, and Emma could invite Maryellen to go with us.

I was frazzled and trying not to show it by the time we crossed the garden to the Messengers' at noon. There was then a discussion of how we would get up to Central Park. There were nine of us plus picnic baskets, and New York cabs could only take five—six if it was a Checker with jump seats.

Sam wanted to call for a limousine; the children wanted to take the bus, and the rest of us thought two cabs would be fine. We ended up in the cabs, Sam and Irwin in one with the three little girls, and Shirley and I with Danny and his true love. They sat in the jump seats, their heads and knees together, and whispered and laughed at shared secrets.

Shirley gave me a look that said, "Aren't they cute? Aren't they sweet, with all that puppy love?" I nodded and smiled, feeling awkward. It didn't seem that different from how I'd felt with Sam in the garden at midnight. Or that different from my feelings for my first love when I was thirteen. If I were simply recapturing the highs of infatuation long past, I really didn't care—it felt so good. But I certainly didn't want to share it with his wife. That was the essence of the awkwardness, which lasted all afternoon.

Sam didn't seem to feel it at all. He seemed to relish the secretiveness. On the carousel, with Shirley and the little girls ahead of us, he stood beside my rising-falling pony and slipped an arm around my waist. When I shivered and turned to him, he was looking up at me with teasing, knowing eyes. During our picnic, on a patch of brown, shaded grass, his hand lingered whenever he handed me something—a paper cup, a chip, a sandwich that I was then too nervous to eat. Shirley and Irwin didn't seem to notice. Irwin had taken an instant liking to Sam, to his humor, to his all-encompassing warmth, even to his star power. Sam wasn't a big star; he was a stage star after all. He could go places freely without attracting too much attention, but he still was stopped and admired and asked for autographs. He loved it, basked in it, and Irwin basked in it vicariously. It was a trait of Irwin's that irritated me. He loved the attention he got when he was with successful friends because he didn't believe that he could be successful himself.

Shirley's attitude toward Sam was one of bemused tolerance: "Oh, Sammy just needs the whole world to love him," she said, smiling at Sam as he charmed a park attendant who was sweeping nearby. "Look at that. He's been talking to that guy for ten minutes. Guy probably doesn't even speak English, but Sammy's going to make sure he loves him. He'll end up giving him free tickets to the show."

"We could use some of those," Irwin said, and I shot him a look. "I can ask, can't I?" Irwin said with a shrug and a grin.

"He gets house seats for every show," Shirley continued. "At a discount, not really free."

"I just gave the guy a couple seats for Friday—it's his anniversary," Sam said as he rejoined us on the grass, and Shirley let out a peal of indulgent laughter.

"I was just saying we'd love some tickets," Irwin said.

"I thought you'd seen it," Sam said, looking directly at me.

"We'd love to see it again," I answered quickly, feeling more uncomfortable than the situation called for.

"Hey, anytime. Just give me a call."

"Thanks," I murmured, as Sam stretched out beside Shirley and put his head in her lap. I watched, mesmerized, as she stroked his dark hair and his closed eyelids. I forced myself to look away toward the rocks where Danny and Annie were climbing, racing each other to the top.

"Quite a little climber you've got there," Irwin said, and Sam sat up, looking toward the small cliff that children loved to climb.

"Should I go help her?" Sam asked Shirley, clearly a bit worried.

"No, sweetie, she's just fine," she said, and turned to me, "Sammy's *so* overprotective." I nodded and smiled, feeling sick of being told everything I didn't want to know about "Sammy."

"Does anyone else call you Sammy?" I asked innocently.

"Just his mama," Shirley said, running her fingers through his hair.

On the way home Sam managed to change the cab distribution. He and I shared one with the three little girls, and Irwin and Shirley took the two older children. Sam's Sandra went to sleep on his lap, and Emma and Maryellen ignored us as they counted cars and buses.

"You coming out later?" Sam asked after a silence.

"It's Sunday."

"So? They'll be out like lights by ten at my house."

"I'll try," I said. "And I've been dying to tell you about my conversation with Laurette. She said, with a perfectly straight face, that the ghost we saw was little Lucy Van Eck. She's very shy, the ghost, I mean," I added, rolling my eyes.

"Is she now?" Sam asked, going along with it. "I can't wait."

There was another silence before I said quietly, aware of the girls, "You and Shirley seem really happy."

"And I hear you and Irwin are the perfect couple," Sam answered.

"In some ways we are."

"And in some ways *we* are," Sam said, and the conversation ended. I had the feeling that with Sam what was left out was often more important than what was said.

"I saw eight yellow buses," Emma said, turning to me, holding up seven fingers.

"That's seven, honey—one more." Emma studied her fingers and held up another.

"Eight!"

"That's right!"

"And I saw nine," Maryellen announced.

"Good for you," I said, and raised my eyebrows at Sam, who laughed and turned away. We were almost at Sullivan Street by then. When the cab pulled up in front of the Messenger house Sam paid the driver, cradled the still sleeping Sandra in his arms, and winked at me over the heads of the girls.

"Later," he said, and I mouthed to him that I would try. But Irwin was wired that evening, so pleased with our new friends, and the prospect of getting house seats for us and his clients, that he stayed up until at least eleven-thirty. We were both reading in the living room, with Joan Baez playing on the stereo, when I saw a tall shape approach our end of the garden. I was on the sofa, close to the bay window, and I watched the shape that I knew was Sam—too solid to be a ghost—wait, sit, pace, then give up and head back to the other end of the garden. I watched until he was out of sight, hidden by the rhododendron bushes.

Sam didn't appear for the next couple of nights. By Wednesday afternoon, when it was time for my session with Pricket, I was jumpy with anxiety.

"That could be it," I said, my voice unusually high. "I may never see him again, see him alone I mean. Shirley may have found out and—"

"Found out what?" Pricket asked, stopping me cold.

"I don't know," I said. "That he's been flirting with a neighbor?"

"Big deal," Pricket answered.

I met Ruthie after my totally unsatisfying session with Pricket, and told her that I didn't want to see the diet doctor; I was too edgy already. She looked at me curiously; I waited while she got weighed and got her uppers, and began telling her about Sam before we even got to the bus stop. On the bus going home, I told her every bit of it, stunned by my need to talk about Sam. It occurred to me that I needed to talk about my crush almost as much as I needed to do anything about it.

"She needs a good lay, if you ask me," Ruthie said.

"She does? Who?"

"Shirley, of course. She's got that look—you know."

"No, I don't. Do I have it?"

"Well, right this minute you sure do," Ruthie said and laughed.

"Oh, God," I said, embarrassed. "So what's the look? What makes people say that?"

"Desperation," Ruthie answered, still laughing. It was a throaty, sexy, contagious laugh, and I found myself laughing with her until I was wiping my eyes beneath my sunglasses.

"And how about you?" I asked, after our laughter dwindled. "You don't look desperate to me, but then again I can't tell."

"Believe me I'm not," Ruthie said, her voice low, her eyebrows dancing.

In the dark living room in the Alta Vista house, I turn off the set, stretch out on the sofa, and try to remember what obsession felt like. I'm older now; I don't have those feelings anymore, thank God. I can only bring them back in dreams. I'll wake in the middle of the night or at dawn with my heart hurting and a knot in my gut. The dreams are similar. They're either about Sam or Kirk, who had unexpectedly dumped me and married someone else. In the dreams either Sam or Kirk is with his wife, and I can't reach him. Shirley is going on about "Sammy this" or "Sammy that" and I try to catch his eye but I can't, or if I do he gives me a secretive kiss, makes a secret gesture, and then is gone. Sometimes, they are leaving with their families, and I have no idea where they're going, or how to reach them. I'm frantic, and wake with those awful feelings of longing and fear. Lying on the sofa, drifting off, the feelings begin to return.

During the months that I saw her Pricket delved deeply into my obsessive nature. She was sure that if I became aware of what had started all this, it would disappear. It didn't. I became aware, but my need and adoration of Sam only grew.

"I never meant for you to fall madly in love," Pricket said, unable to hide her scorn. "I just thought it might be good for you to have an affair."

"And I'd told you up front that I can't do that," I'd practically shouted.

"Fine. Let's look at that again. Why do you think you have to be in love to sleep with someone, and why does he have to be married?"

"Because I'm a total romantic like my father, who wrote love songs for a living, and I was jealous of my mother because she was married to him," I said belligerently.

"So you're still trying to break up your parents?"

"I guess!"

"And they're both dead."

"No shit?"

"So why do you feel the need to project—?"

"I Don't Know!" I'd interrupted.

I'd leave the sessions exhausted. We'd go over and over it—my warm, safe memories of my father, my jealousy of my mother. No, my father had never touched me where he shouldn't; yes, I'd thought at thirteen that my mother was the wicked witch in *Snow White*, but the probing, the awareness, seemed to have no effect on the present. I'd go home with nothing in my mind except how to get in touch with Sam, how to manage to see him again.

We had continued to meet in the garden around midnight a couple of times a week. Sometimes Sam couldn't get out, and sometimes I couldn't. As October turned into November, and all the leaves had fallen, the nights turned cold. We'd keep each other warm on a secluded bench, our breaths misting, and I'd live for the minutes when his arms would go around my heavy coat.

We still talked about the ghosts, and kept an eye out for them. We called Lucy by name now every time a wisp headed for the swings, and we wondered whether the young lovers felt the cold when they met here during the winter, but we mainly talked about ourselves, about our lives.

"I was such a sissy kid," Sam said one moonless night. "All I wanted to do was sing, play guitar and take ballet lessons."

"Ballet? Really?"

"Yeah." Sam laughed quietly. "My mother used to call me faygeleh."

"Like fag? You're kidding."

"No, it's Yiddish. It means little bird."

"Aw, the little bird," I said mockingly, feeling his muscled arms and chest. I was smiling up at him, and he kissed me for the first time. I'd thought it would never happen. I'd told Ruthie that I'd thought we might turn into icicles on this bench before it happened. But then it did, and was as lovely as my daydreams had been.

"That was so nice," I said, catching my breath, and then quickly looking around at the dark garden and the shuttered windows.

"We're going to freeze our asses out here pretty soon," Sam said. "Why don't you come up to the theater one day?"

"When?"

"Anytime. Between matinee and evening is the best time though—that's Wednesdays and Saturdays."

"I thought Shirley took you supper?" I said, without pretending innocence, "because you don't like to be alone."

"Oh, sometimes she does," Sam answered, with a slight grimace. "But not too often, and I'll know ahead of time."

"Then I'd love to come. Can I come this week?"

"Sure, but give me a call first. There's a phone in the dressing room." He told me the number, which I knew I would never forget, kissed me lightly, and we rose at the same time, heading for our separate gardens, separate houses.

Saturday wasn't a good day to get away. Irwin was home, and we usually did something with the children, a trip to a museum, or a visit with friends or family. But on the following Wednesday I called Sam at the theater at about one-thirty. I was scared, and hung up twice before I let the phone ring. A strange voice answered.

"Hello? Dressing room? Clayton here."

"Um, hi, it's Callie. Is Sam there?" There was a shuffling, and I heard Clayton, in the background, giving my name. More shuffling, and then:

"Hey . . . Hi, where are you?" Sam asked gently.

"I'm home," I said. "Can I come up?"

"Yeah, sure. Do you want to see the show?"

"Yes, if it's okay?"

"Sure, I'll leave a pass at the front. Just walk in anytime, stand at the back, or sit if there's an empty, and come back right after. Go through the curtains on the left, where it says exit, and you're on the stage."

"I don't have to go to the stage door?"

"Uh-uh. I've gotta go. See you later." I heard the click and hung up with damp, shaky fingers. Maddy, our sweet, sixty-something cleaning lady, who at times looked after the kids, was in the laundry room when I found her and asked if she could stay later than usual, and give the children supper. She was happy to; she was a lonely widow, and would always rather stay than go back to her empty apartment in Flushing. I thanked her, overpaid her, and then took about half an hour to calm myself down, get dressed and put makeup on.

There was a pass with my name on it at the box office, and I walked into the Schubert Theatre in the middle of the first act. I stood at the back, right behind the last row, and watched Sam with all my senses wide open as he sang, danced and held the stage as Nathan Detroit. I didn't remember him being so graceful, so sensual the first time I'd seen *Guys and Dolls* with Irwin. But that was before our midnight meetings, before that first kiss on a moonless night, and this time I felt as if I were feasting on him. I could soak him in at the back of the dark theater without worrying, for a second, about what he thought of me. I decided, standing there, that I would buy a pair of opera glasses so that I could see him up close from where I stood. I wouldn't miss a single gesture or nuance. Unobserved, I could focus in on his dark eyes, his gentle lips and his beautiful arms.

During intermission I milled around the lobby, smoking, listening to comments and bits of conversations. It was mainly an audience of older women, out on the town on matinee day. Most of their comments were positive—they loved the show, loved Sam, but a couple of them said that they thought he was too old for the part. I grinned inwardly. What would they give for my midnight kiss, I wondered? What would they give, at this moment, to be me?

When the final curtain came down and the applause began I walked slowly down the aisle on the left toward the exit sign, clapping as I went, along with the audience. I even called out a bravo as Sam took his solo bow. Then I slipped between the dark velvet curtains that led backstage. In the dim light actors were hurrying every which way to dressing rooms. I passed a large lighting panel, saw someone who looked like a stage manager, and asked where I would find Sam Messenger. He pointed in the direction I was heading, and stepping over wires and ropes, I reached a flight of metal steps. At the top of the short flight there was a carpeted hallway, and a partially open door with Sam's name on it. I hesitated, then tapped on the door. A tall, thin man with ink-black skin, a shaved head and a gold earring peered around the door and then opened it for me. Sam was behind him at his dressing table, wiping cold cream off his face, and chatting with a young couple.

"Callie, come on in," Sam called out.

"Hi, I'm Callie," I said to everyone, and then thought that was pretty stupid—he'd just told them my name.

"This is Clay Morgan, my dresser, my right hand *and* leg," Sam went on as I shook Clay's hand, "and Mimi and Arthur. Mimi's Shirley's cousin."

"Once removed," Mimi said lightly.

"Whatever that means," Sam said. "I've never figured that out."

"Some kind of cousin," Mimi said and laughed, tossing a full head of blond curls. I shook their hands, feeling even more uncomfortable than when I'd entered, and noticed that Mimi did look like Shirley, just younger and thinner.

"Callie's a neighbor," Sam said, tossing the Kleenex and turning from the mirror. There were still spots of greasepaint around his ears and his hairline. And I was aware for the first time that he was just wearing boxer shorts, an open shirt and gartered black socks. "She came to see the show."

"You hadn't seen it before?" Arthur asked.

"Not really," I said, thinking to myself that that was a ridiculous answer. I really would have to learn how to lie, or I'd never be able to pull this off. "But it was great," I added quickly. "And I guess I should be going."

"No, don't," Sam said. "Mimi and Arthur just stopped by, and Clay's about to get some supper."

"We're in the midst of moving. Boxes everywhere," Mimi said to me as if that explained everything. "Bye, sweetie," she said to Sam, kissing his cheek, and with a wave she and Arthur were out the door.

"Hokay, boss," Clay said. "Tuna on rye and a chocolate shake?"

"Sounds good, but give it about an hour. I'm gonna take a nap."

"You got it. Nice to meet you, Callie." And Clay was gone, closing the door behind him.

Sam leaned back in his chair and smiled up at me, his eyes teasing. "Not really? How do you not really see a show?"

"Oh, God, I know," I said, covering my face with my hands. He laughed then, and reached out, pulling me down into his lap. We kissed, sitting there, and then he jerked his head toward an open door behind him.

"Come into my cave with me?" he asked, dislodging me, and then leading me into the small room behind the doorway. It was dark, with one soot-stained window that looked out on a brick wall. There was a worn sofa, a low table next to it, a clothes rack with old, musty costumes, and that was it. Sam closed and locked the door that led into the dressing room and reached for me again. I could barely see him. We fumbled toward the sofa, fumbled with clothes, and then made love in ways I'd never dreamed of. That was when I became addicted to Sam's body. I'd been obsessed with other aspects of him, but that afternoon I became addicted to his touch, to the feel of him. Not that it was such a great body; he *was* forty-five and looked it, with a slight paunch below the barrel chest, bowed, hairy legs in the socks and garters that never came off.

It was what he did with that body, and with his arms and hands, that hooked me.

There was no thought during our lovemaking, only afterward. After a shared cigarette, he'd given me a sleepy kiss goodbye, and I'd dressed in the dark. As I found my way to the stage door and Schubert Alley, all I could think was that I'd had no idea what I'd been missing. After twelve years of marriage and three children, I'd had absolutely no idea. I kept thinking this as I felt Sam on my skin and inside me. I walked for blocks, not knowing how I could handle the transition. How could I walk in the door and be Mom and Irwin's wife with Sam still within and without? It took me a long time to get home.

Chapter Six

I hadn't been able to see Sam at the theater again during the couple of weeks before Thanksgiving. Either I couldn't make it, or he'd had visitors. We'd met a few times in the garden at midnight, and kissed and held each other, and chatted about nothing, all of which left me yearning for more. I daydreamed a lot, locked myself in the bathroom more than usual, and avoided Irwin physically. I told Pricket that Irwin would have to notice soon, have to say something, and I didn't know what I would do. "Fake it," Pricket had said, which I told Ruthie was no help whatsoever—as usual, Pricket just didn't get it.

Ruthie didn't get it either. She was juggling Josh and Kevin just fine, she said. Of course, Josh was twenty years older, and didn't seem to require that much sex anymore. The person who did understand took me completely by surprise. The angular, aristocratic Diana Lawrence rushed up to me in the garden one wind-blown November afternoon and asked whether I would mind if someone phoned her at my house every once in a while.

"Would you mind terribly running over to get me? It wouldn't be that often?" Diana asked, her cheeks red-spotted from embarrassment and the wind.

"No, if I'm home, of course not. Who—?" I started to ask, and broke off when I saw the anguished look on Diana's face. "Oh, it doesn't matter. If anyone calls for you, I'll come and get you."

"Thank you. Thanks, Callie, so much," Diana said. She squeezed my hands for a second, then turned and walked stiffly back across the garden. I didn't find out what this was about until a couple of days later. It was late morning when the phone rang and a man's voice asked for Diana. I said I'd have to look for her—it might take a couple of minutes. He'd said that that was fine, he'd hold on, and I'd run across to Diana's garden door, called up the stairs to her, and she'd dashed back across the garden to my phone. She'd pulled a kitchen chair close to the wall phone and sat, hunched, her back to the garden and our world, as she spoke softly into the receiver. I went upstairs, to the other end of the small house, knowing what Diana was feeling. She and her lover, whoever he was, were in that enclosed space that held just the two of them. I knew it well.

It took Diana a while to tell me about her affair, and she never told me who the man was. The calls came infrequently, only when he really needed to reach Diana and there was no other way. I listened to his voice when he asked for her, didn't recognize it, and decided he wasn't anyone I knew. Diana confirmed that when she told me about him. And she said that she was in love, torn apart, and didn't know what to do. I had let out a long breath of relief. Finally someone else knew what it was like to be in love with someone other than your husband. I didn't count Ruthie because she was too pragmatic about the whole thing.

Diana and I had our first long talk a few days before Thanksgiving. We were both dreading the holidays. All the participants in our small, but all-consuming, dramas would be separated by various family reunions. We'd be with "families" for four whole days. Both of us said the word as if we couldn't think of anything worse, and then, blushing with shame, burst out laughing.

Our bedroom windows faced the garden, and the backs of the Sullivan Street houses. Getting dressed on Thanksgiving morning, I kept being drawn to the windows, glancing through the gray day and the bare trees to Sam's windows, looking for a light turned on or off, looking for any signs of life that would reassure me. I needed to know that he was there, that I would leave, that he would leave, and that we would both come back, to touch again and kiss again at midnight. It somehow mattered less that we lived in separate houses than that we both lived in the garden, and that we'd both come back.

It took a while to get the children dressed in proper clothes, Emma in a dress and tights, the boys in pressed corduroys and navy blazers. While I brushed hair, found shoes and handled the resistance, Irwin went to the garage on Eighth Avenue to get the car, and then bought pies at the bakery on Bleecker Street to take with us. I took one last look across the garden before we left, saw no one, and we all piled into the Rambler station wagon. We were stopping first at Irwin's mother's apartment, and then going on to Greenwich.

There was almost no traffic on the West Side Highway on Thanksgiving morning; it was all on Central Park West, and we were able to get across to the gated, cavernous building on 79th Street where Dorothy Epstein had lived for the past thirty years. Her husband, Irwin's father, had died of heart failure seven years earlier, but Dorothy had no desire to leave Upper Broadway and the dreary, spacious apartment that faced the inner courtyard. The apartment never saw a ray of sunlight, and barely enough daylight to see by. The lamps, beneath their plastic-covered shades, were always lit, and I could never figure out why the furniture got slipcovers every spring. Habit, I supposed. All in all it was not a homey place, and Dorothy was not a homey grandmother.

We had come for brunch because we avoided other meals like the plague. Dorothy was a terrible cook. She served overcooked vegetables, usually at least three starches in one meal, and as Irwin liked to say, chicken that was raw under the armpits. Brunch couldn't be too badly damaged, so we were delighted to learn that she was going to her sister's for the holiday meal, and could only see us in the morning. We ate bagels and lox and canned fruit salad at the dark mahogany dining table in the dark dining room that looked out on other dark windows that faced the courtyard below.

As I listened to Dorothy complain about the price of meat, the new doorman who spoke no English, how much knitting she had to do, and the children these days—especially mine it was implied—who had no manners whatsoever, I wondered how Irwin had ever chosen me. Dorothy and I seemed to be total opposites. She was cool, critical and narrow. I was overly emotional, overly empathetic and tended to blubber. So, I decided in that moment, that maybe we were the same person, just the flip side—hot/cold, narrow/broad, reserved/effusive. I wondered what our shared core was, and came to the dreadful conclusion that we were both selfish as hell.

The awful thought hit me somewhere on the Saw Mill River Parkway as we headed toward Greenwich. Danny was tormenting Jake in the back of the station wagon by continually rolling over onto Jake's pillow. Jake was possessive about his pillow; he'd brought it along to sleep on in the car and he didn't want anyone, particularly his brother, to touch it. So Jake was yelling, Danny was laughing maniacally, Emma was telling both of them to shut up, and Irwin was threatening to turn the car around and go home.

"Hey, quiet!" I called out to the back of the car, turning in my seat and focusing entirely on my children. I was determined to stop being selfish, to stop thinking about Sam, to stop myself from seeing his smiling face in front of my eyes, reflected from the clouds and the treetops as we passed. I was determined to think only of my children, my husband, my family—it was, after all, Thanksgiving Day.

"Do you want to sing something?" I asked, after they'd grumbled, but settled down.

"Oh, Mommy, no," they said, almost in unison, and Irwin and I looked at each other and laughed. Singing was not my strong point.

"Okay, how about a story?"

"Yes!" they said. "The frog one, the mouse one, the snowman one!" So I combined all three, telling them a story about a frog and a mouse who made a snowman, and for several minutes, as I had their full attention, and they had mine, I felt like a good mother. It didn't last long. Once we reached Greenwich, and Grandma Helen's house on the water, I'd retreated back into my daydreams. I remember wondering what it would be like to be married to someone I loved in the way that I loved Sam. Not that I loved Sam more, just differently. What would it be like to drive the Saw Mill River Parkway with Sam as my husband? To have the children in the back be his and mine? I could barely imagine so much happiness.

I asked Helen about it after dinner, while we were cleaning up. I wasn't giving anything away, not about Sam or my marriage, just asking about love. It was strange because I was drying my mother's dishes at the same time that I was asking her replacement about love. I knew that Helen had been in love with my father before and after my mother's death. And my father, the romantic, who'd brought me up on Keats, Shelley, Gershwin and his own yearning melodies, had left my mother for the younger and softer Helen. But they'd only had six years together before my father's heart had given out. I'd thought, at times, that like Danny's little squirrel, he might have died of too much love.

"What was it like," I asked finally, feeling disloyal because I was still drying my mother's dishes that had been left to Helen, "to live with someone every day, every night, every minute, that you were crazy about?"

"It was heaven," Helen answered, with a curious, sidelong glance. "But you know that. It just—just didn't last long enough."

"I know. But suppose it had, lasted longer I mean—do you think it would have faded, just got comfortable like people say happens?"

"I don't know." And after another sidelong look: "Are you asking about you and Irwin? Is the love fading or—?"

"No, not like that," I said quickly.

"Because I think you were so lucky to have found him." Helen said with an unusual degree of firmness.

"Because I was such a mess?" I asked, laughing.

"Well, yes," Helen said, smiling. "And because he's such a dear man."

"Yes, he is," I said, and we both looked out the kitchen window where Irwin was patiently showing the children what to do with a badminton racket and a bird. The net had been put away for the winter so they were just batting the birds around the backyard. I turned away, and began carrying the dried dishes, the good china, into the dining room to place them snugly in their cabinets. I put them first on the dining room table, the one that had been made for my mother in the forties.

I ran my hand over its veneered surface, saw my mother for a second sitting at this table, smoking, the ebony cigarette holder held close to her face, and then saw a glimpse of her in the small apartment she'd moved to after my father had left her for Helen. She'd been strained, sallow and very thin, barely ninety-five pounds, and I'd urged her to remember to eat when I'd visited from college. I'd looked in the refrigerator in the apartment's Pullman kitchen and seen only some pâté, some olives, a tin of anchovies and a bottle of wine.

With my hand on her beautiful table I promised her that I would never hurt anyone the way that she'd been hurt. No matter how trapped I felt with Irwin, no matter how infatuated I was with Sam, I'd never hurt Irwin the way that she'd been hurt. I'd never tell him about Sam; I'd never leave him. I made a promise that Thanksgiving Day that I found increasingly difficult to keep.

I hear Jake's voice in the middle of a sentence on the answering machine, and make a dash for the phone. I feel as if I'm emerging from underwater as I reach for the receiver, turning off the machine.

"Hi, honey. Sorry I didn't hear the phone."

"Did I wake you?" Jake asks.

"No, I've been up since six. Are you okay? Where are you?"

"I'm fine, back in town. I spent the weekend with Dad and Kathleen."

"Oh? How was it?" I ask, aware of the tightening of my throat as I try to sound natural.

"Fine," Jake says. "A little boring, but fine. So how come you were up at six?"

"I got all involved in our old home movies while I was packing. Remember, the ones I put on video for Danny?"

"Yeah, sure. Hold on to them, okay?"

"Of course. And, Jake, I have to tell you—you were *so* adorable."

"I know," Jake says wryly. "I *used* to be adorable."

"You still are," I answer laughing. "D'you know when you're coming back, any idea?"

"After you move," Jake says, in the same wry tone. Then quickly, "Seriously, how's it going? Do you need anything?"

"No, it's going fine. Friends are going to help this week, then Emma's coming down to finish packing with me over the weekend. The movers come Monday morning, and I drive up to Santa Rosa."

"Not by yourself," Jake says, very aware of my ability to get lost.

"No, I'm going to follow Emma."

"Good," Jake says, "because it could be the Donner Party all over again."

"Very funny. Oh, I forgot to tell you, I'm supposed to see Ruthie. She's in town for the week."

"Say hi," Jake says. "See how Adam's doing. I've gotta go. I love you."

"I love you too," I say. "'Bye." I hang up, warmed by the conversation, warmed by the essence of Jake. The past doesn't matter that much right now. But then I think of seeing Ruthie, of Jake and Adam when they were little, of a snowman they built in the garden at Christmas. It snowed a lot the December of 1967. Snow bent the branches of the decorated pine in the center of the garden, dimmed its lights, and obscured the garden-facing windows, some displaying wreaths, others Hanukkah candles.

The weeks between Thanksgiving and Christmas 1967 were, perhaps, the hardest to get through. We kept being thrown together, Sam and Shirley, Irwin and I, at various gatherings. There was the holiday assembly; we met, by accident, on Bleecker Street on the way to the school, and then sat together—Shirley, Sam, then me, then Irwin. Shirley's cousin Mimi, whom I'd met briefly in the dressing room, joined us, and we all moved over one seat so that she could squeeze in beside Shirley. I prayed that she wouldn't mention our meeting, and sat there trying to think of plausible explanations for my presence at the theater that day. I couldn't think of any, and decided that I'd have to get Irwin out of there as soon as the assembly was over.

The program consisted of holiday scenes from different countries and different nationalities. Danny and Sam's Annie played in the orchestra; Jake and Adam were two of the three kings and belted out "We Three Kings of Orient Are"; Emma, looking like a little Carmen, danced in a celebration of I-wasn't-sure-what. By that time Sam's leg was playing with mine, and we were desperately trying to keep straight faces. It *was* silly, with Irwin and Shirley on either side of us, but at the same time I found it torturous. I wanted to be near Sam, and I didn't want to be near him. I wanted to stay and feel him, breathe him in next to me, and I wanted to run home and hide.

The latter won out. As soon as the assembly ended, amidst cheers and applause from parents and grandparents, I dashed into the hallway where the excited children were gathered, kissed and congratulated mine, and darted out the door. I ran the couple of blocks home, ran past Maddy in the kitchen, and ran upstairs and into bed, where I feigned an upset stomach for the rest of the day.

A few days later Laurette Tompkins called and invited me to a Sunday evening meeting at her house. "You seemed interested in the ghosts," Laurette said, "and a few of us old garden folk meet every couple of months to share ghost stories, fill each other in on any recent activity."

"Ghostly activity?" I asked.

"Pretty much," Laurette answered. "And if your husband wants to come he's welcome, of course."

Irwin wasn't interested, so I found myself sitting on a sofa next to Sam in the Tompkinses' living room, waiting for the meeting to start. Happily, Shirley hadn't been interested either, and Sam and I were able to exchange glances, to touch hands by accident without worrying that we were being watched. Diana arrived, but not Ruthie, being much too practical for things like ghosts. Ninety-year-old Iris Dakin made it across the icy garden with her sixty-year-old daughter, Brenda. Paul and Henry, middle-aged men who lived together in the house closest to Houston, showed up a few minutes late, followed by Susan MacAdams, Jake's friend Joey's young, copper-haired mother.

Hal and Laurette served coffee, cookies and pungent mulled wine, and I noticed that most of the Scientology leaflets and posters had been put away. Everyone talked about the spirits they'd seen, and what their favorite phantoms were up to, as if this were a perfectly rational discussion.

"Have you seen dear little Lucy lately?" Iris Dakin asked the room. "I'm afraid she may have left us."

"Oh, dear, no," said Brenda.

"The little girl who likes the swings?" I asked tentatively. As they nodded, all eyes on me, I added, "I saw her a couple weeks ago. I think Sam did too." I turned to him, questioningly, nudging him at the same time, to remind him that we hadn't seen anything together.

"Yeah, I saw her on the swings," Sam said. "But, come to think of it, I haven't seen her since it snowed. Maybe she doesn't like the cold," he said, looking around hopefully.

"I'd forgotten that," Iris Dakin said quickly. "I used to play with her when we were little, before she got that dreadful fever and passed on. Yes, my dear Sam, Lucy hated the cold, especially the snow and ice. Thank you for reminding me."

"Don't mention it," Sam mumbled, as both Laurette and Brenda talked over him.

"You see, Mother?"

"Not to worry, Iris, the first bright day."

"Does she have any influence on the Captain?" Henry asked. "Because he's been noisier than usual."

"He has," Susan said shyly. "I've noticed too."

"Rattling his sabers?" Iris asked.

"Or swords," Henry said. "Something metal and clanging, anyway."

"And shouting 'Charge' or something like that," Susan added. "You know, like the old guy in *Arsenic and Old Lace.*" Everyone nodded in recognition, and I noticed Sam turning to Susan as if aware, for the first time, that she was pale and freckled and very pretty. I nudged Sam again, distracting him.

"What war had he been in?" I asked. "The Civil War?"

"No, I think the Boer War," Laurette said. "Same as the Captain. He thinks it's still going on."

"Well, can't somebody set him straight?" Paul asked. "Because he's really keeping us up at night. Susan too, it sounds like."

"He does like Lucy," Brenda said. "Maybe when she's

back. And he was in love with Amy Van Eck, but that went nowhere."

"Why not?"

"She was married with three or four children," Brenda answered with a shrug, and I turned to Sam, hoping for a meaningful glance, but he was leaning forward, whispering to Susan.

"Sam," I said, more urgently than I meant to, "didn't you say you'd seen a young couple?"

"What? Oh, yeah," he said, turning back to the group.

"You must have seen Heloise and Abelard. That's what we call them—we don't know their names," Laurette said.

"Such a sweet pair," Iris said, her ancient eyes filling with tears.

At the end of the meeting, which lasted only about an hour, Hal and Laurette, holding hands in front of their fireplace, announced that they had recently opened their church. They'd rented a space, with the backing of the main church, of course, at the corner of 11th and Sixth, right above Blimpie's. It was called Scientology in the Village, and they'd love for all of us to stop by anytime.

"If you want to find out about your past lives," Laurette said, "or find better ways to contact our loving spirits, or if you simply want to be a better communicator, Scientology has the answers." She then handed out cards to all of us, and we pocketed them as we made our way out the garden door. None of us knew all that much about Scientology at the time, so her proselytizing wasn't given a second thought.

"Walk me home?" I asked Sam before he had a chance to

do anything else. I clutched his arm as I started to skid on a patch of ice. Frozen slush had been sprinkled with ashes, but there were treacherous spots.

"Oh, Sam, dear," Iris Dakin called out, "could you help us across?"

"Be right there," Sam called back. They were going over to Sullivan, while I was going to the other end of MacDougal.

"All the ladies love you," I said sweetly.

"Yes, they do," Sam answered. Then softly, "Wednesday? After the matinee?"

"Wednesday," I said, releasing his arm, and then watched him as he went to the rescue of his elderly neighbors.

At home I found Irwin reading a Narnia book to the children. He'd given them baths, and they were shiny-faced in their pajamas as they snuggled next to him on the sofa.

"How was it?" Irwin asked, glancing up at me.

"Creepy."

"Shush," Emma said. "We wanna hear the story."

"Sorry," I whispered, and settled into the stuffed chair across from them. Irwin resumed reading, and I closed my eyes, listening to the drone of his voice, and thinking about Wednesday. I didn't have to go; I could go another time, or end this whole dilemma and not go at all. But I didn't think I could do that. I didn't think I could stand the idea of not seeing Sam again. Or worse, seeing Sam but not being with him again. I'd promised not to hurt Irwin, not to ever let him know, but that didn't mean that I couldn't have another Wednesday. With the holidays closing in, invisible walls of separation, this could be our last opportunity.

I left the house early that Wednesday, telling everyone that

I was going Christmas shopping, which I was. I arrived at the theater with two full shopping bags of wrapped presents, took from my purse the small, inlaid mother-of-pearl opera glasses I'd bought, and feasted on Sam for the last twenty minutes of the show. As the cast took their bows I made my way backstage. I knew where I was going this time, and arrived outside Sam's dressing room without being noticed. I could hear him, as I came up the stairs, wooing somebody, and I remembered Shirley saying that Sam needs to have everybody love him. I waited in the corridor and eavesdropped.

"Hey, bring the kids next time," Sam was saying. "Kids love this show."

"I'll do that, you can bet on it," the man answered. His voice was gravelly, and I could hear a distinct Jersey accent. A woman chimed in, saying what a treat it had been, and then Sam kept them amused, asking questions, listening to the story of their lives for at least another ten minutes. They've gotta love him by now, I muttered to myself. They left finally, after hugs and kisses, and I poked my head in the door.

"Hi, cutie, thought you'd changed your mind," Sam said, rising and opening his arms.

"I was waiting for your friends to leave," I said, fitting myself against him. "Who were they?"

"I haven't any idea," Sam answered.

"You're kidding?" I said, looking up at him.

"I'm kidding," Sam said, and laughed. "You are so gullible. Has anybody told you that?"

"Everybody." I made a face and Sam kissed me quickly.

"You probably believed those nutty old ladies the other night."

"They were so serious," I said, then mimicked, "'Our darling little Lucy.'"

"'We played together before she passed,'" Sam said in a wavering falsetto, and we both laughed and kissed again. He began leading me back to his hideaway.

"Wait a sec," I said, and rummaged in one of the shopping bags until I found a small wrapped present.

"Oh, I don't have anything yet," Sam said, looking dismayed.

"That's okay—whenever. Go on, open it."

"Later," Sam said, kissing me, and leading me again into the narrow, darkened room.

"Later," I echoed, my body craving his. The room smelled of him—sweat, makeup, cigarettes, cold cream, the essence of Sam—and I drank it all in as he locked the door, and we both began shedding clothes. It took me longer since Sam was only wearing an old, checked dressing gown, but Sam helped, removing boots and stockings and sweater so slowly I thought I was going to go out of my mind. Finally we were both naked, except for Sam's black socks and garters, and our lovemaking was even more delicious than it had been the first time.

Sam dozed for a couple of minutes afterward, and I stayed very still against his wet chest, telling myself to remember this moment—the sounds, the scents, the sensations, every bit of it—so I could bring it back at will, days from now or years from now.

Sam woke, playful and hungry. He wanted his lunch, which Clay had said he would leave outside the dressing room door, and he wanted his present. We found lunch for two outside the door, relocked it and devoured our sandwiches. Then slowly, as carefully as my stockings, Sam unwrapped the silver whistle and key chain I'd bought for him.

"I love it," Sam said. "Every time I put my lips together and blow I'll think of you."

"That's the point," I said.

It was still rush hour when I left the theater, impossible to get a cab, so I lugged my packages onto a downtown bus. I didn't want to fight the crowded subway, and the slow bus ride—the stops and starts and waits—gave me time to relive the minutes with Sam, to imprint them on my brain, and then to prepare for the burst of the children at the front door, their excitement over the packages, and Irwin's never-changing, smiling face.

The excitement built each day as we got closer to Christmas. The children were out of school, full of the things they had to do, the secret gifts they had to buy, and I was in my usual pre-holiday panic. I was always sure that I wouldn't get it all done in time. I was busy, and thought I was happy, juggling my family and my silent thoughts of Sam until unexpectedly, at a preposterous moment, I began to sob. We were in the middle of Fifth Avenue, crossing to Rockefeller Center and the bright, giant tree, when I suddenly began to cry so hard I was blinded. Irwin and the children had to help me across to the sidewalk. I continued to sob, sputtering, eyes and nose running, icy against my skin.

"What's the matter? What's wrong, Mommy?" Irwin and the children asked at the same time. Irwin pulled out a handkerchief and I held it to my face as the kids tried to hold me. I shook my head; I couldn't get any words out. They persisted. "What's the matter? What's wrong?"

"It's all a lie," I said finally.

"What is?" Irwin asked, bewildered.

"This—all this," I said, still crying. Irwin looked stunned. I think it was the first time that he grasped the idea that things weren't just fine. The children looked confused and irritated; they were eager to get to the dazzling tree that beckoned, only a block away.

"I'll take you home," Irwin said.

"No, no, I'll get a cab," I said quickly. I blew kisses to the kids, told them to have fun, that I'd be fine, and dashed back across Fifth and into the nearest taxi.

The phone again jerks me back to the present. I hear Ruthie's voice on the machine, and before I can get to it, she says that she's in the car and she'll meet me at the Bistro at twelve-thirty. I would have canceled if I'd reached the phone in time, but I didn't, so I shower, put on a clean shirt and jeans, leave the house and the past, and head for Ventura Boulevard. I walk a couple of blocks, beneath the flowering fruit trees, cross the footbridge over the L.A. River, which is just a stagnant stream at this time of year, and head for the lunch spot Ruthie has chosen, thinking about her.

I start to smile, and then to laugh as I think about Ruthie. I consider her the luckiest of the various women I knew back then in the garden. Her secret affair with Kevin continued for a couple of years, both of them adoring Josh, her husband and Kevin's mentor, until Josh dropped dead one day, leaving everything to Ruthie. She got the money, the Sag Harbor house, the garden house, and in a not-quite-suitable period of time married Kevin. They've been happily married ever since, and I consider her the luckiest because she got everything she wanted without a struggle. The rest of us struggled a lot, and didn't often get what we wanted.

Chapter Seven

Ruthie and I gossip, nibble on salads and kill a bottle of wine. Ruthie looks very stylish, very New York in the midst of the Studio City lunch-hour crowd. Her gray hair frames her narrow face, her suede jacket and platform shoes are just right, and her dimples are still girlish when she smiles. Almost everyone else looks like me, except younger. Young writers, producers, assistants, from the nearby studios, all wearing jeans, shirts, vests, as I am, but none of them over thirty, and most look about twenty. Another reason to leave my sweet, jasmine-scented house, and go north, east, anywhere.

"Where do they put the old people?" Ruthie asks, glancing around, picking up on this. "In New York they're everywhere. Here, they're invisible."

"Hidden behind walls of oleander in Woodland Hills, and other places nobody would be caught dead in," I answer, and shake my head warningly as Ruthie pulls out a cigarette. "Can't smoke in here. In L.A. it's the greatest sin known to man."

"Yeah, yeah, right," Ruthie says, putting the cigarette away. Then she smiles, and begins to laugh. "Do you remember when that crazy dog of yours ate all my pot? In that dumb little house you had with the rented furniture?"

"The Whitsett house," I say, laughing too.

"When was that, seventy?"

"The awful year of 1971," I answer, with a nod, remembering. Ruthie had come to visit during that smoggy, steaming summer, not long after I'd paid off Meekel and the IRS. She'd left her straw bag in the empty living room, chatted with me for a while in the den, and then as she was about to leave, we heard the sound of the vacuum. We found Emma diligently vacuuming the living room carpet, and Blanca howling with delight.

"What are you doing?" I asked, stepping on the switch that turned off the machine.

"Blanca must've brought a bunch of leaves in. I just cleaned it up," Emma said, pleased with herself.

"Oh, my God," Ruthie said, picking up the beach bag and the torn bit of plastic inside. "I had half a pound of marijuana!" We'd laughed then too, even though Ruthie was clearly upset about the loss. The leaves that Blanca hadn't eaten were in the vacuum bag, mixed with a week's worth of spiders and dirt, and irretrievable. Blanca had howled happily for a few more minutes, rolling on the carpet as if it were the softest grass, and then quietly passed out.

"I don't know how you got through it," Ruthie says. "That time, I mean."

"I don't either," I say, and quickly shift the subject to the garden—who's still there? Who has she seen?

"Let's see, you knew Brenda Dakin died, not long after her mother. Some relative got the house and is breaking it up into apartments. Laurette and Hal moved to their place in Bedford."

"Were they still Scientologists?" I ask.

"Oh, I don't know. I wasn't ever into that. And Diana's great. She's a big-time editor these days."

"I know. I hear from her occasionally."

"And Shirley's big as a house," Ruthie continues. "Really, you should come and stay with us, and take a look at her."

"She used to be zaftig," I say, laughing. "That's what Sam said, anyway."

"Believe me, zaftig doesn't begin to cover it," Ruthie says, and we both laugh, though I feel a bit guilty about it. I'm only partly responsible for ruining Shirley's life—only one slice of the whole, lethal pie—but I don't feel that I should laugh about it.

"Really, you should come and visit," Ruthie insists. "You haven't been to the garden in how long?"

"Not since I left," I answer quietly.

"That's right. We'd meet for lunch or dinner, but you'd never come down . . ." She trails off, and there's a pause before I answer.

"Maybe I like to remember it like it was," I say. "Sag Harbor too. I haven't been there either."

"It's so different," Ruthie says. "All the Hamptons, Sagaponack, Amagansett, it's all so different."

"I know. That's why I don't want to go."

"Our house is the same though, our house in the woods. Maybe you'll come one day. Kevin and I would be thrilled."

"Maybe," I answer, quite sure that I never will.

After lunch Ruthie drives me back to my house in her rented sports car. I don't know one car from another, but Ruthie certainly does, and she looks dashing, driving with the top down, wearing aviator glasses that cover half her face. She parks in the driveway, we kiss cheeks, and I'm almost to the porch before she asks if she can come in.

"I'd love to see one of the garden videos," she says. "I don't have any movies from then, just photos of Josh and Adam . . ."

"They're all mixed up," I answer, not really wanting company, not wanting to share private memories. "It might take a while to find one."

"That's okay," Ruthie says, cutting the engine, gathering her purse, phone and keys. "I've got a couple hours to kill."

In the living room Ruthie sits in the rocker close to the television, and by chance I pick a video of the garden at Christmas, the Christmas I'd been thinking about. It's festive, with piled snow, Christmas lights, candles and moonlight.

"It's Christmas," Ruthie says excitedly. "Oh, my God, look at the kids, they're so little! There's Adam and Jake," she says, laughing, and pointing at the screen. "They are so adorable."

"That's what I told Jake the other day."

"And there's Josh and me," Ruthie says, her voice and face sobering. "Oh, my Josh, look at us," she adds quietly.

"Josh was great," I mumble.

"Yeah . . . This must have been Christmas Eve, when the kids sang carols, and we were all around the tree. What year? Wait, don't tell me—'68?"

"Sixty-seven."

"Right. And there you are, and Irwin, and he's carrying

Emma. Look, we're so young—we look like kids ourselves. And so sixties, in our boots and minis. And there's Annie running over to Joey what's-his-name, and Laurette looking like a frump, and Diana like a damn goddess." I simply nod as she gives a running commentary, and then inadvertently suck in my breath as Sam and Shirley appear, coming from their garden.

"There's the Messengers," Ruthie exclaims. "Oh, my goodness, Sammy was awful cute then too."

"Sammy?" I ask quickly, suspiciously. "Did you call him that?"

"Not to his face," Ruthie says, her eyes fixed on the screen. "We used to make fun of Shirley, always going on about Sammy here, Sammy there, Sammy this, Sammy that. It really got obnoxious. Not like he was a big star or anything."

"I dunno. I thought he was a star."

"*You* thought he was a star," Ruthie says with a grin. "More like a second lead. Who did he replace in *Guys and Dolls*?"

"Nobody. It was a revival," I answer, getting annoyed. I'm ready for Ruthie to leave so that I can simply gaze at Sam's young face again.

"It was sad about Sam," she says after a moment.

"Yes . . ."

Finally, she gathers her things, puts out her cigarette, puts on her glasses, and heads out the door. "That was fun! Come see us," she calls from the car.

"Soon," I say and wave, and close the front door with relief. I reclaim the rocking chair, and stop the tape on Sam's smiling face. I look into his eyes, smile back at his image, and then rewind to the shot of Irwin and me. Irwin also looks young and handsome, and I think—poor guy—this was right before I broke his heart and all hell broke loose. Oh, please, it mended rather quickly, or Kathleen mended it rather quickly, so how broken could it have been? I send the tape forward again, watch the children singing, soundless, around the tree, take in the brightness of a clear, city night, and remember a recent dream. It's a dream that I've had often over the years: I'm back in the garden with Irwin, and I'm wondering how I got back here. I feel trapped, and a bit frantic, and I think in the dream, "But I worked so hard to get free. How did I get back here?"

During one of my last sessions with Pricket we talked about freedom. Why did I want it so much? What did I think it was?

"I don't know, I've never had it," I said.

"Let's see, you haven't had success, or a career, or a boat, or a horse either—"

"I had a horse," I interrupted.

"Sorry, you had a horse. My point is there are all sorts of things you've never had, so why are you fixated on freedom?"

"Because I could do what I want," I practically shouted at her.

"Marry Sam?" she asked, curling her lips. "You'd be about as free as a geisha."

"No, I want the choice! I want to be able to be with him or not. I want to be able to walk out the door without everyone having to know where I'm going. I want to be able to have my own money, and spend it without asking Irwin. I want to be able to get up in the middle of the night without Irwin getting up and following me!"

"You don't want to be married," Pricket said flatly.

"Isn't this where we came in?" I asked. We stared at each other for a moment, from over our separate fences, and then both of us burst out laughing.

I watch the Christmas video again, and then a second time—excited children, neighborly hugs and smiles, seeming happiness, and then stop it on Irwin's face, grinning down at me, holding Emma. I know that this was only minutes before my second complete fall-apart. Almost the end of Irwin's age of innocence, I think to myself—good title. "Oh, shut up, Callie," I whisper aloud.

Of course, the fall-apart had to do with Sam and Shirley, and the lie of my happy family, and Christmas, and missing my dead parents, and the sounds of the children's voices, and the carols that always made me cry. But it was as unexpected as it had been in the middle of Fifth Avenue. I was suddenly sobbing—gasping sounds and streaming tears—and I ran as best I could away from the tree and toward our house. I could see Danny through the living room window, putting the camera away, so I veered toward the basement door.

It was dark and warm inside with pipes and heaters, trunks and boxes, and I knew that rats made their way in here from the Hip Bagel. I hated rats, but at the moment there was nowhere else to go. I cried loudly, relieved to be able to, but it wasn't long before Irwin found me.

"Hey, what's the matter? What's going on?" he asked, wrapping his arms around me. I tried to control my sobs, and tried to tell him without lying, which meant that I told him some of the truth.

"Christmas always makes me sad—you know that. I miss

home, I miss Daddy, even Mom. She always made Christmas beautiful, even when I was a stupid teenager, and we were fighting all the time. She taught me how to wrap presents and tie bows—you know all those pretty bows I make?"

"They're really pretty," Irwin said quietly.

"And they're not here," I said, crying over his words. "And I'm the mom, and all I know how to do is wrap presents. I'm a lousy mom, and I want to go home and be a kid . . ."

"Not true. And we're going to Ted and Robin's tomorrow, that's kind of home," Irwin said soothingly.

"Yeah, kind of," I answered, thinking to myself that I'd managed to get through this without mentioning Sam or my longings or my basic dissatisfactions. I'd promised not to tell Irwin, not to hurt him, and I certainly wasn't going to break that promise during the holidays.

My brother, Ted, and his wife, Robin, lived out in the country, thirty miles north and east of Helen's place in Greenwich. Their house was just a couple of miles from the nineteenth-century farmhouse, surrounded by woods and fields, that Ted and I had grown up in. Meedville was the nearest town, and Ted and Robin both taught at the local high school. Ted taught music and led the orchestra, having inherited our father's musical ability, and Robin taught English and history. Ted was ten years older than I, and I'd always idolized him. And Ted and Robin were everyone's image of the perfect couple. They'd fallen madly in love in college, and seemed to have stayed that way, even with kids, money problems and parental deaths.

Ted had been close to his mother, while I had been more my father's girl, so he was angrier at Helen than I was for breaking up our parents' marriage, and he still blamed her for our mother's death. Helen's inheritance didn't help matters, and Ted and Helen hadn't spoken in years. I still adored my brother, was fond of my stepmother, so Irwin and I divvied up the holidays—Thanksgiving with Helen, Christmas Day with Ted and Robin. Fortunately, Dorothy didn't celebrate Christmas, so we were only expected to show up for overcooked latkes.

Irwin led me out of the basement, and back home, where I stayed upstairs on Christmas Eve until the children were tucked away, and then together Irwin and I wrapped the last of the presents and filled the stockings that were hung on the mantel. I glanced into the dark garden a few times; no sign of all the life that had been there earlier, and no flickering spirits around the still lit tree. No Sam either. I stopped hoping that I might get a Christmas present from him.

After all the excitement of spilling out stockings and opening presents the next morning, Irwin got the car from the garage, once again picked up pies, and once again we headed north on the Saw Mill River Parkway. The kids slept, clutching favorite presents—they'd been up before dawn—and I leaned my head against the seat, closed my eyes, and congratulated myself for having made it this far.

I'd congratulated myself too soon. Ted began serving Bloody Marys at eleven in the morning as we sat around the fire in the family room. The children were happy around the tree in the far corner of the room, playing with Ted and Robin's two teenagers. Darren was handsome, athletic and bright, and Nina was beautiful, athletic and bright—in other words they were perfect. Darren was playing Clue with our boys, and Nina was playing with Emma's Barbie, and the miniature clothes Robin had sewn for her. It was all so perfect I thought I would throw up. And I was so envious. Ted and Robin were everything I'd wanted to be, everything I'd tried to be, but couldn't manage to be. And then Ted refilled our Bloody Marys, and I was sure I would throw up. I wasn't much of a drinker and two shots of vodka was enough to make the room go around. By the next one I weaved my way to the guest bedroom, stretched out on the bath mat next to the toilet, and with my eyes wide open, fell sound asleep. Maybe I passed out. All I remember is fixing my eyes on a lavender bathroom tile so that the room would stop going around, and the next thing I knew Irwin was gently shaking my shoulder, saying that it was almost time for dinner.

"Oh, no," I mumbled, and then Jake and Danny appeared behind him.

"Mom, Uncle Ted's carving a goose, and there's stuffing and everything," Danny said. "You gotta come."

"In a minute, okay?" I said, not moving, and they left me to drift off again. It must have been an hour or so later when Ted knelt beside me and stroked my hair. I opened my eyes, and I could see that the winter sky was darkening outside the bathroom window.

"Hey, Cal—hey, Sleepin' Beauty," he said softly. Without thinking, I turned and wrapped my arms around his neck, gripping him, almost choking him.

"I'm so sorry. I had too much to drink and I'm—I'm so sorry."

"That's okay. It happens to the best of us," Ted said, loosening my grip, and then holding both my hands. "Was it just that?

Is anything wrong?" he asked, searching my eyes. I shook my head, then buried it against his chest so that he couldn't see my teary eyes. I couldn't tell him that his marriage was the real thing, and mine, the marriage he'd been so pleased about, was a sham. Not yet, anyway, not on Christmas Day.

Robin packed leftovers because I hadn't been able to eat, and I stashed them in a far corner of the station wagon, behind the children, who slept all the way home. It was dark and sleeting by the time we reached MacDougal, and we went through the ritual of double-parking outside the house, carrying in whatever had to be brought from the car, and then carrying each sleeping child into the house and up to bed. Then Irwin had to return the car to the garage, and walk the few blocks home. I gazed out at the freezing, empty garden for a minute before getting into bed, and was almost asleep by the time I felt the dent in the mattress as Irwin climbed in beside me.

The icy rain froze during the night, and when the sun hit the garden in the morning, it glistened on every branch, twig and bush. All the garden children ran outside, in snowsuits and galoshes, and slid and skidded on the icy, melting paths. I could hear their shrieks and laughter from my bedroom where I sat with coffee, cigarette and the *Times* open in front of me. I was staring at the newsprint, and thinking that I'd made it through Christmas, just barely, and wondering if I'd see Sam this week, and wondering where he'd be on New Year's Eve, and could I make it through to New Year's Day, and how long could I keep this up? I jumped out of bed, silently yelling at myself to stop agonizing, dressed quickly in ski pants, jacket and boots, and joined the children outside.

Diana and Ruthie were already out there, sliding around with the kids, and they waved as Emma rushed up to me, practically knocking me off my feet.

"Watch it, sweetie," I said, kissing her flushed cheek.

"Sorry, Mommy—it's so fun," she said, skidding back to Maryellen. I made my way carefully over to Ruthie and Diana, and we'd barely said good morning before Shirley opened her garden door.

"Anyone for coffee?" she asked, smiling and gesturing. Diana, Ruthie and I glanced at each other—did she mean us? She must have meant us, but none of us had been invited in before.

"Sure, love to," we called back, and followed a path of slush to Shirley's garden door. We took off our boots and jackets and entered the Messengers' sleek living room. The house had been gutted and modernized at some point, and the downstairs was open and sparsely furnished with chrome, glass and black leather. I looked around curiously, and smiled thinking of Sam's musty lair at the theater as we followed Shirley into the bright kitchen.

"Did you have a good Christmas?" she asked, as she poured coffee, and brought it to the white Formica table. "Mine was fabulous," she said, as we nodded and sat. "Here, I made some cookies," and she was up and back again.

"We don't really celebrate," Ruthie said.

"Oh, right, you do Hanukkah. We sort of do both." Then she held out her left hand, displaying a pearl and diamond ring that formed a love knot. "And look what I got from Sammy—an engagement ring, *finally*. He knew I wanted one for the last ten years. We'd just snagged a justice of the peace when we got married, picked up gold bands on the way, so he knew I was just dying for a real engagement ring," she said in a rush, blushing, blond curls bobbing. "I forgot, cream and sugar?" she added, turning back to the counter.

"Yes, please," Ruthie said, and then mouthed to me, "Guilt present."

"What?" I asked, and then realized what she'd said. Diana and Ruthie both looked skyward, and then smiled at Shirley as she returned to the table with a cream pitcher and a bowl of sugar.

"Is there an ashtray?" Ruthie asked, pulling cigarettes and matches out of her pocket.

"I'm sorry, we don't smoke in here," Shirley said. "Sammy's trying to quit. He has to be careful of his throat, you know."

"Of course," Ruthie said, and drummed her fingers on the table as she gulped her coffee. "Thanks, Shirley. Gotta go. Nicotine fit, you know." And before Shirley had a chance to say another word, the three of us were back out in the garden.

"You never heard that?" Ruthie asked me as we lit cigarettes against the wind.

"The guilt thing? I don't think so."

"Husbands give presents when they feel guilty."

"*Men* give presents when they feel guilty," Diana added.

"Do you think she's suspicious?" I asked both of them.

"I think she's totally oblivious," Diana said. "She's just one of those possessive wives who has to let the whole world know that the gorgeous guy belongs to her."

"And she's probably insecure about it too."

"He is gorgeous, isn't he?" I said with a shy smile, and they both laughed as Diana turned toward her house with a wave, and Ruthie and I started to walk across the garden.

"Wanna bet that's the last I ever see of the Messenger kitchen?" Ruthie said, and her dimpled smile was particularly mischievous.

"You weren't your friendliest."

"No shit. But something about her drives me up a wall. I guess it's all that gushing. And the not smoking business—'Sammy has to watch his throat,'" she mimicked.

"He smokes like a chimney at the theater."

"Of course. And if I were married to her, I'd drink myself under the table too," she said, giggling before she even reached the end of the sentence.

"We're evil," I said, giggling with her.

"Ain't it fun? See you later." We separated, heading for our doorways, and I was still laughing at her words as I entered our living room, filled with winter sunlight, and with the remains of Christmas.

The holiday week went slowly. Maddy came from Queens three afternoons a week, as usual, and helped me organize the kids' rooms, clearing shelf space for new games and toys, filling baskets with old toys that we couldn't give away without the children's approval. Jake and Emma were willing to give away whatever they no longer cared about. Danny cared about everything, and most of his sorted things went back in the closet or under the bed.

The boys spent every afternoon with Craig's Winners, a sports group that they loved. They particularly loved Craig, a bearded, vital young man, to whom every one of them was a winner. They went twice a week on school days too, and the boys would wait eagerly out on MacDougal for the Winners' yellow van to round the corner. They had Winners jackets and Winners caps, and once a week Craig gave a special "hurrah" to whichever boy had excelled that week. While Jake wasn't the natural athlete that Danny was, he was far more determined. He'd practice and practice against the backboard at our end of the garden, tossing and catching, tossing and catching, until he was almost as good as his older brother. Determination was his forte, so I wasn't surprised when he bounced in one afternoon and told me that he'd gotten the week's hurrah for guts. I was hugging him when he backed up, looking puzzled, and asked, "Mommy, what's guts?"

That was the high point of the week. The garden froze every night, and softened slightly during the day. No one went out during the evenings, and there was no sight of Sam or the ghosts at midnight. There were only the lights of the now lonely Christmas tree. Diana and I spent quite a bit of time together, killing time really. While the boys were off with Craig, Emma and Maryellen played with their new Barbies, their new outfits and their new Barbie rooms. Emma got a folding kitchen, and Maryellen a folding bedroom.

"D'you think Barbie cooks?" I asked Diana, who had sprawled out on the rug in front of our fireplace, staring at the embers.

"More to the point, d'you think Barbie fucks?" Diana asked. I burst out laughing from my seat in the corner of the sofa; Diana was the most refined-looking woman I had ever seen.

"What's so funny?"

"You. You're so proper, and then—"

"Right, I'm so proper. I'm lying to, and cheating on my husband, pretending to be a good mother while I'm lying on your floor, desperately hoping for a phone call from my lover."

"I know, I understand," I said quietly.

"That's why I'm here," Diana answered.

"I know."

"The fire's going out."

"I'll get a log," I said. I went down to the basement for some precious wood, expensive in the city, and as I gathered it, thought about my Christmas Eve fall-apart. I felt so badly for Irwin, having to work hard to support us, having to be such a good dad, having to deal with me. I said some of this as I reentered the living room, and threw another log on the fire.

"Oh, please," Diana said, dismissing my qualms. "They *have* to work, it keeps them from feeling."

"You think so?" I asked, returning to the sofa. "I don't know. I think maybe they've been working too hard to have time to feel much of anything. Women like us, basically, have nothing to do, so we sit around, feeling useless and dissatisfied, drinking a lot of coffee and talking to each other, and pretty soon there's a movement. If we worked like women used to, milking cows, making butter, growing grain, making bread, sewing wool—"

"Do you sew wool?" Diana laughed.

"I dunno. What *do* you do with it?"

"Maybe knit it?" Diana said, still laughing. "But I get the point. The women's movement is a luxury."

"A luxury of time," I said. At that moment the phone rang,

and both of us tensed. Could it be Diana's unnamed lover? Could it be Sam, calling me from the theater? I looked at my watch. It couldn't be Sam; it was a matinee day, and he was still on stage. I ran to the kitchen phone anyway. It was Irwin, wanting to know what I was doing.

"Just yakking with Diana while the girls are playing," I said.

"Sounds nice. I'll be home in a while. I love you."

"Love you too," I answered, and as I reentered the living room Diana and I exchanged guilty looks, and then resumed our vigil in front of the fire. No one called. It was late afternoon by the time Diana left with Maryellen. Emma was still in her room, and I could hear her Barbies talking to each other. Maddy had put a roast chicken in the oven for our dinner and headed home. Irwin and the boys weren't due for another half an hour. I picked up the wall phone in the kitchen, and with one hand poised to disconnect, dialed Sam's dressing room number.

"Clayton here," I heard, and laughter in the background. I hung up quickly, wondering who Sam was charming today. Maybe even Shirley. Maybe she'd taken "poor lonesome Sammy" his supper. "Oh, stop being a bitch," I muttered to myself, as I walked to the back window and looked across the garden. There were lights on in the Messenger living room, and in the bedroom above, but I couldn't see anyone. I stretched out on the sofa beside the fire, next to the window, and felt myself deflate, all hope and energy leaving me. Sam hadn't called, and now I wouldn't see him until New Year's Eve, *if* I were to see him on New Year's Eve, *if* he showed up at Josh and Ruthie's party.

I hadn't seen much of Ruthie during this dead week between Christmas and New Year's because she was busy arranging their New Year's Eve gala. She and Josh, and Kevin of course, had invited everyone they knew, everyone they worked with, and everyone in the garden. I knew that people tended to party-hop on New Year's Eve, and as I closed my eyes and hoped like mad—not quite praying, but almost—that Sam would show up and give me a special moment, a special dance or a special kiss, I heard the key in the door, and Irwin was home.

The shortest days of the year, just past the winter solstice, seemed like the longest. They began in darkness, turned gray, and were dark again by four in the afternoon. I didn't know what to do with all those hours. Of course, I was waiting, and time goes very slowly when we wait. I played board games with the boys, something I didn't particularly enjoy, took Emma shopping with me while the boys were with Craig, tried to cook, tried to read, tried to think of something to write. But, really, I was just waiting—for a call from Sam, or a clear night when we could meet outside, or at the very least a kiss on New Year's Eve.

I was sick by the time New Year's arrived. I spent New Year's Eve day in bed, my knees drawn up to my chest to alleviate the cramps and nausea. Irwin brought tea, toast and aspirin up on a tray, kept the kids busy, and woke me periodically to ask if I thought I'd be able to make the parties we were supposed to go to. There was a party at his boss's house, the head of the agency, that was important to him, one that a coworker was giving that didn't matter that much, and then the one at Josh and Ruthie's.

We skipped the co-worker's party, and I managed to get up and get dressed for the Cormics' party. We had a garden teenager, Matt Jenning, baby-sitting, and the kids looked upon him as a young god so they didn't mind us going out. We told them they could stay up, and promised a New Year's kiss when we got back. I loaded up on a painkiller that was one of Irwin's accounts, something similar to aspirin, but not aspirin. Going uptown in a cab I thought about that, my big problem with advertising, the thing I didn't understand. They worked so hard, and spent all that money selling something as "the best" that was really no different from something else. It was basically a lie, and I simply couldn't get interested. And here we were going to a party where advertising was pretty much all they talked about.

It was one of the main ways in which Irwin and I had grown apart. We'd both broken unspoken contracts. I had married a writer, someone I could be proud of, and he'd become a businessman in a business that didn't interest me. Irwin had married a potential heiress, who didn't inherit anything except a small amount of ASCAP, maybe enough to pay the laundry and dry cleaning bills.

"How're you doing?" Irwin asked as the cab pulled up in front of 1185 Park Avenue. I shrugged—I was okay—and we followed the doorman to the little gatehouse where a guard checked our names off a guest list, and directed us to an elevator. The elevator stopped at an upper floor that belonged to Oliver and Judy Cormic. We entered the black and white foyer, left our coats, and then separated, Irwin to go charm people, and me to go hide. I took a couple more painkillers in an empty maid's bathroom, sipped champagne in the pantry off the kitchen, then worked up the nerve to act like a proper executive's wife, and went looking for our host and hostess.

I found Irwin talking politics with Oliver, a trim, bald man in his fifties, and another executive's wife, tall with lovely auburn hair, whose name I couldn't remember. I listened quietly as they discussed Bobby Kennedy, the apparent change in him since his brother's assassination, his hatred of Castro, his father's influence, and only chimed in when they got around to Marilyn Monroe. Oliver said that the rumor was that she was Jack's whore, and killed herself over him. I defended her, preferring her to Jackie anyway, and because I'd lived through it with my mother, considered myself somewhat of an expert on suicide.

Irwin pulled me away before I got too argumentative, and I managed to maneuver him out the door by eleven so that we could get back to the garden by midnight. I silently willed the cab to race downtown, and we were home before eleven-thirty. We tucked the children into their beds, kissed them Happy New Year, and I whispered their secret endearments into their ears as I did every night. They were just nonsense words, but they seemed to mean a lot to them, and they never told anyone what they were.

We crossed the garden, the slippery paths newly strewn with ashes, and entered Ruthie's back door at ten minutes before midnight, or the "witching hour" as I remembered my father had liked to call it. The downstairs room was packed. We could hear voices and music on the two floors above, and the air was heavy with cigarette smoke, and the sweeter smell of marijuana. I looked around, passed the bar, passed the food-laden tables, and saw almost no one I knew. Josh owned an artists management company, and this party was much more mixed than the one uptown. There were blacks, whites, musicians, actors, writers. I thought I saw James Baldwin in a corner, smoking a thin cigar, but someone told me it was only his brother.

"They must be upstairs," I said into Irwin's ear.

"Who?"

"I dunno—everyone we know," I said, taking his hand and leading him through small groupings to the staircase, and up to the high-ceilinged second floor. A combo was playing dance music by the bay windows in the front room, and the furniture was pushed back against the walls.

"Hey, drop your coats and join the party," Ruthie called out as she crossed to us between dancing couples. We hugged, and she took our coats, tossing them on a sofa, and then took Irwin by the hand. "Come on, you're good at this," she said, and led him to the dance floor where a few couples were doing variations on the Twist. Irwin *was* good at it, much better than I was, and I watched him for a few seconds, gyrating opposite Ruthie, and then scanned the second floor and the staircase to the third. As yet no sign of Sam or Shirley. I was beginning to be afraid that he hadn't come, that he was at another party somewhere, when I heard his voice at the top of the stairs.

"Aha, it's the beauteous calla lily," he called down, his tone mocking enough so that Shirley wouldn't think he meant it. He was behind Shirley and cousin Mimi, a hand on each of them, as they descended the stairs. He winked at me and pursed his lips in an air kiss over their heads, and I smiled up at him and probably blushed, and might have made more of a fool of myself if the combo hadn't started playing "Auld Lang Syne," and the countdown began—ten, nine, eight, seven. Irwin rushed to me from the dance floor, held and kissed me as I watched Sam over his shoulder. Arthur had appeared and claimed Mimi, and Sam, from the step above, tried to find Shirley's lips and missed, kissing her nose and then her chin. Four, three, two, one, and Shirley was laughing by the time Sam found her mouth, and 1968 began.

Chapter Eight

In early January there was a fire in our house. No one was hurt, but it was frightening. Irwin and I had gone to the theater with my father's friend Ben Cramer and his wife, Sally. They'd moved to Palm Springs in the mid-sixties, were only in the East for a few days, had tickets for *Cabaret*, and asked us to join them. The evening was both nostalgic and festive.

The Cramers loved going to the theater, but I think they loved going to Sardi's afterward even more. They were welcomed home, led to a well-placed table, and ordered their favorites—martinis, cannelloni and snowballs. We toasted them, us, our children, my parents, but I sipped my martini carefully. I really didn't want to end up on the floor of the ladies' room at Sardi's. We listened and laughed as they complained about the desert heat, and their boring neighbors, and they listened and laughed as we told them about the garden and our eccentric neighbors.

Except for a quick glance around the room when we first walked in, to see if he might have come in after his show, I barely thought of Sam. I didn't think of him again until we hugged the Cramers good night, and then hailed a cab to take us home. The weather had warmed somewhat, the ice melted, and it occurred to me that Sam might be lurking out in the garden, waiting for me. I hadn't seen him since New Year's Eve, and it was just past midnight, our time to meet by the garden bench. I found myself wondering if little Lucy were back, now that it wasn't so cold.

The streets were fairly empty going downtown. Matt Jenning was baby-sitting again so we weren't worried until we neared Bleecker and MacDougal. Three fire engines were blocking MacDougal, no right turns, and gray-black smoke was wafting over the houses.

"Oh, my God, what's going on?"

"Is that our house?"

"Oh, my God!"

Irwin handed too much money to the driver, and we raced down the block to our barricaded front door.

"We live here!" we shouted at once to the firemen guarding our doorway. "Our kids! Where're our kids?"

"Everyone's okay," said a tall, heavy fireman, his face and hat smudged with smoke. "Fire was on the top floor, nobody hurt. Can I see a license or something, just to make sure?" Irwin yanked his driver's license out of his wallet, and the fireman led us through the outside hallway and into our duplex. "Seems the tenant up there had too much to drink, dropped a lit cigarette in the sofa, and the whole top caught on fire."

"Where're our kids?" Irwin and I asked again, in unison.

"Over there at a neighbor's," the fireman said, nodding across at Sullivan Street. "That kid was good, your baby-sitter.

He called us, got your kids outside, and your friends over there took 'em in." I followed his pointing thumb to the Messengers' house where all the downstairs lights were on. Most of the other houses were dark. "You got some water damage upstairs," the fireman continued, "but nothin' like the top floor. It's a mess up there."

"Thank you," I said, "thank you so much," and ran out the back door and across the garden. As I ran I could see into the Messengers' living room through the glass doors. Sam was sitting in his glove-leather recliner, his legs stretched out on the hassock, with Emma dozing against his chest. I couldn't see the boys right away, but as I stumbled in the garden door I could see that they were both on the floor, involved in a card game with Matt.

"Go fish," Danny said happily.

"Oh, thank God!" I said, running to them, holding them, sending their cards flying. Irwin was right behind me, and as he gathered his boys in his arms, I crossed to Sam, and scooped Emma up in my arms. "Sam, thank you! Oh, Matt, you angel, thank you!"

"No problem. It was pretty exciting," Matt said, as he gathered up the cards.

"The fireman carried me on his shoulder," Emma said sleepily.

"It was so neat," Jake said.

"Yeah," Danny echoed. "And there were hooks and ladders and hoses and smoke and everything!"

"You weren't scared?" Irwin asked.

"No," the boys said.

"I was," Emma said. I laughed with relief, hugging her, as

Shirley appeared from the kitchen, wearing flannel pajamas, and with pink curlers in her hair.

"I've always wondered about those curls," I said silently to myself, realizing that it was the first time I'd given a thought to either Sam or Shirley. They were both so inconsequential at that moment.

"I was just making some hot chocolate," Shirley said. "Goodness, what a scare. It was so lucky Sammy was getting home just then."

"No, Matt's the hero," Sam said. "I just happened to get here when the trucks did, so I told 'em to bring the kids over here."

"Well, thanks everyone, especially Matt."

"Yay, Matt!" Danny said. "Can we go home now?"

"No hot chocolate?"

"We'll make some at home."

"Come on, Matt, we owe you baby-sitting money. And we owe you big-time."

As we traipsed back across the garden, carrying the children, I felt that I had my priorities in order for the first time in months. Nothing in the world mattered but the safety and welfare of my children. My wonderful perspective, my gratitude for what was, for everyone's well-being, for the here and now, lasted for a few days, maybe even a week. As it dissipated, as I began missing Sam, longing for just a minute with Sam, I called Pricket for an emergency session.

"I don't get it," I said, frustrated with myself. "This always happens."

"What always happens?" Pricket asked, leaning forward, hands clasped on her desk.

"Every time I'm grateful, every time I see a child in a wheelchair, or a child injured in the stupid war, a leg blown off or something, like I'll see on the news, or a kid in the South trying to go to school and getting shot at, I'm so grateful for about two damn minutes, and then it goes. I forget to be grateful. I get all wrapped up in my own stuff. Then I'll see or hear something else awful, going on out in the world—starving babies, starving animals, a whole village wiped out in Vietnam, and I'll be grateful again, so grateful that we're okay, that we have enough to eat, that we're not being bombed, and then I forget again. I long for what *I* want, care about what *I* feel, and it's so selfish!"

"You're being philosophical," Pricket said with a sigh, leaning back in her desk chair.

"So what's wrong with that?"

"Nothing. It just has nothing to do with therapy. Our personal drives have a way of taking precedence over our philosophical concerns."

"Oh." There was a pause during which I fidgeted. "Well, I don't like it," I said finally, petulantly. "I don't want to care so much about what I want. I just want to stay grateful, and maybe, like you, care more about somebody else."

"Who says I care more?" Pricket asked.

"You don't?"

"I'm the most important person in the world to me. I'd like for you to say the same about yourself."

"Really?"

She nodded, and there was another pause.

"I'd like you to love yourself," she said, leaning forward again.

"Oh, please," I answered, with a wave of dismissal. "I mean I get the concept, but feeling it is a whole other thing. I can't imagine loving myself the way I love the kids, not all the time, of course, but there are times when love seems to just pour out of me. I can't imagine feeling that way about myself."

"I'd like you to give it a try," Pricket answered. "Try going home, pouring love into yourself every day, and then come back and tell me about it."

"All day, every day? You're kidding."

"No, not all day, just a few minutes every day."

"Sure, why not . . ." I said, knowing that I wasn't about to. Pricket knew it too.

There were two garden meetings during the last week of January and the beginning of February. The first was about evicting the drunk who rented the top floor of our house, and had accidentally set the fire. He had moved out temporarily while the place was being fixed, and no one wanted him back. This fire had been quickly contained, but we certainly didn't want another. The garden home owners, and their lawyers, could have him legally evicted; we were there to back them up.

Sam and Shirley showed up a few minutes before the meeting was to start with cousin Mimi and her husband, Arthur. I thought of leaving, still worried about their seeing me in Sam's dressing room, but I was more concerned with getting rid of the fire hazard. Hopefully, they would have forgotten. We were gathering in Josh and Ruthie's downstairs living room, and Ruthie began plying them with questions. I tried to catch her eye, to ascertain her motives—Ruthie's chitchat often had a hidden agenda—but she ignored me, and served drinks and asked questions at the same time.

"You're in law school, Arthur? Columbia? NYU?"

"Columbia," Arthur answered, stroking his newly grown beard. "That's why we moved from Madison. I got accepted, better late than never."

"But you're young?"

"Twenty-eight," Arthur said. "But I only decided last year that I want to be able to do something legally, instead of just protesting."

"And he's brilliant," Shirley chimed in.

"No, but thanks," Arthur said shyly. "And Mimi wants to act, so here we are."

"I tried law school, many years ago," Josh said, joining us. "I couldn't hack it."

"Well, you did just fine," Ruthie said, gesturing around at their sumptuous townhouse, and as we laughed other garden couples arrived, and the meeting began.

Irwin and I sat across the room from Sam and Shirley, and I tried hard to pay attention, but the lawyers' voices droned as they presented suggestions and contingencies. I avoided looking at Sam because my insides stirred at just a glimpse of those beautiful arms, and his strong fingers reminded me of pleasures I'd told myself not to think about. The couple of times that I glanced at Sam I found that he was looking at me, his lips slightly curved, a teasing light in his lidded eyes. I tried to remember what Pricket had said, something about human drives being stronger than philosophical notions, and I tried hard to hold on to my dwindling perspective.

When the meeting broke up, and we were heading home

through the garden, Sam and Shirley invited us to join them, and Mimi and Arthur, for coffee and brandy. I said that we should really get home, but of course Irwin wanted to go. I then said that I had a headache, wanted to take something and get to bed, at which point Shirley said that she had stuff stronger than aspirin, and Sam said that he was known for his healing hands, that he could toss my headache away in less than three minutes.

"Healing hands?" I muttered, as I brushed up against Sam, and all six of us headed across the garden. Inside their sleek living room, Arthur laid a fire, Shirley and Mimi went to get drinks, and Sam positioned me in his recliner, head back, feet on the hassock, and began kneading my forehead, my scalp, the back of my neck. He sat on a stool behind me, and when Mimi and Shirley returned, and everyone talked at once, whispered behind my ear.

"Where've you been? You avoiding me?"

"Trying to," I murmured.

"We've missed you."

"Who's we?"

"Me and little Lucy," Sam said, and I couldn't help laughing.

"Feeling better?" Irwin asked.

"Oh, I forgot the painkiller," Shirley said.

"That's okay. Yes, I'm better," I said quickly.

"What'd I tell you," Sam said, and drew his index finger down my spine in a way that chilled and warmed me at once. I sat straight, feet on the floor, and half turned to him.

"Thanks, Sam, I'm fine, headache's gone," I said, as I rose, crossed the room, and joined Irwin on one of the sofas.

Sam smiled, tilted his head in a kind of bow, and reclaimed his recliner. I let out my breath, found a cigarette in my bag, and lit it.

"Oh, God, sorry," I said to Shirley. "I'll take it outside."

"Don't worry about it," Sam said, but I'd already grabbed my jacket, and was out the door. In their private garden there was a table and wrought iron chairs, and I smoked and looked out at the garden to see if any ghosts were lurking. The air was warmer than it had been, the sky clear, a quarter-moon rising—a perfect night for little Lucy and her friends, but I could only see real trees, real bushes, no flitting spirits. I turned back to the Messengers' glass doors, and glimpsed Sam smiling at me, the same amused look in his eyes.

It occurred to me that the more I tried to stay away from him, since the fire and my refound values, the more interested he became. Well, of course, it was always like that, but I wished he wouldn't be so obvious in front of his wife and my husband. He seemed to enjoy flirting with the edge, seeing how far he could go. I'd seen it that first day in Central Park, both families at the carousel, picnicking on the grass. Sam had seemed to enjoy the intrigue, and I hadn't at all.

I put out the cigarette, stuck the butt in my jacket pocket, and reentered the living room. Arthur was in the middle of a speech. I sat on the rug in front of the fire, and listened as he told the room why it was important for all of us to become activists. We had to get out there, he said, make ourselves seen and heard in whatever way possible. We had to join the war protesters, march against segregation, do more than donate money and give lip service. He was fired up, and I glanced around at the listening faces. Mimi and Shirley were nodding, intent upon his words, seemingly ready to march out the door after him at any moment. Irwin looked skeptical, Sam bemused.

"We have families," Irwin started to say.

"I'm forty-five, Art," Sam said. "I've sung and danced for more good causes than I can remember."

"I know, that's great," Arthur answered. "But this is a different time. We're in a terrible, unjust war."

"What war isn't?" Sam asked.

"Right, but we need action now to stop this one," Arthur said, rising, starting to pace.

"Fine, you kids go act," Sam said with a smile. Irwin tried to stifle a wide yawn, and Sam and I both laughed. The others kept their serious expressions.

"Sorry," Irwin said, rising, getting into his coat, "but I'm an early-to-bed, early-to-rise kind of guy. Thanks, Shirley, Sam. Hon?" I nodded and followed him, calling back a good night, and once outside took Irwin's arm, my head on his shoulder, so that Sam could see us through his window.

My good intentions continued for a whole week. I wiped away images of Sam, resisted yearnings that caught me by surprise, went to bed early so that I wouldn't sit in the dark and gaze out at the garden. I even made love to my husband one night. Or, rather, he made love to me. I didn't ask for anything so it was like the way it used to be, passion for him, closeness for me. We talked for a while afterward, first about the kids, if they'd recovered from the night of the fire, then about the evening at the Messengers'.

"That fellow, cousin what's-his-name, has no sense of humor."

"Arthur," I said. "Arthur and Mimi."

"Right, Arthur. He doesn't know who he's talking to—a bunch of liberals who talk a good game, but wouldn't dream of breaking a rule."

"Or a law."

"God forbid a law. Hey, we'd all hide under the bed before we'd go out and march for what we believe in." He then mimicked Arthur's serious tone, "Follow me, friends, as we all go get our heads blown off in Mississippi." And in a tremulous voice, "I'll write a check from under the bed, okay? How about Vietnam, you wanna go march with Jane? No, I think I'll just stay here under the bed, thanks." I laughed, and asked Irwin to turn off the light that was on his side of the bed. He did, and I kissed him quickly, and turned on my side with my face to the wall. After a moment, I felt Irwin's arms come around me in a tight grip.

"I wish I could keep you like this all the time," he said. "Every second of every day and night." As I took deep breaths, and tried to wriggle free, he whispered, "I wish I could lock you in a closet when I leave for work in the morning, and open it every night when I come home."

"That's sweet," I said, as I tried to take deeper breaths, and unlocked his arms.

That night I dreamt about Sam, over and over, throughout the hours. We were in places I'd never been, in houses I'd never seen, at parties with people I didn't know. I'd wake briefly and think, "I don't want to go back there, I don't like that party, I couldn't find Sam there." Then I'd be back in the dream, back at the party, searching for Sam. Sometimes I'd find him, sometimes not. Once I found him in an upstairs hallway; he gave me a sad, gentle kiss, and we heard Shirley calling him. In another dream he had a son, a beautiful boy about ten, and Shirley was going blind. I heard someone say, "That's the poor blind woman."

The last time that I awakened, at dawn, I was exhausted, and felt that my soul hurt. I'd been searching for, and finding, and losing Sam all night. When Irwin got up, humming to himself—he was happy that morning—and began his rituals, I kept my eyes closed, my face to the wall, and tried not to cry. Sam's dream kiss had been so sweet, and why was Shirley going blind? I wondered what she wasn't seeing, and if Sam cared for me more than I knew. Then I wondered if it was Sam I missed so much. Maybe it was just my dead parents, my melancholy, loving father, but they were dead and unreachable, and Sam was here across the garden, sleeping still because he would have come home after midnight.

Of course, Irwin was here too, now doing his Canadian Air Force exercises on the bedroom carpet. Why couldn't this longing be for him, my best friend, my roommate? Sam had been a sexual awakening, as Pricket had said, but it was more than that. It was my soul that was crying, not my body.

The second garden meeting, early in February, was another get-together of the ghost lovers and keepers. It was on a Sunday evening, and I dreaded and hoped that Sam would be there. It was still mild for this time of year, the city sky clear and sparkling as I crossed the garden. I made a secret wish on the evening star, a habit from childhood, as I walked slowly toward the Tompkinses' back door. Diana caught up with me as I neared their garden.

"Ah, the eternal romantics, still wishing on stars," she said, linking her arm in mine.

"You did too?"

"Of course. Every little wish helps," she answered, and we were both laughing as Laurette opened the door for us. The Dakin ladies, old and older, were already sitting by the fire, sipping wine. Susan MacAdams was standing and chatting with Paul and Henry, and as we entered Sam appeared from the kitchen, carrying a tray of cheese and crackers. He winked at me, and I felt a second's relief before I noticed cousin Mimi right behind him. She came right over and hugged me as if we were old friends, and I wondered what that was about, but then Sam was beside us and I forgot about Mimi. He put the tray down, and beckoned toward the love seat, which had room for three. Diana shook her head, settled in the rocking chair, and Sam, Mimi and I managed to sit three in a row—Mimi, then Sam, then me.

Just as Hal began the meeting, and everyone took seats, Josh came in without Ruthie, which surprised me, but everyone knew him and greeted him so I assumed he'd been before.

"Hi, Josh," Hal said. "Get a drink, have a seat. Had any visitations lately?"

"Thanks, I will," Josh said, pouring himself a glass of wine. "And, yes, I saw my late ex-wife again, pushing the little Van Eck kid on the swings."

"You saw little Lucy?" Iris Dakin asked, her wrinkled eyes wide with excitement.

"Yeah, she was having a great time," Josh answered, as he found a seat near the fire and the Dakins.

"We knew she'd come back when the weather turned," Iris Dakin said, clasping her hands gratefully. "Didn't you say that, Sam?"

"Yeah, I guess I did," Sam said, as he shifted his weight so that his thigh was against mine.

"We all said it," Henry said shortly, and I hoped that no one had noticed my slight gasp. I tried to see how close Sam was to Mimi on his other side, but I couldn't look without being obvious.

"I just wish Rachel would move on, and stop hanging around here," Josh said. "I look out there, and there she is, and I want to just be with Ruthie, and I can't because I feel like I'm cheating on Rachel . . . Oh, hell." And he threw up his arms for a second.

"Does Ruthie see her too?" I asked.

"No, you know Ruthie. She doesn't believe in anything she can't see and touch."

"We know," Diana said, and we both laughed.

"So I want to know," Josh continued. "Can't we talk to Rachel somehow, and convince her to just move on?"

"We can try," Hal answered. "Some of us are better at it than others. And she's probably just dropping by, Josh, checking in, because she was happy here. That's why most of them visit."

"The old Captain sure isn't happy here. He's fighting some goddamn war every night," Paul said.

"And he's still waking me and Joey up at least three times every night," Susan added. "Can't we talk to him and Rachel, and ask them to go—I don't know—go trip the light fantastic somewhere else?" She gave a jittery laugh and ran her fingers through her copper hair. I glanced at Sam next to me, saw that he was appreciating Susan's charming bashfulness, and made sure that my thigh was firmly pressed against his.

"We could hold a séance," Laurette answered. "But it's tricky because we could attract other spirits that are worse than the ones we've got already."

"And some, like darling Lucy, we don't want to lose," Iris Dakin said, a dreamy look in her ancient eyes.

"True," Hal said. "Probably the best thing is to just go out there and talk to them, tell the Captain he's keeping you up, and please cut it out. Josh, tell Rachel you'll always love her, but you have a new wife now, and she's interfering with your sex life."

"I didn't say that," Josh said laughing, and we all laughed with him.

"Just kidding," Hal said, then added, "And if any of you want to drop by our center . . ." He winked at Laurette, and she began passing out leaflets that were stacked on the tables. "We can teach you how to contact those who have passed on better than any séance could."

"Really?" I asked, suddenly more interested in the discussion than in the feel of Sam's leg. "Could I learn how to reach my father, who I loved more than—more than anything?"

"Probably you could," Hal answered. "It depends on where he is now. There are a lot of different levels on the other side, some harder to reach than others. But we can certainly teach you the basics of communication, both on this plane and the ones beyond, and you can learn a lot about your past lives and, say, why you loved your dad so much. Maybe you had a bunch of lifetimes together, maybe he was your husband, your son, your best friend, even your mother once. You can find all that out."

"Really?" I said again softly, intrigued. I'd never believed in much of anything before this night, and I saw a door opening just a crack. This was my first inkling that perhaps those I'd loved weren't completely lost after all. I only half listened during the rest of the meeting, most of me trying to imagine a conversation with my father—what would I say to him? What would he say to me? Would I still love him as much? Would he still love me?

I was still only partly there by the time the meeting ended. Maybe Sam sensed my absence as we walked out the back door together. Mimi had left earlier to get the subway back uptown; the Dakins didn't need help across the garden tonight; Susan took off toward Houston, and Diana waved discreetly as she headed for her townhouse.

"I've got your Christmas present," Sam said, a few paces behind me.

"I thought you forgot," I said, turning back.

"Now how could I forget?" Sam asked, with a slight smile and a tilt of his head.

"I don't know. Where is it?" I said, laughing.

"At my house. Come on." His tilted head jerked toward his glass doors across the garden.

"Where's Shirley?"

"Protesting something with Art in Washington Square. Marta's asleep with the kids on the top floor."

"Oh." He beckoned again, and I followed him, too curious and happy to consider any consequences. We entered his garden door, he closed it behind us and picked up a guitar that was leaning against the fireplace. He sat in his recliner, leaning forward, tuning his guitar, and patted the hassock where he wanted me to sit.

"I've been practicing this," he said, as I took my place, and then he began to play and sing a little known song of my father's from the forties. It was about love and loss—what else?—and Sam sang all three verses, each followed by the lilting chorus. As he sang, he glanced at me with tender eyes, and I felt that this was the most beautiful moment of my life, more beautiful than Shakespeare, or great sex, or "Kubla Khan."

Tears were in my eyes and spilling over as he finished, and then I saw, through the blur, Irwin's face on the other side of the glass door. Sam and I weren't touching, and Sam's back was to him, bent over the guitar, but Irwin's face was stark white, drained and transfixed. He saw, through the glass, my tears, nostalgia and obsession all wrapped up together—my belated Christmas present from Sam.

Chapter Nine

Irwin seemed in shock as he walked back across the garden. I followed him, aware of what he had seen and its impact. Sam wasn't, or if he were it didn't show. He'd waved and smiled at Irwin, said something about a song of my father's, and I guess thought that, as long as we weren't touching, there was nothing to see. He was wrong. I knew that Irwin had seen it all in my eyes and on my face. He entered our garden door, and stared at our living room as if he'd never seen any of this before—it was all new, all changed. He slumped into the rocking chair beside the fireplace, still white and frozen, and I ran for a blanket as if this were really someone in physical shock. I draped the blanket around him, over his chest and across his back, and began to light the fire, shoving paper in beneath blackened logs.

"You don't love me anymore," Irwin said, a statement rather than a question. I lit a match, lit the paper, before answering.

"No. I do. I love you, just—just I love Sam. It's different. I'm so sorry, so sorry." I was crying again, miserable tears this time. Irwin remained frozen, immobile.

"For how long?" he finally asked.

"I don't know." I shrugged and fudged, "A couple months—I don't know."

"Okay," Irwin said, after a minute.

"No, it's not okay."

"It's okay," Irwin said again. "I'm going to bed now." And he rose, stiffly, like a mechanical toy, and walked toward the stairs. I watched him climb the stairs, heard him in the bathroom above me, and then listened to the creakings of the silent house. Beside the now blazing fire I tried to figure out what to do. After an hour or so with no answers, I went into the kitchen and dialed Pricket's number. Her answering service said to leave a phone number, and if it were an emergency to call Bellevue. I didn't think either Irwin or I were ready for Bellevue so I left a message, asking Pricket to call me in the morning. When the fire died down to smoldering coals, I turned off the downstairs lights, looked in on the sleeping children, and crept into bed beside Irwin, being careful not to touch him or wake him.

In the morning I kept my eyes closed and listened to Irwin go through his morning routine—several minutes in the bathroom, a half-hour of Air Force exercises, a shower, a shave, downstairs for coffee, putting out the children's cereal boxes, a different one for each. I opened my eyes as he entered my bedroom with a mug of coffee for me. He placed it on the coaster on the night table, and I half sat up and looked at him. He had done all of this by rote, and his brown eyes, which were usually warm and amused, magnified by his glasses were the dead agate of a mounted deer's head.

"Have a good day," I said, also by rote.

"You too," Irwin answered, turned, and was gone. I lit a cigarette, and smoked it, sipping the coffee before rising, putting on a robe, and going downstairs to see how the children were doing. It occurred to me that, in his robot frame of mind, Irwin could have set anything out on the kitchen table—a box of dry macaroni, a box of baking soda, a sack of flour. But, no, as I came into the kitchen I saw that each of the kids was eating his or her favorite cereal. They were also racing matchbox cars around their bowls, creating crashes with sound effects.

"Hi Mommy. Daddy forgot toast," Danny said.

"I'll get it."

"No, we'll be late," Jake said. Jake hated to be late.

"Daddy forgot my hair," Emma said.

"I'll do it." I got the tangles out of Emma's curls, pulled boots, mittens and winter jackets out of the closet, and ushered them out the front door. "Hold hands crossing," I called after them, and watched as the three of them crossed MacDougal, the one street between us and school. I reentered the house, picked up the kitchen phone and tried Pricket again. This time the service put me through. I told her that it was an emergency, and she agreed to see me during her lunch hour.

"I can't see Irwin alone, and I can't see you and Irwin together," Pricket said, from behind her desk. "It's unprofessional."

"Why?"

"Because you're my patient, I know too much, I'm biased, and I'm not a marriage counselor. But I can recommend—"

"Oh, God, I don't know what to do. He looked dead. I feel like I killed him."

"Is he walking and talking?"

"Come on, you know what I mean."

"Yes, I do, but I don't think it's fatal, and I started to recommend someone I think is good that you and Irwin could see together." She opened the top drawer of the desk, and hunted for a card. "I've sent other couples to him with good results."

"Like the suicide pact went off without a hitch?" I said gloomily.

"Ah, here it is. Don't be snide. Couples found clarity, either one way or the other."

"That's promising."

"Dr. George Kleiner," she said, handing me the card. "And not far from here, East 86th."

"German?"

"Hungarian."

"Okay. How do I get Irwin to go? I've hurt him so badly why would he want to go?"

"He'll want to go. He'll do anything to make you happy, remember?" There was a slight sneer in her voice, but it turned out she was right. That evening, still running on automatic, Irwin said he would be glad to go with me to Dr. Kleiner. He then began mimicking Freud with a thick, Hungarian accent:

"Ve vill vork out dis farce so dat each body iss to feel goot again. How iss dat?"

"It's not funny," I murmured, from my end of the sofa.

"Ah, but, liebchen, you must to see dat it iss a farce. Irvin want you, you vant dis Sam person, dis Sam person vant his vife and his vife vant—who does da vife vant? Ah, perhaps dis Arturo person. And dis Arturo person, perhaps he vant—"

"Oh, come on, stop," I said, but I was starting to laugh. I couldn't help it, and Irwin continued his monologue until we were laughing together, and thereby managed to get through the second miserable evening.

We met in Dr. Kleiner's office the following afternoon. He was short, round through the middle, and he did have an accent, but it was slight compared to Irwin's Hungarian/German/Yiddish of the night before. Dr. Kleiner sat in an armchair with doilies on it, and spoke gently to us across an antique coffee table. His gentleness immediately induced tears from me. While Irwin remained calm and charming, his eyes still looked dead to me. I wondered later if that was when his soul left, and the walk-in found him and took him over. At any rate, I was a guilt-ridden, sobbing mess, and Irwin was fine. He told Dr. Kleiner that he was sure that all this would blow over, that my Sam crush would dissipate, and that he would take care of everything until I regained my senses.

I was crying too hard to get much of a word in edgewise, and the session ended with Dr. Kleiner writing a prescription for me. I still don't know what it was—this was way before anyone talked about antidepressants—and the doctor said that it would calm me down and lift my spirits. Irwin and I filled the prescription at our corner pharmacy, and I began taking half a small orange tablet in the morning and the other half in the evening. After the first week I had gained six pounds, and felt nothing at all, not for Sam, not for Irwin, not for anyone. I began writing again, and found that I could write disguised versions of personal experiences without hurting. I was fine; Irwin, or the walk-in, was fine, and for a month or so the children had two zombies for parents.

Then I threw out the pills. I'd picked up the refilled prescription, left the drugstore, saw a wire trash basket on the corner, and like Peter Sellers's automatic arm in *Dr. Strangelove*, my right arm jerked the bottle of pills into the basket, joining the newspapers, pizza crusts, crushed cigarette packs and empty cans. I'd looked at it for a moment, almost fished it out, then realized that I was sick of being this person that felt little, had no desires, few interests, and whom I barely recognized.

It was the beginning of March, the first hint of spring visible in the parks and the garden. Willow branches were a light green, and bulbs were sending small green shoots up through the soot. I loved the spring, always had, and wanted to feel that love again, wanted the thrill of the first magnolia blossoms, the first daffodils, without the dampening, dulling effect of the pills. It took about a week for the weight to come off, and for the dullness to wear off. I told Irwin that I was fine now, that I clearly didn't need the shrinks and prescriptions anymore, and optimistically, and with a grain of salt, he believed me. It took another week or two for the desires to return.

Where was Sam? Had he missed me? More importantly, who was he screwing besides Shirley, if that actually happened? Had he been in the garden at midnight, while I'd been enjoying a drugged sleep? Had he seen our ghosts, little Lucy, and Heloise and Abelard? I suddenly had to know. On a windy afternoon in mid-March I called the dressing room number. Clay answered.

"Hey, Calliope, little muse, how you been?"

"Did Sam tell you that?" I asked, laughing.

"Of course he did. When you comin' up?"

"I don't know. Is he there? Can he talk?"

"Where else would he be? Sam?" he called out. "You got time for the muse? And don't you go askin' which one."

Sam and I were both laughing by the time Sam took the phone.

"Where've you been?" he asked gently. "I froze my ass off out in the garden, hoping."

"Drugged," I said. "I'll tell you when I see you. Can I come up today, or—?"

"Aw, shit." Then loudly to Clay, "Is Shirl bringing supper up today?"

"I think today," I heard Clay answer. "Maybe next week."

"It looks like Shirley's coming today. Can I call you back, or if not, next week?"

"I guess so."

"Okay, baby, glad you called." And he was gone.

My first reaction was happiness. Then, as I paced from the kitchen to the living room and back, and back again, waiting for the wall phone to ring, I felt anxiety return, and longing, and then fear, feelings that had been absent during the previous weeks. I spent a few minutes weighing the calm of the pills against my escalating heartbeats before the phone actually rang. I grabbed it. It was Diana. Her voice was excited.

"Have you heard from Lorraine yet?"

"Who?"

"Your agent, the one I got for you," she said, as if to an imbecile.

"No. Should I?"

"She's probably calling you right now. You sold a short story!"

"Really?"

"Yes, really, to *Collier's*, but she'll—"

"To *Collier's*? You're kidding! For money?"

"I assume so. But she'll be calling. I'll talk to you later."

I hung up, sat in one of the kitchen chairs, and again waited for the phone to ring. Maybe Sam would call and say that Shirley wasn't coming, and the coast was clear. Maybe the agent that Diana had found would call and say that I'd really sold a short story. I had fun for a few minutes, trying to decide which call I wanted more, or which call I wanted first. If Lorraine called first, then I'd be able to tell Sam the news in his lair at the theater. If Sam called first—well, then I'd be out the door.

During the weeks that I'd been able to write without hurting, Diana had read some of my short stories. She'd liked them a lot, and asked if she could show them to a college friend, Lorraine Geller, who had joined a small literary agency. Lorraine also liked them, and asked if she could send them out to a few magazines. That had been about three weeks before.

Sam didn't call during the next half an hour so I figured that Shirley was taking him a care basket, and I'd have to wait another week. But Lorraine did call, very excited, as only agents can be when they've sold something. Yes, she had sold one of my short stories to *Collier's* for twelve hundred dollars, and it should appear in the May or June issue. She needed a Social Security number, and by the way, did I want to put Calliope Hyde Epstein on it, or just Calliope Hyde? I gave her the Social Security number, and told her that this was all so new that I wasn't sure about the name. I'd have to talk to my husband and call her in the morning.

My first thought, after saying thank you and hanging up, was about the money. This would be the first money, since I'd been married, that would belong to me. The small royalties that I'd received from my father I'd turned over to Irwin. He handled the finances, paid the bills, and gave me whatever I asked for, but this twelve hundred dollars would be mine. I could put it in the bank under my name, and do whatever I wanted with it. I had no idea that I'd be so thrilled. Money hadn't meant very much to me. Why would it? I'd never earned it, and never had to worry about it.

By the time Irwin got home I'd decided that my maiden name, my father's name, was the one that I wanted in print. It was all mine, just like the twelve hundred dollars. Irwin didn't know what had gotten into me, and I didn't either. I was adamant, and Irwin terribly upset. The children were in bed and asleep before we closed the bedroom door and started yelling at each other.

"You didn't give a damn about my stories before I sold one!" I shouted at Irwin. "What, I sold one so it's suddenly got cachet?"

"Not true. I said they were good."

"Bullshit, you glanced at one and said, 'You're writing about your mother again?" Well, they bought it, the one about my mother you didn't even want to read."

"I know all about your mother."

"No, you don't. I don't either. Which is beside the point. I wrote the damn thing, and I can put my own goddamn name on it!"

"It's not your name anymore," Irwin shouted back. "You changed it when we got married, remember? Or do you want to throw out the marriage too, along with the name, the husband and the kids?"

"Don't be ridiculous!" At which point I lunged at him, wanting to shake him, but he ducked, and I knocked off his glasses instead. "Oh, I'm so sorry," I said, picking up the pair of glasses that he was groping for. Irwin looked crestfallen as he put his glasses back on, and I reached for him, trying to put my arms around him.

"It tells everybody you don't give a damn about our marriage," he said, pushing my arms away. "If you did you'd be proud to be Mrs. Epstein—you used to be."

"I still am. That has nothing to do with it," I answered, frustrated by the fact that I couldn't explain, but Irwin had retreated behind his replaced glasses. He'd stepped back, his chest slack, his face masked, and then turned and walked out the door. He didn't come home that night, and didn't call, the first time that that had ever happened. I was worried, because this was so unlike him, hoped he was all right, but took the opportunity to wander the garden at midnight.

I walked the path, past the dark houses, only an occasional night-light visible, past the swings where I didn't see little Lucy or any of her friends, and then past Sam's house, as dim as the others. I ended up on the bench at our end of the garden, and waited. Maybe Sam would still come out; maybe Irwin would still come home. It was damp after a spring rain, and I shivered in my slicker as I watched the houses and tried to decide whether or not to see Sam on Wednesday. I'd already broken my promise to myself about Irwin. He'd been hurt, devastated, by just the sight of Sam and me. What difference would it make if I went to the theater and Irwin never knew? Irwin had never asked about Sam. He hadn't asked if I'd slept with him, or loved him, or anything. I guess he didn't want to know. He seemed to think, as he'd said to Dr. Kleiner, that it would all blow over.

In the midst of my indecision, I thought I spotted the lovers, the shades that they called Heloise and Abelard. It was only a glimpse, and only lasted a second or two, but they were parting, painfully moving away from each other, their arms reaching forward as they moved backward. Then they were gone, and I felt it in my own heart, and wondered how many times they had gone through this pantomime of parting. Once they disappeared I wasn't sure whether I'd seen them or dreamed them, but their image made up my mind. I didn't want to live eons of longing and leaving. I wanted to grasp it now, to hold on to it with clenched fists, and to hell with the rest of my life.

Irwin came home early the next morning, said he'd gone out with an office buddy, and slept at the buddy's apartment. He went through his morning rituals, put on his suit, and was gone. I got the children off to school, called the agent and said that I definitely wanted my maiden name on my story, and then called everyone I could think of to tell them I'd sold a short story to *Collier's*. Ruthie was as pleased for me as Diana, and the two of them conferred, and arranged to take Irwin and me out for a festive evening. They picked us up in a town car, husbands in tow, took us to a recent production of *The Little Foxes*, and then to an after-theater dinner at the Algonquin.

We toasted, ate, and gossiped about the garden, but no one mentioned Sam and Shirley. I was grateful, but wondered if Ruthie had clued Josh in, and wondered whether Diana had had a word with her husband, Cliff. I assumed that I would do the same for them if the occasion arose. I had a good time (and stored up tidbits for Sam), but Irwin had an even better time. As I've mentioned, he enjoyed the company of successful people, and Josh was certainly successful. I haven't mentioned that he was also fascinated by wealthy WASPs. Diana, Boston gorgeous, and Cliff, tall, silvering, and taciturn, seemed to fit the bill. Irwin asked questions about the Cape, about who summered where, about the pitfalls of inherited money, and about Edith Wharton and John Cheever until I began to be embarrassed, and shifted the subject to our various summer plans.

Josh and Ruthie were going to their Sag Harbor house as usual, and Diana and Cliff had a place in Sagaponack. Cliff became almost animated as he talked about the old stable that they were in the process of turning into a guesthouse. Irwin and I had rented different places each summer, didn't have one set yet, so of course Irwin asked if the stable would be ready, and could we rent it for a couple of months? Diana and Cliff glanced at each other, and said that they'd have to see how soon it could be occupied. I found that I was even more embarrassed by Irwin's pushiness, and said that I was worried about our baby-sitter. Shouldn't we be heading home?

After paying the sitter, and finally alone in our living room, I lit into Irwin, "Don't you think that was putting them on the spot? Don't you think if they wanted to rent to us they would let us know?"

"I've got a great idea," Irwin said, his eyes bright for the first time in a couple of months, "and I wanna do research."

"What?"

"There's this old Edith Wharton story—1910 New York—in the public domain, and I want you and me to turn it into a musical."

"What?"

"You and me together—I want us to write a musical."

"Irwin—dear," I said slowly, "I sold one story, which does not make me a writer, and I'm not the least bit musical."

"But you write poems sometimes, which is almost the same as lyrics, and I've met this guy at the agency who writes jingles. He's dying to do a musical."

"I'll bet he is."

"Don't be that way—he's good."

"So write it with him."

"We need you too," Irwin said. "And I want to spend more time with Diana and Cliff, see how the upper crust lives. That's why I jumped on their rental."

"I don't really know Cliff, but Diana's not like that," I said. "And I'll be damned if I'll use my friend for research. What's gotten into you anyway? For years I've tried to get you to work on your own writing in your spare time, and you wouldn't touch it."

"It's lonely that way," Irwin answered with a shy shrug.

"Not really. Not for me anyway."

"I've been thinking about it a lot," Irwin said, after a moment. "I want us to do something together." I simply looked at him. What could I say to that? He thought he'd found another way to save our marriage.

We tried to work that weekend, when we weren't doing things with the kids, and tried again on Monday night and

Tuesday night. Our different styles became quickly apparent. Irwin wanted to plan everything out—the scenes, the dialogue—leaving nothing to chance, or the imagination, as I told him heatedly. I didn't write that way, when I wrote at all. I thought up characters, or took them from life, let them move around and talk, and put it all down. Irwin thought that was nuts, which I supposed it was, but I countered with the fact that he wrote nonfiction and I wrote fiction. They were entirely different. On top of that I could only write dialogue in a room by myself where I could listen to the characters. Irwin could only write dialogue by playing out a scene with somebody else, hopefully me. And on top of that, I couldn't write a lyric to save my life. Everything I came up with was so sappy we couldn't stand it.

By Wednesday afternoon I was dying to get away, and yearning for Sam. I'd called the theater. Yes, he was expecting me after the matinee. I took a cab uptown, stood in the back, watching Sam as Nathan Detroit, feeling that my whole body was in knots. He hadn't touched me in so long. My anticipation built during the curtain calls, during the long walk to his dressing room, and once there, Sam seemed to feel the same way. There were no visitors, and he shooed Clay out the door as soon as I came in. We went straight into his cave. He didn't even remove his makeup, which meant that I ended up half covered with greasepaint.

"Look at me, I'm a disaster," I said laughing.

"You're gorgeous," he said, backing up and squinting at me. "Two-toned, but gorgeous."

"Thanks, you too," I said, and then told Sam about the

short story I'd sold, and about Irwin deciding that we should write together, a musical no less. Sam was happy about the short story, and then quiet for a minute.

"D'you think that has anything to do with me? Wanting to write a musical?"

"I don't know. It hadn't occurred to me."

"I'm starring in a musical, after all." And after another pause, "What's this musical about, anyway?"

"New York society, circa 1910."

"Is it now?" Sam asked, in a snooty accent. He then rose, and proceeded to go into a song-and-dance takeoff of a drawing room comedy. I was laughing so hard that I didn't even know what he was singing. He was singing and prancing, wearing nothing but his garters and socks. He couldn't keep a straight face after a while, and we both laughed until our tears smeared the greasepaint. We took a shower together in the small bathroom that was hidden behind the musty costumes, laughed some more, made love again, and then devoured the sandwiches that Clay had left outside the dressing room door. By then it was time for Sam to get ready for the evening performance. We kissed, promised to be together soon, and I left knowing that I couldn't give this up. Pricket had been right—desire was winning out over good intentions, over philosophical notions, over any damn thing I could think of.

At home that night, as Irwin read aloud an article he'd found at the library about the Astors and the Vanderbilts, I unexpectedly started laughing. I was seeing an image of Sam, very upper-class, prancing around in nothing but his socks and garters.

"What's so funny?"

"Nothing. Sorry." I wished I could tell him. Under different circumstances Irwin would have thought this hilarious. Of course, I couldn't tell him, so I excused myself, controlling giggles, and went to bed early. Bed felt wonderful, the sheets like silk against my skin, every bit of me awake and alive. I luxuriated for a minute or two before drifting into a dream about Sam.

Chapter Ten

April was explosive, inwardly and outwardly. The assassination of Martin Luther King shocked us, and devastated the children. They'd been too young when Kennedy was killed to really understand. I remember the boys watching the funeral with me, at moments, and then carrying large blocks down the hallway, chanting, "We're burying President Kennedy, we're burying President Kennedy." But Martin Luther King was different; they'd grown up with him. The Little Red School House, in the heart of the Village, was a progressive, integrated school. In assemblies they sang "We Shall Overcome" and "Where Have All the Flowers Gone?" King was a hero, his dream and his movement embraced, so his killing was their first run-in with insanity and injustice. They tried to make sense out of it, and couldn't, and we weren't much help. All we could do was to grieve with them, and try to hide the fact that our lives were in shambles, and getting worse by the day.

The best part of early April in New York was the shedding

of winter clothes. Snow pants, mittens and galoshes were happily discarded by the kids, overcoats and parkas by the grown-ups, and we could walk outside in just sweaters, jeans and sneakers. Bare branches were coming alive, the forsythia was golden, and the first robins were darts of red between the garden trees. The garden mothers began gathering again on the benches, and on one of these perfect afternoons I found Diana sobbing on the bench nearest our house. She was turned away, hiding her face, but her shoulders were shaking.

"Diana, sweetheart, what's wrong?" I asked, sitting beside her, trying to get an arm around her.

"I can't talk," she said, between sobs, shaking me off.

"Sure, you can. You can talk to me," I said gently. She twisted further away, and pressed her forehead on the top slat of the bench. "I'm the one that gets it, remember?" I said.

"Not this," she said, and after a minute turned her ravaged face to me. "I told Cliff, and he said he'd take the children—he'd take everything."

"Told him what?"

"Told him I wanted to leave him, told him I loved somebody else."

"Oh, God . . ."

"Oh, God is right," she said bitterly. "I can't lose my kids—I'd die—and Cliff controls the money—I turned it all over to him!"

"I know, I did that too," I said quietly. "Not money like your money, but still—I did it too."

"Fucking idiots," Diana muttered, and I tried not to laugh. "I don't know what to do, Cal . . . I have no idea."

"Maybe he'll change his mind. Maybe if you give it some time."

"You don't know Cliff," Diana answered as she wiped her face and blew her nose. "You don't know how stubborn, how totally self-righteous—"

"No, I don't."

"I can't lose my kids," Diana said again, her voice desolate.

"Then you won't," I said, and reached out and held her, one hand stroking her hair. I knew that she'd made a decision. She would tell her lover, whoever he was, that it was over, and stay with Cliff and the kids. How would she do that, I wondered? How could she?

"Can I use your phone?" Diana asked.

Diana stayed with me for a couple of hours after her wrenching phone call, and then stayed out of sight for a few days. She didn't show up at the next meeting of the garden ghost-hunters, but Sam didn't either, which made me uneasy. The meeting wasn't that different from the previous one: the old ladies carried on about Lucy, Josh was still trying to rid himself of the presence of his first wife, and the old soldier was still rattling his sabers. I told them about my glimpse, or what I thought was a glimpse, of the young lovers parting, and Brenda Dakin, the sixtyish maiden daughter, burst into tears. I knew the feeling. Hal and Laurette again pushed their new Scientology church above Blimpie's.

I left a bit early, and went looking for Sam. It was one of his nights off, and he usually jumped at the chance to get out of the house. I circled the garden, going the long way round, and walked past his picture window. He was on the phone in front of the window, and he gestured for me to come in. I shook my head, but his next gesture was urgent, harried, and he was shouting into the phone. I pushed open the glass door in time to hear the tail end of his tirade.

"What do I pay a goddamn fortune in taxes for if you can't tell me what the hell's going on up there? Yes, my wife was protesting but she's not a kid, she's thirty-five for Christ's sake—they could be holding her hostage or something! Yeah, let me know, fine!" And he slammed down the phone.

"What's going on?"

"Like I know," he said angrily. "Shirley and Arthur went up to Columbia for some peaceful protest, something about the blacks and the new gym—"

"Oh, I read about it. The back door faces Harlem and the kids are all upset."

"They're more than upset, they're taking over the fucking campus, and the police are there, and they're calling the fucking National Guard." He grabbed his keys and jacket, and headed for the front door. "I'm going up there."

"What are you going to do?"

"I dunno, find Shirl."

"Is someone with the girls?" I called after him.

"Yeah," Sam called back, and banged out the front door.

I left through the garden door, and walked home slowly. I was startled by Sam's concern, and then thought that that was really naive of me. Shirley was his wife, the mother of his daughters. Hadn't I been willing to give everything up the night of the fire? Hadn't Sam been almost invisible when I was so worried about my kids? Yes, but that was my kids, not my husband. Sam had been so worried about Shirley he'd barely noticed me. I was still distracted as I entered our living room, and saw that Irwin was listening to the news on the radio.

"Damn kids are taking over Columbia," he said, glancing up as I came in. "How were the ghosts tonight?"

"Fine." And indicating the radio, "What's happening?"

"They're throwing chairs out the windows, stuff like that. It sounds like they don't even know what they want."

"Any real violence?"

"Not yet, but there will be. Peaceful protests seem to be a thing of the past. Anyhow, I wrote some dialogue I want you to hear." He picked up a yellow pad from the coffee table and began to read aloud. "Esther: I can't possibly stay at Lady Mayberry's. Jane: But why not, my dear? . . ."

As I listened to Irwin's voice, I realized that the strange feeling in my chest was fear. Maybe it was the idea of going the way of Diana, giving up my dreams, and spending the rest of my life stuck in this moment, listening to Irwin, smoking the same cigarette, hearing the same voice on the radio—forever. Maybe it was that violence had come to our city. There had been plenty of it elsewhere in recent years, uprisings and brutality in the South, in Chicago, in San Francisco, and now it was in New York. No, that wasn't it. Our part of the Village was like a small town. Sure, there were hippies, head shops and antiwar protests, but the storekeepers knew the children by name and kept an eye on them. Even the grizzled drunk, who sometimes slept in our doorway, clutching his paper bag, looked up and smiled at the children as they stepped over his feet on their way to school.

The fear that clenched my chest was closer to home. Sam

cared a great deal about Shirley and very little about me. His behavior tonight made that obvious. So if I managed to get free, he probably wouldn't. But freedom was what I really wanted, or so I'd told Pricket. Maybe it was a lie; maybe I just wanted Sam.

Irwin continued to read aloud—"Esther: Even if I managed to get an invitation, I couldn't possibly go. Jane: If it's a matter of the proper clothes, dearest, that's hardly a problem at'll." As I listened to Irwin, and the monotone of the radio, the sense of being stuck in this moment forever increased to the point of seeming an endless nightmare.

"Irwin, I'm going insane!" I shouted suddenly. "In one second I may go upstairs, and like those kids, start throwing all the furniture out the window!" Irwin put the pad down slowly, and studied my reddened face.

"Is it Sam?" he asked, for the first time since the night of my Christmas present. "I saw you come from there."

"No, it's nothing to do with Sam!" I lied. "Sam was just scared about Shirley. She's up at Columbia with Arthur, maybe in danger—"

Irwin cut me off with a short laugh. "Shirley and Arthur in the midst of the melee." He shook his head, and there was a silence before he looked at me directly. "If you really want him, I'll help you get him," he said.

"What?" I asked, staring at him—gaping would be more accurate.

"I'm good at thinking up campaigns," he said. "So if you really want Sam, I'll help you get him."

"Is this part of 'getting it out of my system'?" I asked with disbelief.

"I guess," Irwin answered.

"That's the craziest thing I ever heard," I said.

We left it at that. I went to bed, wondering which one of us was crazier, and the next morning I went looking for Diana. I couldn't find her, but I had to talk to someone. I wasn't about to call Pricket—I could hear her response to this in my head—so I sought out Ruthie. She was heading for the markets on Bleecker, and I joined her. As she fingered outdoor produce I told her what Irwin had said about helping me get Sam.

"Sounds good to me," she said, without missing a beat, as she squeezed a cantaloupe.

"I don't believe you," I said, laughing. "You are so—so—"

"Tough?"

"Yes, tough."

Ruthie shrugged. "It wouldn't hurt you to acquire some toughness yourself."

Those words echoed in my head in the two weeks that followed. I was a wreck. Sam and Irwin both seemed to be withdrawing, my fears escalating, and my explosions occurring more frequently. During the early evening, after returning from the walk with Ruthie, I'd tried Sam at the theater to ask if he'd found Shirley, and if everything was all right. It wasn't a matinee day, but he should have been there. Clay said he wasn't, but that Sam, Shirley and Arthur had managed to get home okay. I heard voices in the background so I told Clay to just tell Sam, whenever it was convenient, that I'd been worried about them.

At home Irwin continued to be dead-eyed and jovial. He stayed up later than usual, working on the musical—I had pretty much dropped out—and increasingly I felt imprisoned in a moment that would never end. I'd wait for Irwin to go to bed, hoping to be able to go out into the garden, praying for a sweet look or word from Sam, but instead we'd sit there, me in the rocker, Irwin on the sofa, and I'd be living my nightmare—this particular second would go on and on and on.

It was to break this stasis that one evening I bolted out of the house. I'd grabbed a jacket, my shoulder bag, and fled toward Eighth Avenue. I got our car out of the garage and headed north, wanting to go home, and at the same time knowing that my childhood home wasn't there anymore. It started to rain somewhere in the Bronx, and I discovered that the windshield wipers were worn, and just pushed the water around like used mops. I slowed down, hunched over the steering wheel, and watched ugly brick buildings being washed by an April shower. I speeded up on the parkway—I knew this stretch so well—and felt enclosed by the dark woods I loved so much on either side of the road.

It was close to midnight when I pulled into my brother's driveway. Ted and Robin were waiting for me, in pajamas and robes. Irwin had called, frantic they said, and thought that I might be on my way to them. I started to cry as soon as I sat down at their kitchen table, and spilled out the whole miserable story of my marriage and affair. They hadn't heard any of this; I hadn't told them, but they'd known at Christmas that all was not well on MacDougal Street. They fixed me a hot toddy with bourbon and butter that was lethal, and proceeded to sound like all my former psychiatrists. It was a phase. A few of their friends had reached this crisis, and managed to stay together. They'd had crises themselves, which I found hard to believe, but were so glad that they'd been slow to react, hadn't split up, and had found that their marriage was stronger for having been through a tough time.

I kept shaking my head, drunker by the second, and saying that I couldn't do it. I just couldn't do what everybody thought I ought to do. "I'd rather die," I said drunkenly, dramatically, but I knew that I meant it. Ted and Robin glanced at each other, very aware of the family history, and then decided to let it be.

"You'd better call Irwin," Ted said. "He sounded really upset and worried."

"You call him," I muttered. "Can I sleep here?"

"You'd better," Robin said.

I fell into their sofa bed, and once the guestroom stopped spinning, slept for ten hours. Ted had calmed Irwin down the night before, and again in the morning. After breakfast, a lot of coffee and thank yous, I got in the car and headed home. The sky was clear, the greening trees glistened along the parkway, and my marriage was almost over. It only took another couple of days. Irwin had been frightened by my bolt into the rainy night, and began to offer solutions. I couldn't figure it out; why couldn't he let it be over? Why was he holding on to a sham? Maybe it was pride, maybe it was love of the children, maybe he needed me, or someone, so much that he was willing to make any bargain to save us.

It seemed to be all three as he offered solutions, propositions, to get us through. He'd brought home travel brochures, and spread them out on the coffee table after the children were in bed. He said that we needed to get away, for at least a couple of weeks, have the honeymoon that we hadn't been able to have. Like so many lonely children who married, we hadn't been able to afford a honeymoon, and then the babies had come, so close together, and we hadn't been able to get away together for more than a weekend.

Irwin spread out the Paris brochure, then the literary tour of Great Britain, then the cruise around the Greek Islands. I kept shaking my head.

"I really don't want to go anywhere with you, Irwin."

"How about India and the Taj Mahal?" He was only half joking.

"Irwin, you don't understand."

"What? What don't I understand?"

"I don't want to go anywhere with *you.*" This silenced him, and he seemed to be taking it in, but then, just to be sure, I said the worst thing to him that I've ever said to anyone in my life: "Irwin, my nightmare is the two of us growing old together."

He got it then. His eyes went from pained to dead again as he slowly gathered the brochures and headed for the stairs.

"I'll leave tomorrow," he said.

"We have to talk to the kids."

"Tomorrow," he repeated.

Irwin went to work, and came home at the usual time the next day. The children and I were waiting for him; I'd told them that we needed to talk, all of us together. It was a warm spring evening; the boys had been playing ball, and they sat on the sofa, tossing balls into mitts as Irwin began to speak. He was in the rocker opposite us; Emma was snuggled next to me.

"Your mother and I have decided—" Irwin began, in a mournful tone.

"But you promised," Danny interrupted.

"What?"

"You promised you'd never get divorced like everybody else!" It was true. Irwin and I looked at each other—yes, when marriages were busting up all around us, we'd promised Danny that it would never happen to us.

"I've told you too," Irwin said, "that grown-ups can't always keep their promises. We thought we wouldn't but—"

"You can't," Danny said, starting to cry. "You lied."

"We didn't mean to," I said, reaching for him, but Irwin was already there, holding him.

"It's going to be okay," Irwin said gently to all three of them. "Actually, it's going to be better than it is now."

"How?" Jake asked suspiciously. Emma simply looked confused.

"Well, you'll see more of both of us," Irwin answered. "You'll have a lot of time with your mom, and be able to do the stuff with her she likes, like reading and telling stories. And you'll have more special times with me to go to ball games and the Automat—"

"I don't like ball games," Emma said.

"But you like the Automat," Jake interjected.

"And your dad and I will always be best friends, and talk to each other all the time," I said.

"On the phone?"

"On the phone, and here."

By the time it was over the kids believed, and I believed, everything that we'd said. We'd all love each other, see each other, and it would be much more fun than it had been before. In the morning Irwin gave the children breakfast, kissed them at the door, and waved as they went off to school.

They seemed fine; their world wasn't really changing, or so they thought. They still had their home, their school, their parents as much as before, only separately. Irwin had told them that he'd come by later, and take them on a fun trip during spring vacation, so they left for school, excited, arguing about where they wanted to go. Danny wanted to visit a jungle, any jungle. Jake wanted to see a Pirates game. Emma wasn't sure, but she wanted to go to Grandma Helen's for Easter and find a lot of eggs and candy.

I helped Irwin pack his two suitcases, handing him shirts, and finding things that he was forgetting. He said he'd get the rest later. I followed him downstairs as he carried his bags, and stood beside the stairs as he reached the front door.

"Do you know where you're going?"

"Maybe my old room at the cave on Broadway."

"Oh, please."

"Maybe the Y, and fend off the bugs and the fags."

I laughed, aware that he was still making me laugh. Then there was a moment, a brief moment, when Irwin smiled at me, all the old warmth back in his eyes, and I wanted to call him back. I wanted to run to him, tell him how much I loved him and say, "Don't go, please don't go." But the moment passed. I didn't say anything, and he was gone.

The house was wonderfully quiet. I went back upstairs, into the boys' room, said hello to Danny's gerbil in his cage, and then began spinning, my arms over my head, my head thrown back. I spun and spun until I collapsed on the floor, dizzy with relief and freedom.

Chapter Eleven

"You're the happiest separated woman I ever saw," Diana said, when I finally found her a couple of days later. She was doing spring cleaning, tossing everything out of the linen closet on the third floor, wiping the shelves, refolding and replacing. She looked relaxed, her face and arms freckled by the spring sun, not a sign of the distraught woman who'd sobbed in my house after giving up her lover.

"Who told you?" I asked.

"Let's see . . . Ruthie, Susan, Brenda, Laurette and, oh, yes, Shirley."

"Shirley?"

"The one and only."

"God, I haven't told Sam yet. I haven't seen him."

"He probably knows."

"Yeah, I guess, seeing as the whole garden seems to."

Diana shrugged, and snapped a sheet in my direction. "Can you take the other end?" I nodded, grabbed the ends of the sheet, and walked it toward her. "As I was saying," she continued, "you look great, really happy."

"I am," I said. "And relieved."

"Me too," Diana said, as we started on another sheet.

"What happened? The last time I saw you—"

"I know, I was a blubbering mess."

"So, what happened?"

"I went to the beach for a few days, just me, and walked on the sand, through the fields—it was still freezing—and slept, and ate a lot of chowder, and came back and got a job."

"Really?"

"Really. With your new agent, my old friend Lorraine. I'm starting at the bottom, of course, learning about contracts, negotiating, reading the manuscripts that come in. I love to read, and find talent, as you know—I found you—"

"I don't count."

"Yes you do. Lorraine's about to sell another story of yours. You should call her."

"Really?" and then I wondered how many times I could say "really" in a conversation. I thought I'd try again. "Are you really happy, Diana, really?"

"Yes. I was just bored, that's all. That's what it was all about. That's what I realized in Sagaponack. Now I'm just excited about getting up early, putting on snazzy clothes, spending my days doing what I love to do."

"Really?" I asked again, feeling like an idiot. I couldn't imagine a job, any job, making me happier than hopeful dreams of Sam.

"You look dubious," Diana said, as she confronted me with another sheet.

"No, not at all. I'm happy for you," I answered, as I walked the sheet toward her.

"By the way," Diana said, "I talked to Cliff, and we'd be happy for you to rent the stable this summer."

"Really?" Shit, I'd said it again.

"Yes, really," Diana said in a light, mocking tone.

"I know, I know, I sound like an idiot. How come?"

"Well, we always liked you better than Irwin, and now you're on your own—"

"Really?" And we laughed at the same time. "I'll have to talk to him, see if we—he—can afford it. What are you asking, do you know?"

"No, I'll have to ask Cliff, but we'll give you a break because it's right next door. We can baby-sit for each other."

"It sounds wonderful."

"Good. And if you want to come for a weekend with the kids, and check it out—it's almost finished—let me know."

"Thanks, I'd love to," I said, and left Diana's house baffled, pleased and surprised.

There were other surprising reactions. Dorothy, Irwin's mother, thought it was a good move. She'd been stuck in an Epstein marriage for forty years, and was now enjoying her widowhood. Helen, my stepmother, thought it a dreadful move—Irwin had saved me, and now I'd be all alone. Pricket, when I called her, was cautious. She said again that she'd thought I'd needed an affair, not a divorce. Ted and Robin were disappointed; they thought I could have worked it out. They also emphasized that it wasn't an irrevocable decision. They knew several couples who had separated for a time, then gotten back together. Ruthie was predictable: why shoot yourself in the foot? She was perfectly content with Josh *and* Kevin. Shirley had large, blue, bloodshot eyes when I ran into her in the garden, and told me how terribly sorry she was. She added that she'd be available at a moment's notice during my time of pain. Laurette offered a free Communication course at their new church/office, Scientology in the Village.

When I called Sam at the theater, two days after Irwin left, he was putting on his makeup for the evening performance. I asked, excitedly, if he could meet me after the show?

"Anywhere," I added.

"How about Blimpie's?" he said.

"Blimpie's?"

"Yeah, I've been dreaming about their ham, cheese and pickles. The one on 11th Street. Then we can walk back."

"Sure. What time?"

"I ought to get there between eleven-thirty and twelve, depending on traffic."

"You're sure? I mean I asked Maddy to stay."

"I'm sure, I've gotta go," he said hurriedly, and I heard Clay in the background telling him that it was the half-hour call.

Irwin came by that evening, as he'd promised he would, gave the kids their baths, read aloud the next chapter of *The Lion, the Witch, and the Wardrobe,* and asked the children what they thought about a ski vacation in Vermont for their spring break?

"We don't know how," they pretty much said at once.

"We'll learn," Irwin said. "We'll rent skis, get a teacher, and start on the bunny slopes."

"Are there bunnies on it?"

"No," Irwin laughed, "it just means the slope for beginners. Hey, I've never done it either. A nice Jewish boy from Upper Broadway? I'm gonna learn right along with you."

That made them all happy, and the children jumped up and down on the sofa cushions, and said that they couldn't wait for spring vacation. It made me happy too. I thanked Irwin for being such a wonderful father, said good night to him, and tucked the children in bed. As I sat alone in the living room, waiting for it to be eleven and time to walk slowly up to Blimpie's, I felt grateful that it was all going so well. The children didn't seem too upset; Irwin was being sweet, and seemed cheerful, considering. I heard later that it was an act, that he was trying hard, that he was devastated, but I didn't know it at that peaceful moment.

I found that I was too excited to walk slowly. My feet kept accelerating, along with my heartbeat. I tried to focus on the night life that I'd rarely seen—the dimly lit basketball game in a playground on Sixth Avenue, the beaded children high on love or something, the NYU students looking for some action, the blind musician with his dog, the leftover Village intellectuals heading for the in bar, the right poetry reading. I wanted to savor it all, having lived the sixties in a continual state of motherhood, but I couldn't concentrate. I told myself that I had plenty of time to take it all in, and hurried toward 11th Street.

The lights were bright in Blimpie's, the Naugahyde booths more crimson than maroon, hardly a place for a rendezvous. I was the first to arrive, naturally. I got some coffee, sat in a booth in the back, facing the door, and waited for Sam. There were only three other people in the restaurant, two a few feet away from each other at the curved counter, and another in the front booth. I tried to amuse myself by imagining what they were waiting for, but I was too anxious for Sam to appear in the doorway to indulge in musings about strangers.

Then there he was, wearing a light trench coat, the rim of a fedora tipped over his forehead. I laughed as he approached, and settled into the booth across from me.

"What's funny?"

"You look like Sam Spade," I said, still laughing.

"I'm in disguise, sweetheart," he said in the Sam Spade accent that we'd both heard as kids. "And I'm starving," he added as he rose and went up to the counter. I watched him as he described in detail the sandwich he wanted, then turned back to me. "You order?"

"I ate before," I lied, much too nervous to eat, and waited as he made small talk with the guy making his sandwich. Probably giving him tickets to the show, I thought, then realized that I was sounding like Shirley. I began to wonder how long it would take, living with Sam, to become as jaded as Shirley about his incessant need for adoration. But as soon as he returned, slid into the booth, gave me a melting smile, and lifted his sandwich to his lips with those beautiful hands, all such thoughts flew out of my head.

"You look great, glowing," he said, between mouthfuls.

"I am. I'm excited. You heard about me and Irwin?"

"I heard that he left, not more than that. How come?"

"It was mainly me. I've been wanting to get free for so long. I was going around to shrinks saying 'I just don't want to be married.'" I looked down at the grainy Formica of the table, at the pale circle on my left hand where my gold band had been for years, then back up at Sam. "And it had something to do with you," I added.

Sam chewed slowly, swallowed, and wiped his mouth before he reached over and covered my left hand with his right. "If it's a good thing, then I'm proud to have had something to do with it," he said.

"Thanks," I answered shyly. Was that all he was going to say?

"How are the kids doing?" he asked.

"Pretty well. Irwin's being great."

"Good." Sam nodded, squeezed my hand and let it go before saying quietly, "I couldn't ever leave my kids."

"I don't think I could either," I said.

"You don't have to. But me—well, men—I'd lose everything." It was quiet for a minute as Sam finished his sandwich, and I listened to his chewing, and tried to hide my disappointment. I'd sensed that Sam wasn't about to leave his family for me, but I'd hoped for something more, more than I was getting at any rate.

"What are you going to do with yourself?" Sam asked finally, his flirtatious look back in his eyes. "With all that spare time?"

"I don't know. Write more, cook less." We both laughed, and I added that it would be easier to see him now, if that was all right with him.

"All right? You're damned right it's all right," he said, and again covered my hand with his.

After Sam had paid, had another lengthy conversation, this time with the cashier, and we began to walk east on 11th Street, I noticed Hal and Laurette's new Scientology office/church on the floor above Blimpie's.

"Look. I'd forgotten they'd said it was here. Up there, Sam." He followed my pointing finger to the dark space above the restaurant. The entrance, a nondescript doorway at street level, was on 11th, but "Scientology in the Village" was painted in black letters on the tinted windows of the second floor.

"Looks empty," Sam said, as we both stopped and looked up.

"It's after midnight."

Sam pulled his hat down further over his eyes, and asked in his Sam Spade voice, "You wanna raid the joint, sweetheart?"

"What for?"

"Secrets, sweetheart," he said, grinning.

"You're kidding? Whose?"

"No, I'm not kidding. It's like going to a shrink. You pay money, you use this lie detector thing, and you tell them all your secrets. Come on, let's go." Sam took my hand and pulled me toward the doorway.

"Sam, I don't think it's a good idea," I said slowly, pulling him in the other direction. "We could get arrested!"

"Nah. I've broken into lots of places."

"As a grown-up?"

"Who says I'm a grown-up?" Sam asked innocently, and we were both laughing, and playfully shoving each other as I linked my arm in his and led him down the quiet street of brownstones.

"Did I tell you Laurette offered me a free Communication course, whatever that is?" I asked.

"Do it. See what their game is."

"Maybe sometime," I said. "I was intrigued, remember, when she talked about learning how to contact the ghosts, not just the garden ones, but people we loved?"

"I remember. That's why I go to their meetings, and sit out in the garden waiting for ghosts—and the calla lily, of course," he added quickly. He pulled the hat brim down further, and gave me a quick kiss.

"D'you want to try their course with me?" I asked, feeling bolder, aware that I was blushing.

"Hell, no, I've got too many secrets," he said with another grin. We turned the corner, heading down Fifth Avenue toward the park, and Sam pulled away slightly, removing his arm, as we approached the kids beneath the arch in Washington Square, still strumming and singing at one in the morning. Sam left me at the corner of MacDougal, and headed for Sullivan. We mouthed "soon" to each other as we parted, and I stepped over the drunk in my doorway as if on a cloud. There were possibilities; anything was possible, for the first time in years.

I locked the front door, looked for messages, tiptoed up the stairs, and checked the quiet rooms. Maddy was asleep in the fold-out bed in Emma's room. Emma was holding her Snoopy, pink-cheeked, moist hair on her pillow. I kissed her and went into the boys' room. The gerbil was still, the boys breathing deeply. I kissed Jake's forehead in the bottom bunk, and ran a hand across Danny's forehead as he slept on the top.

In my double bed, facing the trees and the lights of the garden, I spread my arms and legs and luxuriated. No one was going to latch on to me during the night. No one was going to jump up, like a startled owl, if I crept out of bed. I could walk out into the garden at midnight, free as the nesting birds. This was what I'd dreamed of, and it was delicious.

The following weekend the children and I went to Sagaponack to check out the nearly remodeled stable that Diana had offered to rent to us for part of June and all of July and August. Spring was in full bloom in Sagaponack that weekend. Apple, peach and cherry trees sweetened the ocean air. Acres of corn and potato fields stretched to the beaches. Cliff and Diana's house, the family plot, was a mile from the general store where milk was sold and mail picked up, and a curved, rutted road led to the shingled farmhouse, the ancient barn and the newly renovated stables. The children and I stayed in the house with Diana that weekend because the stables weren't quite finished, and Cliff had decided to stay in town.

We loved our summer home on sight. Part of the downstairs was a garage, separated from our living room and large pine/country kitchen. Upstairs there was a bedroom, mine, and a long, low attic room that had been a loft of some sort. Aside from the fact that the children weren't sure they all wanted to sleep together, in dormitory fashion, we were delighted. I told Emma that we could put up a screen, or hang a curtain to separate her from the boys, and besides she'd be spending most of her time with her best friend, Maryellen.

We went to the Bridgehampton ocean beach in the afternoon because it was much too cold to swim—no need for a fly-infested bay beach—and walked through the dune grass down to the wet sand and the pewter waves. The children played chicken with the surf, running out with the tide, and then scampering back, just ahead of the foam. We picked up sand dollars, bits of sea glass, pieces of gray driftwood, and the children popped clusters of seaweed with their bare heels. I told Diana that I'd never felt so happy, or loved my children as much as I did at this moment.

"How come?" she asked, frowning slightly.

"How come I love my kids so much?"

"No. How come right now?"

I tried to light a cigarette against the wind before answering, but the match kept blowing out, and I gave up. "I guess because they're no longer symbols of my trap," I said finally. "I can just love them now." Diana still looked confused, but I couldn't find the words to explain further, and we walked in silence until we heard the children shouting—they were freezing and starving—and we turned back, laughing at their delight in exaggeration.

Diana drove her station wagon to the old-fashioned soda shop on Sag Harbor's main street, and we all stuffed ourselves on sandwiches and milk shakes. Afterward the children dozed in the back seat while Diana drove across the long, low bridge over the bay to see if Ruthie and Josh, or Ruthie and Kevin had come for the weekend. But as we left the bridge, Diana pulled over and pointed at the first house on the left, almost hidden from the road by trees and hedges. I could make out a wide porch, the length of the house, an ancient wisteria vine just beginning to flower, and a widow's walk above the trees.

"Whose house is that?" I asked. "It's beautiful."

"Sam and Shirley's. I thought you knew."

"No, I didn't. I didn't know them last year," I said, and as Diana laughed, I cut her off with a glance at the back seat. "Let's not get biblical, shall we?"

"Where are we?" Danny asked, sitting up.

"Oh, that's Annie's house," I said, without turning.

"Neat. Can we go back now?"

"Sure. I don't feel like Ruthie's," I said to Diana, and she nodded and turned the car around.

"It's an old whaling captain's house," Diana said, as we drove back across the bridge, catching the last lavender colors of sunset over the bay. "It's supposed to be haunted, of course."

"The ghosts just follow Sam around," I answered, smiling, and then turned away, wanting to be quiet. I wanted to think about the summer, to dream really. I'd be in Sagaponack, Sam just a few miles away. Maybe we could meet at the beach at night, steal time on his widow's walk, commune with the ghosts as we did in the garden. Then I remembered that he wouldn't be here that much, he'd still be in the show, but he'd be here part of the time, and I'd be able to go into town for a day or two. It was still summer in my mind as we pulled into Diana's driveway.

Easter fell on the first Sunday of spring vacation, so Irwin and I arranged with Helen that he would bring the kids to her house for the traditional egg hunt, and then continue on to Vermont for their ski trip. They were all packed on Saturday, and I sent them off on Easter morning with baskets filled with chocolate bunnies and jellybeans. I didn't have to bother with the eggs—Helen would do them in Greenwich—a relief because I was never any good at the artsy-crafty things that mothers were supposed to do, decorating eggs or making Halloween costumes.

It felt strange to be alone on Easter, a family holiday, but I recovered quickly. I took the bus uptown, watched a bit of the parade, stopped by St. Patrick's to pay my respects, and window-shopped my way up to Bergdorf's and the park. Every once in a while I'd stop and look at my watch, thinking I had to be somewhere, then realize, with lovely relief, that I didn't have to be anywhere. It was the first time in my life, since school vacations, that I could do whatever I wanted, or do nothing at all. My one responsibility was to feed and water Danny's gerbil. I relished every second of that week. It was a good thing that I did too because I remembered that week later with longing.

Irwin called a few times from Vermont, said the trip was going well, and put the children on the phone. They said that they were having a great time, not fighting too much or too often, and that they missed me. I lied and said that I missed them too, thanked Irwin again for being such a good father, and headed for Figaro's, writing pad under my arm, to drink coffee among the Village artists, and pretend that I was one of them.

I had another fun day, pretending to be a writer. My agent

actually had sold a second short story. I went up to their office on Lexington to pick up my check—all mine, made out just to me—and Diana and Lorraine took me to the Pen & Pencil for an expense account lunch. They wanted to know what I was working on, taking me seriously in a way that I didn't at all. I told them that I was thinking about a novel, which was sort of true.

On matinee day I went to the theater to spend Sam's "rest time" with him. After some passion and a sandwich, we smoked in his lair, and I told him about selling another story, and being treated like a writer by my agent.

"Why don't you write something for me?" he asked.

"How about a turn-of-the-century Edith Wharton musical?" I asked, keeping a straight face in the dim light.

"Oh, that one, great!" Sam said, and tried to jump up and dance, naked as usual except for the damn socks.

"No, Sam, no," and I threw myself on him, and we rolled around and laughed for a minute. As I caught my breath, I said, "Sam, I have a huge favor to ask."

"Yeah?"

"Please show me your feet."

"Never," he said, in some kind of accent. "Never do I show you my feet!" We laughed some more, shared another cigarette, and I thought how wonderful it was just to have fun.

"Why don't you stay for the show? I'm craving Greek tonight, and there's this dive on Tenth—"

"You don't have to get home?"

"No, Shirley took the girls to Washington so they'd know what she's protesting about."

"That doesn't quite follow, but I'd love to stay."

I sat through all of *Guys and Dolls* that night, in an unused house seat, treasuring every second of Sam on stage, hung around the stage door afterward while Sam took off his makeup and chatted with visitors, then jumped in a cab with him that the doorman had hailed. The Greek restaurant on Tenth Avenue in the 50s *was* a dive, but it was authentic—the food, the dancing, all of it. Everyone knew Sam, of course. They brought us ouzo from the back room, plied us with delicacies, and urged Sam to dance. Only the men were allowed to dance, in proper Greek fashion, so I sipped the potent, milky drink, and watched Sam as he and a few other men danced the backwards-forwards-sideways steps, arms around each other's shoulders.

It was three in the morning before I sank blissfully into bed. The rest of the week continued to be carefree, and I was happy to see the children when Irwin brought them home on Sunday. They were tanned, bubbly and tired, but wanted to tell me all about the trip. Once they were fed, bathed and in bed, Irwin and I sat in the living room, and talked for a bit about nothing.

"I met someone there," Irwin said suddenly.

"You did? Who?"

"Her name's Kathleen Riley. She's great—the kids liked her." His eyes were half closed, the expression that meant he was uncomfortable.

"That's wonderful," I said, meaning it, and wanting to ease his discomfort.

"It doesn't bother you?" he asked, his eyes opening.

"No. I'm happy. I want you to be happy."

"Good. Thanks," he murmured.

"Tell me about her."

"Not right now," he said as he rose. "I'm late already." As he left I noticed that his eyes were half closed again, but aside from a twinge of separation in my chest, there were no intimations of anything to come.

Chapter Twelve

The changes were incremental, barely noticeable. I was surprised that Irwin was spending so much time with Kathleen so quickly. She had a one-bedroom, terraced apartment in Carnegie Hill, and spent most weekends at the family compound in Cape May. They hadn't moved in together, but Irwin seemed to be spending a lot of time at both places. This didn't interfere with our lives, the children and mine, and Irwin was happier than he'd been in months. He was cheerful, and joking, when he picked up the kids, and my guilt lessened considerably. I was also surprised when the children told me that Irwin had taken Kathleen with them one Saturday to meet Helen. She was my stepmother, after all, but then I realized that Irwin was fond of her, and it was natural for him to want to introduce Kathleen to her.

When Helen called to report, I found out that Kathleen was a divorced, childless interior decorator, who specialized in imported fabrics, rugs and antiques, and worked occasionally.

"She does it for fun," Helen added. "Her family owns Delaware."

"Pretty small state," I answered, laughing.

My mother-in-law, Dorothy, added to all this when she called with the news, "And they're all Catholics, the whole family!"

"You're kidding?"

"No. And Irwin's talking about converting! His father would sit shiva if he was still here."

"He won't do that, Dorothy. Irwin's not religious, but he's proud of his whole Jewish heritage."

"From your lips," she said, and hung up because she was starting to cry.

The first change that affected us involved the children's visits. There were no formal arrangements yet, no separation agreement, although Irwin said that he would see a lawyer soon, and get one drawn up. Irwin still visited frequently, and picked the kids up to do whatever they wanted to do—a movie, a game, Central Park. But by mid-May, early June, Irwin was spending most weekends in Cape May with Kathleen and her family, which included grandparents, sisters, aunts and cousins. He invited his mother for one weekend, but that didn't go too well because the family priest showed up on Sunday morning to conduct a private mass.

Then he and Kathleen invited our children for a weekend. I packed their clean clothes carefully, told them to be good and not to fight, verbally or physically, over every little thing. But, apparently, it wasn't enough. Kathleen's house on the compound was small, a two-bedroom cottage, filled with fragile Americana, too small for three rambunctious kids. The boys barely missed a Tiffany lamp with a softball, and Emma screamed her head off when Kathleen wouldn't let her wear her Danskins to the family dinner at the main house.

The result of all this was that Irwin told me, as tactfully as possible, that Kathleen could only handle a visit about one weekend a month, if that often. The first mention of money came after Irwin had sat down with the Riley family business manager. Irwin sent me a list of all the expenses that the business manager suggested I cut down on.

"Flowers?" I said to Ruthie, as I showed her the list in the garden. "He wants me to stop buying flowers!"

"Just not every week. It says right here." She pointed with her nail file. We were sitting on a shaded bench, and Ruthie was giving herself a manicure. "You can buy flowers once a month, what's the big deal?"

"Flowers make me happy."

"Aww," was all she said.

"And the Winners, the boys' favorite thing, and Maddy—they want me to cut Maddy down to once a week."

"Did you expect your life to stay just the same?" Ruthie asked between filings.

"And laundry and dry cleaning?" I said, talking over her. "It was Irwin's shirts that went out, anyway."

"So cross out laundry, cut down on flowers, and you'll be fine. And Maddy doesn't come during the summer, and the boys don't go to Craig till fall, right?"

"Right."

"So stop fretting—until September, anyway."

I put the list in a drawer, and stopped buying flowers at the stands on Bleecker. We'd be in Sagaponack soon, and there'd be wildflowers everywhere—daisies, black-eyed Susans, Queen Anne's lace. I spent a lot of time dreaming ahead to the days and nights of the summer. I'd always daydreamed while doing mundane things like cooking and washing dishes, but I had more time now. I didn't have to really cook anymore—no dinners for Irwin, no elaborate dinners for clients or agency friends. One of the first things I'd done after Irwin left was to throw out my whole file of gourmet recipes. The children were happy with Maddy's warmed-over roast chicken, hamburgers, hot dogs and even TV dinners.

The other thing on my mind during the first long days of June was what could I write for Sam? He'd said, "Write something for me," and I wanted to, but I couldn't think of a thing. I couldn't write music or lyrics; I knew very little about the theater, and I didn't think he'd appreciate a new short story all about him. But then, as I had coffee alone in the mornings, showered, shopped on Bleecker, waited for the kids after school, bits of dialogue started going through my head. I heard Sam's voice, saying things that he might say, things I hoped he'd say, things that were cleverer than anything he'd actually said. I started jotting them down, thinking that I might be able to do a monologue for him, or a one-act play like *Zoo Story*, which I'd seen off Broadway.

I'd hoped to mention the idea to Sam after the last garden ghosts meeting before the summer, when everyone took off for various beaches, but he showed up at Hal and Laurette's with Mimi and Arthur in tow. I couldn't even manage to sit next to him. All in all, it was a frustrating meeting. Arthur, young lawyer and activist, was also a skeptic, and proceeded to sneer at the recent ghost sightings. I felt bad for Brenda and her aged mother, who seemed to live for seeing little Lucy, and for Susan, who was so pleased with a conversation she'd had with the raucous Captain, but then Arthur started in on Josh, who was older and smarter, and Josh shut him up with a lecture on paranormal studies that Arthur clearly knew nothing about. It was uncomfortable and the meeting broke up earlier than usual.

Sam gave me a slight, apologetic shrug as he headed home with Mimi and Arthur, and I walked back to my end of the garden and sat on the bench alone. I was looking up at the pinkish clouds over the city when Josh approached, lighting a joint.

"I needed this," he said, breathing out slowly, "after that asshole. Want a hit?"

"Um, sure," I said, after deciding not to tell him that I'd never tried the stuff before. I took a drag, held it in the way I'd seen people do, and it wasn't long before I got a fit of the giggles. Josh was going on about "Arthur Asshole" as if it were Arthur's given name, and I chimed in, imitating Mimi batting her long, blackened eyelashes.

"Why, I don't know why you boys have to fight over the ghosts. Why don't you just fight over me?"

"Happy to, ma'am, but I don't think your hubby, Andrew Asshole, is all that interested in you. He's too busy poking holes in our illogic."

"It's Arthur Asshole," I said, and it went on like that for a few minutes, both of us laughing, both of us thinking that we were much funnier than we were. Then Josh kissed me—awkwardly, unexpectedly—in the midst of a giggle. I backed away, sobering quickly.

"What?"

"Sorry."

"We were kidding around."

"I got carried away. Sorry."

"Ruthie's my best friend."

"I know. It's just—you looked lonely."

"I'm not lonely."

"Good. Just forget it."

"I will." I stared at him for a minute. This was a new, startling experience. "Good night," I said, and turned quickly, hurrying toward my back door.

It was never mentioned again. Obviously, I couldn't ask Ruthie for advice this time, and after a while I became less shocked by the advances of friends' husbands. Most of them seemed to think that a separated woman, or divorcee, was lonely, and they might as well give it a try. One garden husband, whom I'd only met casually, would call in the morning, after the children had left for school, and start describing body parts. I was shocked; I'd never heard of phone sex. If I sound naive, I was. This was a whole new landscape. I kept hanging up on the morning caller until he gave up, and learned how to avoid the attentions of married men. Except Sam of course; he was the only one I wanted.

During the first week of June, Irwin called to say that he and Kathleen would like to come by and pick up his dresser, leather chair, stereo and other odds and ends of his. He'd come with movers and a small truck—would noon be convenient?

"Of course, it's fine," I said, feeling nothing more than curiosity. I straightened the house as best I could, considering that the kids' rooms were hopeless, put on a clean shirt and some makeup, and answered the door cheerfully. Irwin was equally genial as he introduced me to Kathleen, who was all smiles as we shook hands. I offered coffee and sandwiches, but they said that they had to get this stuff moved during their lunch break. I didn't ask where it was going—it was obvious.

I waited in the living room while they went upstairs with the movers and critiqued Kathleen in my head. She was younger than me, but didn't look it. She was a couple of inches taller, making Irwin look shorter, and her hips looked rather wide as she climbed the narrow staircase. Aside from that, I decided, she was pretty and seemed pleasant.

They left in a flurry of activity, movers banging against the walls, horns honking at the double-parked truck on MacDougal, Irwin waving as he hailed a cab for him and Kathleen. I shut the front door with relief, and went upstairs to inspect. No noticeable damage, and I liked the way the bedroom looked without the bulky leather chair and the large bureau. I vacuumed the dents in the carpet where the chair had been, and the colony of dead bugs behind the dresser, and glanced around appreciatively. Except for the double bed, everything in this room was now mine.

School ended for the summer and it was at last time to go to Sagaponack. Maddy and I did laundry and packed for days, and Irwin agreed to get the car from the garage and help us fill it. I was grateful to have the car for the summer, but figured that Kathleen probably had a car or two. Finally the Rambler was loaded with bags, games, beach balls, Barbies, baseballs and bats, Danny's gerbil and cage, and the bicycles tied on top. The kids squeezed in, and blew kisses to Irwin and Maddy on the sidewalk as we pulled away. It seemed to me as I looked back that Maddy had tears in her eyes, but Irwin didn't. He waved happily as we turned the corner.

We settled contentedly into the renovated stable. The farmhouse, the barn, the stable were shaded by elms and willows, the grass was patchy, crisscrossed by paths, and petunias, geraniums and snapdragons spilled out of window boxes. Hammocks were hung between trees, a tire swing from a heavy branch, and all of it was surrounded by fields. We couldn't see the ocean, but we were close enough to catch whiffs of the salty, fishy air, and to share the fog that drifted inward from the sea. We rarely went to the ocean beach because the children couldn't swim there. So nearly every summery day we packed up all the crap—rafts, beach balls, picnics, thermoses, towels, blankets—and headed for Sagaponack Pond. The pond was really a large tide pool, fortunately without the bay's biting flies. The beach sloped down to the quiet water's edge, the pond was shallow for a few yards, perfect for paddling and rafts, but then dropped off suddenly. A rope barrier had been strung across the beginning of the drop, but still the children were warned not to go past it, and the beach mothers watched closely while the children were in the water.

The kids were happy, barefoot and quickly tanned. Mornings were spent playing around the compound, and afternoons at the pond. A week after we arrived, Ruthie and Josh settled into their Sag Harbor house for the summer, along with Adam, Jake's best friend, and shortly after Shirley and Sam moved into their whaling captain's house with Annie,

Sandra and their mother's helper for the summer, Grace. Grace was a smart, chunky nineteen-year-old, between her freshman and sophomore years at Sarah Lawrence. Sam, naturally, referred to her as zaftig. She became friends, by proximity, with Ruthie's mother's helper, Gull Mai, whom Josh and Ruthie had brought over for the summer from Sweden. Gull Mai was blond, bosomy and full of fun, and all the children adored her.

I didn't have a mother's helper that year. It was one of the non-necessities that Irwin had asked me to cut out, and I'd agreed. Having one made sense when the kids were little, and one or two of them in diapers, but not anymore.

The days were without drama. Time had a rhythm. Cool mornings at the compound, lunch and afternoons at the pond, except when it rained. Then we'd head to the library, or the toy store in East Hampton, and come home with new Colorforms, crayons and drawing pads to keep everyone busy for the rest of the day. Diana took the month off from her new job, so she was around for morning coffee, afternoons with the children, and an occasional movie. When Ruthie arrived she and Adam joined us at the pond.

I was excused from the Friday evening ritual at the East Hampton station because I didn't have a husband that year. I'd done it the previous years, waiting in the car beside the tracks and the covered platform, the children in pajamas, watching the fathers descend, still in their seersucker jackets or blazers, arriving from the week's work in the city. On Sunday evenings we'd take them back to the station and wave goodbye. I didn't miss the ritual. I was still savoring my free time, weekends included.

The assassination in early June of Robert Kennedy had been the second shocking, inconceivable death of 1968. The children weren't as devastated as they had been by the death of Martin Luther King. They didn't have the heart connection with Kennedy that they'd had with King. The rest of us, the so-called grown-ups, were stunned by the murder, but ambivalent about Robert Kennedy. He seemed to have changed, seemed to be a better person since his days as attorney general, but we weren't yet convinced.

Shirley and Arthur were the exceptions. Along with their various protests, they had campaigned for Kennedy. Shirley had arranged fund-raising dinners, and pressured Sam and his theatrical friends to perform at benefits. She had been as idealistic about Robert Kennedy as she was about ending the war, feeding the hungry and eradicating prejudice. All of which was admirable, but I had a feeling of not quite believing her. I put it down to the fact that I barely knew her, that she was Sam's wife, and I was jealous as hell. But then she decided to bring her disillusionment to Sag Pond, and to be our friend.

It was perfectly natural. Annie and my Danny were best friends; Shirley and Ruthie were neighbors, and it was easy for them to come to the pond together. Shirley began to show up regularly, still in grief. Talking over sandwiches at the water's edge, she poured out the pain of her shattered idealism. She had so believed that she could make the world better, and now she had given up. Day after day, she squeezed her well-rounded body into our small, tight circle, and unburdened herself. We sympathized, but it was disconcerting; we didn't know her that well, and weren't sure that we wanted to. But there she was, on the beach, or on the phone, or dropping by, or making plans with us.

"I'd so wanted to believe that people are good," she'd say, her red-rimmed eyes tearing. "But I can't anymore. I'd so wanted to work for peace, and all the starving children, but we get killed for being good."

"Not everybody."

"No, the leaders, the saviors, Jesus, the Kennedys, the Kings, leaving us nowhere to turn, and nothing to believe in anymore."

"You can still do good, Shirl—protest the war, work for civil rights, raise money to feed the children?"

"No, I can't. I can't go through this again."

This conversation was repeated, variations on a theme, a few times, before Diana, Ruthie and I broached the subject to each other. Annie had an ear infection, and Shirley had stayed home with her on a particularly nice beach day. The children were in the water, or building in the wet sand, and we kept an eye on them as we shared iced tea and potato chips.

"There's something off with Shirley," Ruthie said, looking questioningly at Diana and me.

"What do you mean?"

"I don't know. She doth protest too much?"

"She doth," Diana said. "I'm always suspicious of people who want to save the world, but don't see what's going on right around them."

"Well, don't look at me," I said, aware that they were both looking at and through me.

"We're not," Ruthie said, laughing. "Sam's doing whatever

he's doing, you're doing whatever you're doing, and Shirley's blind as a bat."

"No, she's got blinders on," Diana said. "Like tunnel vision."

"And she's so bloody innocent," Ruthie said. "*She* tried to save the world, and it didn't work—poor baby. '*I* can't go through this again,' like it was her husband who got shot."

"You're right. There is something off," Diana said thoughtfully. We were quiet for a minute, then Ruthie jumped up, trotting toward the water. Diana followed her, while I lit a cigarette against the breeze, and watched a sand crab scurry into a small, wet hole.

Sam wasn't around too often. He'd arrive on Sunday, and head back to the city on Tuesday, early enough so that he'd have plenty of time before the evening performance. I missed him, but there wasn't a chance to be alone with him, and it was uncomfortable to be around him in the midst of his family. Besides Shirley and Grace, the mother's helper, Arthur and cousin Mimi were often there when he was, and Annie and Sandra wanted as much attention as he could spare.

As part of her desire to be our newest, dearest friend, Shirley invited all of us—me, Ruthie, Diana and whichever husbands and children were available—for a Sunday afternoon barbecue. I brought my children, and a potato salad, Ruthie came with Josh, son Adam, and Kevin, and Diana brought Maryellen and homemade brownies. Cliff was playing tennis at a club that none of the rest of us belonged to.

Sam, Shirley, Arthur, Mimi and Grace were drinking gin

and tonics on the wide porch that faced the harbor. Sam rose from the porch swing, where he'd been sitting with an arm around Mimi, approached, and hugged all of us. He looked wonderful, wearing just bathing trunks and sandals. His olive skin had become a reddish brown, emphasizing the thickness of his chest and the dancer's muscles of his arms and legs. I felt a spasm of longing as I handed him the potato salad, and walked quickly up the porch steps to greet Shirley and the others. Everyone hugged everyone as the children ran across the lawn, down to the water and the pier—this was going to be pure hell.

"You can't go in the water," I yelled to the kids.

"We know, Mommy," they yelled back, and I watched them for another minute to be sure. The lawn sloped down to the bay, but you couldn't swim there. It was too close to the harbor, and high, sharp reeds grew along the shore. The weathered pier came with the house, but the Messengers didn't have a boat, so except for play and sunbathing, it was mainly unused. The western sun was golden on the water, and on the rocking sailboats, and I had to force myself to turn and follow Shirley into the house. She was saying something about the men tending the barbecue, and the women putting out the salads and the paper plates. We were to serve ourselves from the dining room table, just off the porch, and take our plates wherever we liked—there were wicker chairs and tables on the porch, and a picnic table by the water.

I mumbled to Diana, as she followed me through the narrow pantry into the kitchen, that I thought I might find a spot under a rock somewhere. She laughed, gave me a light shove, and we helped Shirley and Grace with the table and the display of salads. Back on the porch, I noticed that Ruthie had stayed with the men and the barbecue. I was on my second gin and tonic by then, and the red coals of the outdoor fireplace seemed to dance and blur as I tried to focus on them from the porch steps. I was looking at Sam, and aware of Ruthie as she grinned her adorable grin at Josh, then at Kevin, and back to Josh. I was full of admiration for the aplomb with which Ruthie handled her ever present triangle.

As Sam carried the platter of ribs and burgers into the dining room, I spilled the rest of my drink onto the gnarled roots of the wisteria—this was no time to end up on the bathroom floor—and joined everyone in the dining room. I helped my children with their plates, barely filled mine, and escaped into the kitchen where it was quiet. I sat in a kitchen chair for a minute, and gazed out the open back door where the bay and the white sails were being tinted by the sunset. I rose, poured some milk into a paper cup, took a deep breath and started back through the pantry just as Sam entered. We both stopped, and looked at each other with the same intensity, the same sense of longing that I'd felt when I'd first arrived and handed him the potato salad. There was no time to say anything. Children pushed in behind him, and we laughed as we bumped each other and passed each other in the narrow hallway.

I wanted to leave, and I didn't want to leave. As evening set in, Shirley lit candles and hurricane lamps on the porch, and the grown-ups sat on the steps, the swing, the wicker chairs. The children didn't want to leave the lawn and the beach, so Grace and Gull Mai organized a couple of games of Dodge Ball and Red Rover. They soon tired and joined us on and around the porch, and it seemed to me, as I sat on the steps, that Sam was managing to put a beautiful arm around every single woman. He sat on the swing with one arm around Mimi, and the other around Shirley. Then he moved to the porch railing where he put an arm around Diana and then around Grace, who I could see was blushing in the candlelight. He tried to get an arm around Ruthie's waist, but she gave him a look that made him back off, so he returned to the porch swing and Mimi and Shirley.

The by now bored children went inside, and with Annie instigating, began running and screaming through the large attic, which connected the upstairs bedrooms and the back stairs.

"It's haunted up there!" Danny said, breathless, as he appeared for a moment on the porch, and then ran up again.

"They love that game," Shirley said indulgently. "They're convinced that widows of the lost whalers are holed up in our attic."

"Maybe they are," I said.

"Oh, you and your ghosts," Shirley laughed.

"Let's not put down the garden ghost-hunters," Sam said, with a wink in my direction.

"Do you think they've followed us?" Shirley asked.

"No, I think they're different," Sam said. "They live here, not there."

"Cut the crap, Sam," Arthur mumbled.

"Now wait just a minute," Josh said, but he was interrupted by Mimi.

"There's a ghost in the guest apartment, Art, sweetie, you know there is." And as she turned to us, Arthur shook his head derisively. "He crosses the bedroom in the middle of the night—we can hear his footsteps—goes into the bathroom, flushes the toilet, then recrosses the bedroom and leaves."

"You're kidding?" most of us said at once.

"Obviously, a weak bladder," Arthur said.

"But that's fantastic," Josh said. "What did the apartment used to be? Does it have a history?"

"It was the carriage house," Sam answered. "It's a garage now with an apartment above it."

"Fantastic," Josh said again. We were interrupted by the children, red-faced and sweating, as they rushed back onto the porch and into various parental arms.

"It's so scary," Emma said, her head buried in my lap.

"Really scary," Jake said.

"Really, really scary!" Adam said.

"Come on, let's go back!" Annie said.

"No," all the grown-ups seemed to say at once. "Time to go home, time for bed." The children groaned, but acquiesced as we herded them into the cars. My three were asleep by the time we crossed the bridge into Sag Harbor.

The evenings were long. Diana returned to her new job, and she and Cliff arrived on Fridays, and left on Sundays. Ruthie was around part of the time, and in the city with Josh and Kevin part of the time. Shirley was around more than I'd hoped she would be, and either Sam was rarely in Sag Harbor, or Shirley kept him to herself while he was there. The children tended to go to sleep with the sun after long days in the water and on the sand, and I was left with the evening hours to myself.

I had a stack of books from the library piled next to my favorite chair in the living room, but nothing held my attention for long. I wrote a short story about Shirley and me sitting on the beach together, both unknowingly in love with the same man, but decided that I couldn't possibly publish it. I started the one-act play for Sam about three times, and each time threw it out.

Irwin called the children a couple of times a week at suppertime, and usually asked for me after they'd said good night. He mainly wanted to fill me in on his conversations with Bob Malcolm, our lawyer, who was working out our separation agreement. In late June Irwin said that the agreement was ready for me to sign, and he'd bring it with him when he visited the children on the July Fourth weekend.

"I didn't know you were coming," I said.

"I told the kids. Kathleen's going sailing with her family, so—"

"You hate boats," I laughed.

"I coitainly do," he said in a Catskills comic's accent.

"Well, why don't you stay here, and I'll go check on things in town?"

"I could stay at a motel."

"No, stay here," I insisted. "I'd love a break."

We all looked forward to the long holiday weekend, but for different reasons. The children would spend time with their father, Irwin would avoid sailing with the Riley family to the Cape and back, and I would get to have four whole days in the city by myself. I called Sam at the theater the day before I was to leave, and arranged to meet in the dressing room at five the next afternoon. It wasn't a matinee day, but it would give us time together before he had to get into costume and makeup.

Late that same day Irwin drove up in a Mustang convertible. As he got out of the car, and the children ran to him, I could see that he was wearing Bermuda shorts, dark sunglasses, and was sporting new, bushy sideburns.

"Well, look at you," I called across the grass. "Aren't we snazzy?"

"I try," Irwin called back as he hugged the kids, and lifted his overnight bag out of the back seat. Danny insisted on carrying the bag, and each one held a hand or a shirtsleeve as they crossed the lawn. Irwin kissed my cheek in the doorway, and let the children lead him through the kitchen and into the living room. While they hovered, Irwin opened a bag, handed each a new book, and tossed an envelope on my worktable.

"I brought the papers so you could take a look, and sign it."

"Good, I will. Want a drink?"

"Gin and tonic?" As I nodded and turned, he glanced at the notebooks on my desk. "You been writing?"

"Yeah, some," I called from the kitchen. I had been careful to put away anything that I didn't want Irwin to see.

We ate hot dogs and corn in the shade of the willows, their slim leaves whispering in the ocean breeze, and while it was still twilight Irwin helped the children with their baths, read one of the new books to them, and tucked them into their dormitory beds. When I went up to kiss them good night, they told me excitedly that their father was going to take them to see the fireworks at the East Hampton beach. They were asleep by the time I got back downstairs.

Irwin fixed another drink for each of us, and brought the separation agreement to the kitchen table for me to look at and sign. While Irwin sat across from me, trying not to drum his fingers, I lit a cigarette and read as much as I could stand of the legal paragraphs. The main points appeared to be that I would have primary custody of the children, and receive almost twenty thousand a year in monthly installments. It seemed like a lot to me then.

I signed the agreement, we clinked glasses, and I went upstairs to pack.

Irwin and the kids dropped me off at the East Hampton station, and as the train pulled out, I settled into a revolving lounge chair and sighed with pleasure. I was alone and anonymous. No one knew me, no one could reach me, no one would yell "Mommy" in the midst of my wandering thoughts. I observed the few other passengers, and made up stories about them, as I'd done with the ghosts in the garden. They were no more real than that. After an hour or so, I turned my chair to the window, heard the motion of the train like a lullaby, and drifted into anticipatory dreams of Sam.

From Penn Station I took a cab straight to the theater. The stage doorman was asleep as I entered, his chins resting on his open newspaper, and I slipped past him and up the metal stairs. It was dark backstage, lit by a single work light, and silent, but then I heard a laugh, unmistakably Clay's, and Sam's voice answering him. The dressing room door was open, and I walked in, and into Clay's embrace.

"Where you been, Miss Muse?" he asked, then held me at arm's length. "You almost as black as me."

"Just at the beach," I said, laughing. I turned and jumped into Sam's open arms, and I don't think either of us were aware of Clay leaving and closing the door behind him.

In Sam's lair a rotating fan sent an intermittent breeze across our naked bodies as we laughed about our white bathing suits, and slowly made love. There was nothing remarkable about this time together, except that we hadn't seen each other, without wives and neighbors around, for over a month, and every pleasure was heightened. After exhausting ourselves, dozing, waking, then smoking—the ashtray on Sam's chest—we lay there, wet body against wet body, and filled each other in on the month of June. Sam asked how Irwin was doing, and I told him about Kathleen.

"I think he's on his way to marrying an heiress," I said.

"Shit," Sam said, snapping his fingers. "How'd I miss out on that? Well, too late now. Shirley likes you, by the way."

"Yeah, I know."

"What's that tone?"

"It makes me uncomfortable," I said with a shrug.

"Don't worry about it. Shirley never puts two and two together."

"Okay," I answered, wondering what other twos-and-twos Shirley hadn't put together. I decided to change the subject. "I've been working on that one-act for you, but I've been having trouble. I'm not used to the form."

"You'll get it," Sam said. "What's it about?"

"You're all three characters," I answered. "You play you, your father and the ghost of his father."

"Sounds good," Sam said. "And we can call it—let's see—*Hamlet*!"

"Don't make fun of it," I said, punching him lightly. "You'll stop me cold."

"Sorry. It sounds interesting—really. And you're a terrific writer."

"What makes you think so?"

"I read the short stories."

"Really? You think I'm good?"

"I think," Sam said, cupping my face in one large hand, "that you're a great writer, and a great lay."

Chapter Thirteen

Sam said that I could watch as much of the show as I wanted to, from the back or from the wings, but he couldn't get together afterward because he'd arranged, before he knew that I was coming, to meet with his agent to discuss a couple of offers. I was disappointed, but had fun watching the first act from the wings. Sam made a point of winking at me offstage with the eye that the audience couldn't see, and I relished the sense of being his "chosen one." I blew a kiss goodbye at intermission, another to Clay, another to the doorman, and took a cab down to MacDougal Street.

It was a bright, dark night, moonlight blending with street lights, as I opened our outside door. I turned the key to our duplex, pushed open our front door, and was struck by the worst smell that I'd ever smelled in my life. My first thought was that someone, maybe our friendly wino, had broken in and died in our living room. My second thought was rats. I didn't know which was worse. I was terrified of dead bodies, and terrified of rats. The apartment had been empty for a while—it could be either one, or something worse. For the first time since we'd separated I really wanted Irwin. I really wanted *somebody*.

I flicked on the light switch next to the front door, still gripping my overnight case, ready to make a run for it, and looked first toward the living room—nothing. Then I looked to my left, through the open kitchen door, and saw a disaster zone. I heard scurrying at the same time, and trying not to breathe in the stench, took a tentative step forward. I didn't bother to turn on the kitchen light; I could see enough by the light that spilled from the doorway. Rats had apparently eaten themselves to death in our kitchen. Two were dead in a pile of white flour. Sugar was everywhere, empty canisters and nibbled boxes all over the floor and the counters. They had dragged whatever they could out of the pantry—cereal boxes, cookies, something too moldy to be recognizable. I reached gingerly for the doorknob, and slammed the kitchen door shut. I then ran to the back door, opened it, and dashed into the garden where I tried to breathe, and not be sick.

The garden was eerily empty. It seemed that no one had stayed in the city over the Fourth of July weekend. A few outside lights were on above the garden doors, but all the windows were dark. I dropped my bag outside our door, and walked the path that circled the garden. I tried a few back doors—Ruthie's, Laurette's, Diana's—hoping that someone had forgotten to lock a garden door, but no one had. I saw a white flicker, like a large firefly, beside the swings, and simply said, "Hi Lucy" as I headed for Sam's. I was much too frightened of the inside of my house to worry about the ghosts at that moment. Sam's door also was locked, and drapes were drawn across the picture window.

I forced myself to reenter my house. The downstairs lights blazed, and the kitchen was quiet as I ran past it and back out the front door. I started to cry, helpless tears, as I turned from MacDougal onto Bleecker. I wanted to call someone, but I couldn't use the wall phone in the kitchen, and I couldn't work up the courage to go upstairs to the bedroom. The rats could be up there too, disgusting bears in Goldilocks's bed. Tears ran down my face, and I was making gulping noises as I pushed open the door of the Hip Bagel. No one was there except a large man in a long, stained apron, holding a broom, staring at me.

"Your rats came into my house next door, and I don't know what to do," I cried. After denying that they were *his* rats, or belonged to his establishment in any way, the large man, who told me his name was Jack, sat me down at the counter, gave me a cup of coffee, a phone book and a phone.

"You want the twenty-four-hour service," he said, as I looked up exterminators. "That way you can leave a message, and tell them to come first thing." I did as he suggested, finished the coffee while he swept, thanked him with a sizable tip, and left feeling calmer. But I couldn't go home. I wasn't about to sleep there with the possibility of rats in obscure places, like under the bed or in the toilet. I stood between MacDougal and Sullivan, the block nearly deserted, trying to decide what to do. I could wait in the garden for Sam to come home, but then I realized that I might not see him come in his front door. I could wait beside his door on Sullivan as long as no one else saw me. I looked at my watch; he should be home within the hour.

I turned down Sullivan just as *The Fantasticks* ended in the small theater across the street. Perfect, I thought, I could blend with the exiting audience, possibly the only crowd on a Village street during this holiday weekend, and watch for Sam. I hung around in front of the theater posters, having a cigarette, looking as if I were waiting for someone, until everyone had dispersed, the lights been turned out, and the doors bolted. The street was silent as I crossed in the middle of the block to Sam's doorway. I wasn't sure why I wanted so badly to see him. It was too late for him to help me with the rat problem. I'd already done whatever I could. I had a distant hope that, because I didn't want to sleep with the rats, he might ask me to spend the night with him, but I wasn't counting on it. Maybe I just wanted him to take me in those warm, beautiful arms and tell me that it would all be all right. I started to cry again, just thinking about his arms, thinking about how alone I felt with my house full of rats, and no one to help or comfort me.

A cab turned down Sullivan, and I ducked into Diana's doorway, right next to Sam's and hidden from the street. I wanted to make sure that it was Sam before running to him, and to make sure that he hadn't brought his agent, or whoever, home with him. He'd told me that Shirley was at the beach, but you never knew with Shirley. Sure enough, a bunch of blond curls jumped out of the cab after Sam. I peered from my hiding place. It looked like Shirley, but it wasn't Shirley. Oh, shit, it's cousin Mimi, I almost said aloud. What was she doing here? Was he having a thing with cousin Mimi too? No, that was a ridiculous idea. She was family—

she was probably just staying over. It was a townhouse with four floors, after all, and she was Shirley's cousin.

Sam had closed and locked the door behind them by the time I'd convinced myself that Mimi was harmless, and I was imagining things because of the rats, and that I had nowhere to go. I walked down to Houston and back up MacDougal. I stood staring at our house for a while, the downstairs lights slicing the sidewalk through the inside shutters, and decided that I could probably sleep on the living room sofa if I kept all the lights on. I opened the front door and went in. The kitchen was quiet, and the sofa inviting. I opened the windows and the garden door, and turned on the exhaust fan to diffuse the smell. I was tired, angry and disappointed—angry that Mimi was at Sam's, disappointed that Sam couldn't hold me and take me in, and angry that I had to deal with things like a disgusting kitchen and exterminators. I lay on the sofa, shoes on for protection, and by the time it occurred to me that I'd been wrong, that I probably couldn't do this alone, I was asleep.

The next day wasn't much better. I'd left a desperate message for the exterminators, and they arrived early, for which I was grateful, but I couldn't make coffee or shower until they were finished. They cleaned up the worst of the mess, spread their poisons, but said that I'd have to get a cleaning service to deal with the rest of it. They gave me the number of an emergency service that they recommended, and I spent more hours getting ahold of the cleaners, and waiting for them to arrive. It was dark by the time they finished. I'd hoped to see Sam again that night, but I was too disgruntled and sorry for myself to even call the theater to see if he was free. Instead I called Irwin to say that I was taking an early train back, that I'd been through a minor hell, and would he please pick me up at noon at the East Hampton station.

My family was waiting for me as I got off the train. Irwin smiled beside the children, who were tanned, bleached, sandy and happy to see me. All their small arms came around me at once, and as I glanced at Irwin, it crossed my mind again that I'd possibly made a mistake. Maybe I should ask him to come back. Maybe I wouldn't be able to handle all the crises to come by myself. But I still wanted freedom, and I still wanted Sam. I vacillated during the drive to Sagaponack while Irwin and the kids told me about the fireworks on the beach, and I told them about the rats in the kitchen. I left out the details, but they still reacted.

"Yuck," yelled Emma.

"Dithgusting," said Jake, with a trace of his former lisp.

"You didn't kill them, did you?" asked Danny.

"No, I found them a good home," I said, with a look. "Of course I did. They can't live in our kitchen."

"You could have taken them to the park!" Danny grumbled.

"Your mother did the right thing, Danny," Irwin said, and I gave him a grateful glance. When we arrived back at the stable Irwin gathered his things, and said goodbye as soon as possible. The children and I waved from the lawn, and as I watched him jump in the car, with new sideburns and new sunglasses, and tear down the driveway with the Mustang's top down, I knew that if I'd had the audacity to ask him to come back, he simply would have said that it was too late—he was on his way to a whole new life.

As I unpacked, and took a load of laundry over to Diana's

kitchen, I wondered again at the suddenness of Irwin's new life. He'd loved me so completely; he'd been so devastated, and there he went, rushing into the future, with the top down.

The peaceful routine of Sagaponack mornings and beach afternoons was shattered in the middle of July when I received a letter from our lawyer, saying that under the terms of the separation agreement, I would be receiving the first monthly check of $1,650 on August 1. This, however, included all my expenses. I would be responsible for the August rent in Sagaponack—$2,000—and the children's school tuition, which came to $500 a month year-round. Just as I thought that I could put some of this on a credit card, I read that Irwin would assume the balances, but that all joint credit had been canceled. I was sure that the lawyer had made a mistake, and called Irwin at Kathleen's that evening.

"I thought you paid for the whole summer," I said, when Kathleen put Irwin on the phone.

"I paid for half," Irwin said.

"But I don't have enough to stay here for August!"

"Then I suppose you'll have to go back to town."

"Irwin, you know there's nothing for the kids to do in town! No one's there, and it's hot as hell."

"Well," Irwin said, drawing out the word, "why don't you talk to Diana? Maybe she'll give you a break."

"Yeah, maybe she will."

"Okay, I've gotta go."

"Wait a minute. The letter also says I'm responsible for the kids' tuition. When was that decided?"

"When we drew up the agreement."

"I had no idea that was in there," I said. "I assumed you'd be fair—I didn't even read all of it."

"Didn't your mother ever tell you about fine—?"

"Don't be funny right now," I interrupted. "If I'm supposed to pay the rent, and monthly tuition, there's not enough left to live on."

"It's the agreement we both signed," Irwin said steadily. "What's more, it's all I can afford."

"So what am I supposed to do?"

"You're smart—get a good job."

"I sure don't feel too smart right now," I answered. I hung up without saying goodbye, went upstairs to make sure that the children were asleep, then, leaving the back door open, walked across the rutted lawn in the moonlight and tapped on Diana's screen door.

"Diana, you home?" She was, and we sat in her kitchen so that I could hear the kids in case anyone had a nightmare, and I told her about the lawyer's letter, and my conversation with Irwin.

"That's really shitty," Diana said, as she poured a glass of wine for each of us.

"I guess, but it's my fault too, I didn't even ask—"

"Of course, you assumed."

"Yes, I did, but here's the thing, Irwin said maybe you could give me a break. Maybe I could pay some, and pay it off out of my monthly check? Or maybe I'll get a small royalty from—"

"Oh, I don't know," Diana said, shifting her eyes to the knots in the old floorboards. "If it were up to me I'd say of course, but you know Cliff . . ." Her voice trailed off into a quiver as she looked back up at me. "He handles the finances, and he's, you know—"

"Careful?" I asked aloud, a more negative term in my mind.

"Very careful," Diana said. "But I'll ask him, and try because it's great having you here."

"I love being here." We hugged—unusual for Diana—before I left and recrossed the lawn. Outside my door I looked above the willows to the Milky Way, a web of stars in the clear night, and wished and hoped that Diana would be able to soften Cliff's tightwad heart.

Diana spent the next couple of days in the city. I'd taken the children to the pond early that Friday, and was joined first by Shirley and her girls, a bit later by Diana and Maryellen. I could tell by the way Diana kept studying the sand at her feet that her talk with Cliff hadn't gone well. I didn't want Diana to mention August in front of Shirley, but Shirley was practically on top of us, and I couldn't catch Diana's eye. As the three mothers put the right sandwiches on the right paper plates—no mustard for Jake, no tomato for Annie—and poured lemonade, Diana looked at me for the first time.

"I'm really sorry, Cal," she said quietly, "but Cliff says he's really counted on the August rent, and he's got people lined up who want the place. He can get a lot for just the month."

"Oh, hell," I said, and felt unexpected tears prick, then spill out of my eyes.

"I'm so sorry," Diana said again as she pulled a handkerchief out of her beach bag, and handed it to me.

"What's wrong?" Shirley asked, putting a hand on my shoulder, her blue eyes wider than usual.

"Mommy, what's wrong?" Danny asked, wet and panting, as he ran up to me. Jake was right behind him.

"It's nothing terrible," I said as I cried.

"Is Daddy okay?"

"He's fine. It's really not that bad."

"So why are you crying?" Danny insisted.

"It's just that we can't be here in August. See, it's really nothing," I added quickly.

"Where are we going?" Jake asked.

"Nowhere. We'll be in town."

"That's awful," Danny yelled. "That's the worst thing!" Beside him Emma started to cry, and Annie and Maryellen echoed that it was the worst possible news.

"We can go to the Winners every day," Jake said hopefully.

"There's no Winners in August, stupid," Danny said, kicking sand in the air.

"Ow, you stupid head, you got sand in my eye!" Emma cried.

"Okay, okay, let's sit down and eat," I said, wiping Emma's eye with the wet handkerchief that was clutched in my hand. "We'll work it out."

"I'm not hungry," Danny mumbled.

"I've got an idea," Shirley said, squeezing in beside Emma and me. I simply looked at her. "Our garage apartment is empty in August—you could stay there!"

"We couldn't possibly," I said instantly.

"Why not?" Danny shouted.

"Yeah, why not?" the other children asked, in a chorus.

"Because." I couldn't think of a plausible "because," and my eyes pleaded with Diana for help.

"It's probably too expensive," Diana said, "or too small."

"No," Shirley said. "Arthur and Mimi have it for July, but they won't be there in August, and we don't rent it out—it'll be for free."

"I'm sure it's too small for all of us," I said.

"It's got two bedrooms," Annie said, clutching Danny's hand, "and a living room with a fold-out bed."

"It's the place with the ghost who flushes the toilet," Danny said excitedly.

"I don't want ghosts!" Emma cried.

"Emma doesn't want ghosts," I said desperately.

"Oh, that's just a story, make-believe," Shirley said to Emma.

"I don't want ghosts either," Jake said.

"None of us want ghosts," I said. "Thanks, Shirley, but I really don't think it would work."

"Why don't you think about it?" Shirley asked gently.

"Yeah, Mom," Danny said in a disgusted tone. "Why don't you think about it."

"Good idea. Okay, let's go home, and I'll think about it." I would have said anything at that moment to leave the beach, and leave Shirley far behind. The argument continued in the car, and back at the stable. Danny was angry, and taking it out on Jake, who preferred to sulk rather than hit back, and Emma was teasing both of them, pretending to be the toilet-flushing ghost in order to lessen her fears. While that was going on, I made supper, got the kids to the kitchen table, and thought about borrowing or stealing the two thousand dollars. I decided that I couldn't borrow it from family or friends because a desire to stay at the beach was a decidedly minor problem in the scheme of things. I wasn't about to steal it because knowing me I'd get caught and go to jail.

After they ate, the children took off to look for baby corn cobs in the field next door, and I buried my face in my hands. A few minutes later I peeked through my fingers at my watch. It was early evening; Sam would be putting his makeup on in the dressing room. I dialed the number. Clay answered, and put Sam on the phone. I filled him in, as efficiently as possible—I knew that he didn't have much time.

"So stay in the guesthouse," Sam said. "What's the problem?"

"It'll be so—awkward."

"It'll be fun," Sam said. "The kids'll have a ball, and I won't be there that much anyway. The show's supposed to run another few months."

"Are you sure?"

"Sure, I'm sure. I know Shirl offered, but look at it as a present from me."

"That's so sweet."

"Nah, it's not sweet. It'll be my pleasure."

"I'm working on the play for you," I said.

"You can read it to me on the porch," he said. "Clay's makin' faces at me, gotta go. Tell Shirl you'll be there."

As I hung up this time, I felt my predatory instinct kick in, like a squid's ink, black and oily, seeping through my veins. If I were close to Sam, really close, maybe I'd have a chance. Maybe he'd see me, and then see Shirley, and know that I was the one he wanted. Through half-closed eyes I pictured Shirley, tearing out her curls as Sam and I left together for parts unknown. I pictured Sam sweeping me up in his arms and carrying me over some threshold. I saw my children, running happily to him across an imaginary lawn.

"Mommy, he hit me again!" Emma shrieked, running in the door, Jake and Danny right behind her.

"Oh, stop it!" I shouted, not wanting to leave my fantasy, but I opened my eyes and stood, smiling to myself as I thought that my dream was marginally possible. And If not, at least I'd be near Sam for a time. Suddenly, being near him was what I wanted more than anything. I could wake up on a Sunday morning and have coffee with him. I could cook something special for him. I could read to him the pages that I was writing for him. I was still smiling as I calmed the children down and told them that I'd changed my mind. We could stay at the Messengers' for the month of August.

Before we moved, probably out of guilt, Diana gave me an old Royal typewriter that had belonged to her mother. She knew that I was writing the play for Sam on yellow pads, and thought that I might want to type it up for him. I did. I'd never been so inspired to write anything. I stayed up way into the night, plucking away at the keys. I got a bit faster with my two or three fingers, but it was still tedious work, transferring the scribbled pages to the typewriter.

By the time we moved our belongings from the stable to the carriage house I had a sheaf of typewritten pages. The move was easy. The stable was furnished, including linens and dishes, and the guest apartment was furnished, so it only took a couple of trips in the station wagon to move our clothes, toys, rafts, bicycles and the gerbil over to the Messengers'. Shirley greeted us ecstatically. You would have thought that she was adopted, and we were the real family that she'd always yearned for. It was disconcerting, to say the least.

The apartment over the garage, which used to be the carriage house, had a living room, a compact kitchen, a bedroom, a den and one bathroom, where it was said that the ghost liked to flush the toilet in the middle of the night. I put the boys in the bedroom, Emma in the den, and I took the sofa bed in the living room. The apartment was charmless, filled with leftover furniture, but that didn't matter. We were at the beach, outdoors most of the time, and only returned to the apartment to wash off the sand, have a bite and sleep. On rainy days all the children played on the wide porch that ran the length of the main house.

The main house was dark and cool downstairs, sheltered by the porch and the vines, and hot and cramped upstairs. Shirley and Sam's bedroom and bath were downstairs, off the dreary living room. Upstairs there were three narrow bedrooms and another bathroom. Annie and Sandra shared a room and a bunk bed; Grace had a room, and upon our arrival I was surprised to find cousin Mimi in the guestroom.

This was explained later as Shirley, Mimi and I sat on the veranda, tired by the day, drinking something chilled and lethal. The children were finally asleep, Grace had gone to her room to study, and we sat in the late twilight, watching fireflies appear and disappear, and listening to the crickets and the tree frogs. I asked Mimi about Arthur, more out of something to say than any real curiosity.

"He's working like mad for Gene McCarthy, getting ready for the convention."

"Which convention?" I asked, feeling stupid, but then again none of us had television sets during the summer, and weren't paying much attention to the news. It continued to be bad—the war, the riots, the student protests—and as parents we felt that the children had been exposed to enough violence for one year. Besides, except for Arthur, and Shirley's brief excursion into liberal activism, none of us cared all that much. We cared, but not enough to go do anything about it.

"The Democratic convention," Mimi said, as if to one of the children. "Arthur really thinks McCarthy's got a shot at the nomination."

"God, I miss Bobby," Shirley said suddenly, her eyes welling up.

"Bobby? Oh, Bobby Kennedy. Yes, that was terrible."

"I just couldn't care that much after that," Shirley continued. "I decided to just give all my attention to my family—my babies and poor Sammy."

"Poor Sammy?" Mimi asked, before I had a chance.

"Ready for a refill?" Shirley asked, rising, bumping through the screen door.

"Sure," we answered, and I whispered to Mimi, "Is something wrong with Sam?"

"Not that I know of," Mimi whispered back, as Shirley returned with a chilled bottle of gin. I waved my hand over my glass as Shirley offered to pour. I hadn't known that we were drinking gin. I could end up on the bathroom floor drinking vodka, but gin had a way of loosening my tongue. I could easily blurt out the wrong thing at the wrong time, and this wasn't a moment to do that.

"Is something wrong with Sam?" I repeated to Shirley.

"Poor baby's forty-five, almost forty-six," Shirley said, settling back into the wicker rocker, and taking a long sip. "He's getting old."

"He's not old," Mimi laughed.

"But he's getting old men's problems," Shirley said, "and I'm trying to help him, I really am, but I don't seem to be able to. And you know Sammy, he won't go to a doctor."

"About what?"

"Oh, you know, his *problem*," Shirley answered, reddening beneath her tan.

"No, we don't know."

"For a while now, he's had a hard time—" Shirley stopped and started again, her voice low. "He's had a hard time—he's impotent." As I gaped at Shirley, I caught a glimpse of Mimi, stifling laughter. Shirley saw it too.

"It's not funny," Shirley said stiffly. "He feels so bad about it."

"I was just laughing with relief," Mimi said quickly. "I'm just so relieved there's nothing really wrong with him."

"Me too," I managed to say.

"I'm doing everything I can think of to help, but it's just not working," Shirley went on innocently. I rose. I couldn't take any more.

"I'm off to bed, I'm bleary-eyed," I said. "Good night, and thanks."

"Good night, sleep well," they both called, as I walked down the porch steps and crossed the driveway to the carriage house. Once out of sight I stood still, watching the moonbeams patterning the bay, and wondering what in the world Mimi was laughing about. Maybe she was embarrassed for

Shirley. Maybe Shirley going on about "Sammy's problem" struck her as funny. I thought it funny and embarrassing, but that was from my point of view. Maybe Mimi knew something; maybe Sam had confided in her. I couldn't consider the other explanation—Sam and Mimi—it was unthinkable. I climbed the stairs to the guest apartment, and went to sleep in the midst of a question.

The next day my first so-called alimony check arrived from the lawyer, along with a bill for my part of his fee. He said that I could pay it in installments, which was helpful, but I realized again that after rent, tuition and bills there wouldn't be much to live on. I deposited the check in the Sag Harbor bank, and stuck the bill in my suitcase. It was August 2; I didn't have to worry about it, or anything for that matter, until September.

Feeling as free as the gulls that were swooping and diving around the harbor, I joined Ruthie, Diana, Shirley and all the children at the pond for the afternoon. I'd stopped wondering about what Mimi knew, what she didn't know, and was quietly delighted that Sam wanted me, and not his wife. The air was warm, the water clear and cool, and I paddled around with Emma on a raft, working on my tan, and my overall desirability. I couldn't wait for Sam to arrive, but at the same time the anticipation was delicious.

Shirley picked Sam up at the station on Sunday, and the rest of us—Mimi, Grace, the children and I—waited on the porch as the rain hit the roof, and spilled down onto the steps and the grass. The fog hid the bay and formed a cloud around the house, so that we could barely make out their shapes as Sam and Shirley arrived and approached across the long porch. I could tell as soon as their faces became clear that something was wrong. Shirley's face was wet with rain, and possibly tears, and Sam's whole body was mournful. His shoulders slumped as he wiped his head and neck with a bandanna, and carrying his bag, walked right past us into the house. The children ran after him, but Shirley sank into the wicker rocker and gazed at the fog.

"Looks like he's playing *Death of a Salesman,*" Mimi said, after a silence.

"The show's closing," Shirley said quietly.

"What's so awful about that?"

"I don't know," Shirley answered. "But he's upset. They expected it to run through Thanksgiving at least. Now it's closing after one more week."

"I don't get it," Mimi said. "It's not like he needs the work."

"I think it's all part of the same thing," Shirley said, her voice full of sadness. "He feels old, he feels like a failure, and this just makes it all worse. He says he's not going to be able to sit here, like his grandfather, on the porch all day."

"I'd think he'd want a vacation," I chimed in. "He's been working so hard."

"Well, he doesn't seem to. Would someone be a dear and get me a gin and tonic? I'm beat."

"Sure," I said, eager for the chance to catch Sam alone and find out what was going on. "Mimi?" Mimi shook her head, and as I passed through the dining room I checked out the empty living room and the closed bedroom door.

Grace was in the kitchen with Sam and the children, dishing out ice cream. She'd left the porch so quietly I hadn't noticed.

"Gracie's making sundaes with chocolate," Emma announced as I entered.

"Would you like one, Callie?" Grace asked, reaching up for another bowl. As I smiled a "no thank you" I noticed how young she was. I hadn't paid much attention to her before, but with her arms raised as she reached, almost on tiptoes, I saw how smooth and honey-colored her arms and legs were. She was wearing shorts and her T-shirt was still damp from being out in the rain. She wasn't just the intense, studious, college girl I'd seen her as.

"I told Shirley I'd get her a gin and tonic," I said, more to Sam so that I could try to read his face. I couldn't. His face was bent over a bowl of ice cream and chocolate syrup. He managed to look at his watch.

"It's a bit early for mother's milk," he said.

"What?" Grace and I asked at the same time.

"Gin was mother's milk to 'er," he answered in excellent Cockney, then added, "*Pygmalion.*"

"Well done." Grace laughed.

"It's a rainy Sunday," I said with a shrug. "Almost anything goes." Sam glanced up at me as I emptied an ice tray and poured the gin, but as I started to say something he shook his head and went back to his sundae.

"Gull Mai and I were talking about taking all the kids to *Chitty Chitty Bang Bang,*" Grace said, as I was about to leave the kitchen.

"Yes!" the children shouted.

"Again? How many times have you seen it?"

"Three," Emma said.

"Four," Jake corrected.

"Sure, thank you. I'll get some money."

"It's on me," Sam said, reaching in his pocket, and handing Grace some bills.

"Thanks, that's sweet of you."

"Don't mention it," Sam mumbled, and smiled briefly, his eyes still mournful.

On the porch Shirley and Mimi were leaning toward each other and talking softly. They stopped as I appeared, and handed Shirley her gin and tonic.

"You're a lifesaver," Shirley said, raising her glass.

"Grace is the lifesaver. She's taking all the kids to *Chitty Chitty Bang Bang.*"

"Again?" Shirley asked, and the three of us laughed.

After their ice cream Grace and I herded the children into Shirley's station wagon. They would go first to Ruthie's to pick up Adam and Gull Mai, and then to the movie theater in East Hampton. They looked adorable in yellow slickers, clutching dollars for candy, and I was glad to see them go. I wanted time to think, and I hoped for a moment alone with Sam. Something was obviously wrong, and I didn't think that it was just that the play was closing. But as I returned to the porch, Mimi yawned, said that it was naptime, and Sam and Shirley agreed. They retired to their rooms, closed the door, and I was left on the porch, watching the rain dripping from the eaves, beginning to shiver in the fog and not knowing what to do. I got a sweater and my yellow pad from the apartment and tried to work on the play for Sam, but I kept listening for sounds from the downstairs bedroom. Was Shirley trying to comfort Sam, help him with his problem? I didn't want to know.

After an hour or so, I left a note on the kitchen table, and drove the five-minute drive to Ruthie's glass house in the woods. It wasn't far, but it was a different environment. The house was glass and cedar, deep in the woods, and far from the water. Ruthie was alone when I arrived, and glad to see me. She didn't like rainy days with nothing to do; it wasn't her style. We sat in the glass-enclosed living room, aware of the rain and the clouds that surrounded us, and talked of everything except ourselves, until Ruthie rolled a joint and shared it with me. She showed me how to hold it in, and I had about three good hits before I found that it loosened my tongue even more than gin. I began to discuss "Sammy's problem."

"Do you believe it? She really thinks Sam is impotent, and she's trying everything she can think of to help the poor baby." Ruthie started to laugh, that wonderful, devilish laugh of hers, and I laughed with her.

"Sammy, sweetie, booby," Ruthie said. "Let me suck little Sammy and see if he won't get happy for little Shirley-poo."

"And Sammy, poor baby, you're just getting old, you poor, old thing—kiss, kiss, booby."

"Is poor little Sammy tired?"

By this time we were laughing with tears streaming. We kept it up until we could barely breathe.

"But it's sad, you know," I said, catching my breath.

"Aw, it's so sad," Ruthie said, with a drawn face, and then burst out laughing all over again.

"But it is," I said, higher than I'd ever been before. I liked this stuff. It didn't make me sick, and it made all of our problems seem absolutely ridiculous. "I can't tell you what it's like to sit there and listen to her go on about poor Sammy."

"Sammy sweetie-pie," Ruthie giggled, "mama's here," and we were off again, only to be interrupted by Adam and Gull Mai, as they returned from the movie. I realized that my children would be back by now, and still laughing every time I remembered something that Ruthie had said, I drove very carefully back to the Messengers'.

Chapter Fourteen

It was still raining, and the fog still shifting in waves as I parked and entered through the kitchen door. Grace was giving the children supper, bowls of reheated spaghetti, which they loved, and salad, which they barely touched. I was still high, and hungry, and started to dish out some spaghetti for myself.

"Don't you want to wait for the lobster rolls?" Grace asked.

"What lobster rolls?" Danny asked eagerly.

"They're for the grown-ups. Sam and Shirley—"

"Not fair!"

"Danny, don't interrupt. I'm sure there'll be a couple of extras." And to Grace, "They went all the way to Amagansett in this weather? You can barely see the road."

"I think they wanted to talk."

"What about?" Annie asked.

"Probably about something they didn't want ten little ears listening to," Grace said.

"Not fair," Danny said again.

"Danny, they can do whatever they want."

"Besides, Sam's going back tomorrow, and they probably wanted some time," Grace said.

"He is? He usually goes Tuesday."

"Something about a reading," Grace answered. "Come on, kids, let's finish up."

"Where's Mimi?"

"On the phone with Arthur."

"Oh, okay. Thanks," I said, putting my bowl in the sink. "My gang, come on over when you're done. Time for baths and pajamas."

I left the kitchen amidst groans from the children, and ran through the rain to the guest apartment. I turned on the tub, lit a cigarette, and stood by the window that overlooked the driveway. My drug-induced sense that all of this was absurd had left me, and I watched for Sam's car while I feared that Sam and Shirley had reunited, that behind their closed bedroom door little Sammy had performed perfectly, and they'd driven off for lobster rolls as if on a second honeymoon. The tub was close to running over by the time I remembered it. I turned it off and went back to the window, my stomach knotting as my anxiety increased. It was the not knowing, the inability to reach him that was so awful. I decided that staying here had been a really bad idea, and that we should pack up and go back to the city, heat, rats and all.

Then I saw, or thought I saw, my first Sag Harbor ghost. She was there in the fog—or part of the fog—in the driveway, waiting as I was, except that she'd been waiting a hundred years or more. Her skirt was long, a shawl covered her head and shoulders, and she seemed to have no feet. Sam had told me that he'd seen her once up on the widow's walk, that she was probably the captain's wife, still waiting for him to come home. That would be hell, I thought, to wait for years, not knowing. I didn't want to wait another day, another minute.

She vanished as the children pounded across the lawn and up the outside stairs. I shooed them, one at a time, into the tub, and once they were in pajamas, read a story from *The Happy Prince*, at the same time that I listened for the sound of Sam's car in the driveway. I only heard the rhythms of the rain, falling gently, then in streams, then in drips. Once the children were in bed I stretched out on the sofa and fell deeply asleep. I didn't hear the crunch of the gravel when the car returned. I didn't hear the silence after the rain. I didn't hear anything until our toilet flushed. I turned on a light; it was almost midnight. I walked cautiously to the children's bedrooms. They were sound asleep, arms spread, hair sweaty, sheets bunched. They could not have gone to the bathroom, flushed the toilet, and been back in bed and asleep that quickly. Besides, they didn't flush the toilet during the night.

Jesus, two ghosts in one night. I grabbed a sweater, cigarettes, and stepped outside, leaving the door open. The rain had stopped while we slept, the fog lessened, and the stars were becoming visible. I walked down the steps, lit a cigarette, and heard Sam's laughter coming from the porch. I smoothed my hair, crossed the lawn, and saw Grace perched on the porch railing.

"Hi," I said softly, before reaching the steps. "I just heard the toilet-flushing ghost."

"Join us," Sam said from the swing, patting the seat next to him. "You're pale as, you know—"

"I'm spooked," I said, sinking onto the swing beside him.

"Poor baby," Sam said, putting an arm around me. The contact felt incredible. Not being able to touch him was almost worse than not being able to reach him. I playfully put my head on his shoulder, then lifted it quickly.

"Sorry, am I interrupting?" I asked both of them.

"No, we were just gossiping," Grace said.

"Great, what about?"

"I'd much rather hear about the ghost," Grace answered. "I haven't seen or heard anything."

"They're drawn to Cal and me," Sam said. "We saw them—or thought we did anyway—in the garden too." I smiled at him. There was more intimacy in this moment than there'd been in weeks.

"I think I saw the widow earlier too," I said. "But it was so foggy, I don't know."

"Now I'm getting scared to go up to bed," Grace laughed, "and I'm really tired."

"I'll escort the lady," Sam said, rising, showing muscles. "Hell, I'll escort both the ladies."

"I'm fine, I was kidding," Grace said, jumping lightly from the railing. "Walk Callie over, and scare her ghosts off." She smiled, opened the screen door, and Sam and I walked down the porch steps, and across the lawn together.

"I've almost finished your play," I said as we reached the carriage house.

"*My* play?"

"The one I've been writing for you," I said.

"Oh, that play," Sam said with a grin. "I hope it'll be my play. I wanna give it to my agents."

"But it may not be any good."

"It'll be good."

"How d'you know?"

"Because," Sam said, and glanced back at the dark windows before whispering, "Like I told you, you're a great writer and a—"

"Yeah, yeah, I remember," I interrupted, laughing.

"Give it to me next week," Sam said, turning. "This week's jammed up already."

"Okay. 'Night." I blew a kiss, but Sam didn't see it. He waved over his shoulder without looking back.

I worked that week like one possessed, which of course I was. On a folding table in our small, hot living room I struggled with the typewriter and the carbon paper, typing with three fingers and blackening my hands. On sunny days I went to the beach with the children, but I didn't see that much of Shirley, Mimi or Grace. I surprised Shirley one morning by coming in their kitchen door, looking for more coffee, right at the moment she was pouring gin into her orange juice. I pretended that I hadn't seen anything, fumbled with the coffeepot, and left before she could see my smile. Maybe there hadn't been a second honeymoon after all.

Ruthie invited me over for a late dinner one night with Josh and Kevin, no kids, and after dinner introduced me to hashish. Josh passed a pipe around as we sat on the back terrace beneath the birches and maples, gazed at the sky beyond, and laughed a great deal. I have no idea about what. By midnight we were starving, and Josh decided to make pizza from scratch. I tried to last until the dough rose, or did whatever it was supposed to do, but by two in the morning I was exhausted, and took half an hour to manage the five-minute drive home. The next day was lost, but I did have the play finished by the following Sunday when Sam was supposed to arrive, but didn't.

If they knew, no one told me what was going on. Shirley was walking around all day with glasses of orange juice, closing the bedroom door at intervals, and having long phone conversations. I could hear her voice rising, falling, breaking, but couldn't make out a sentence, or even a phrase. I was dying to call Sam, but the show had closed on Saturday night. I couldn't call the dressing room anymore, and I wasn't about to call the house in town. About halfway through the week I asked Grace, as casually as possible, if she knew what the problem was. She shrugged, and hurried outside. I finally asked Mimi, who was understandably distracted.

"Whatever the problem is, nobody's in danger," Mimi answered, more harshly than I'd expected.

"What? Who's in danger?"

"I can't reach Arthur. He's on his way to Chicago with McCarthy, and everybody's saying there's gonna be protests and riots, and God knows what."

"I'm sorry, I hadn't heard. Who's saying?"

"The papers, the radio. All the student radicals are converging, and the Black Power people, and it could get really ugly."

"I'm sorry," I repeated. "I've been kind of out of it."

"Yeah, me too," Mimi muttered. "I want to try Arthur again if I can get the damn phone away from Shirley."

"Well, good luck," I said, as I retreated out the back door.

Thinking that that was an insensitive thing to say, I called back, "I hope he's okay."

The last week of August passed slowly. It rained again, and there were dreary afternoons on the porch, playing Clue and Go Fish, and trying to prevent the children from screaming through the attic after ghosts. Grace and I tried to keep them from disturbing Shirley, who continued to spend a good deal of time in her room, or Mimi, who still hadn't been able to reach Arthur. During times alone I fiddled with the one-act for Sam, and fantasized about working with him in the theater. The play would be a success off Broadway, and he and his agents would want a full-length play for the next season, and we'd both win Tony Awards, and he would thank me, and I would tearfully thank him, and later we'd fall into each other's arms.

"He's okay, I talked to him," Mimi screeched, interrupting a reverie. We ran into the living room—me, Grace, Shirley and the kids—and hugged Mimi as she babbled, "He's at the Hilton with the McCarthy boys, and he says they're fine, but the streets are full of crazies and the cops are everywhere. He says there's already a layer of tear gas over downtown. The hippies, Yippies, whoever, are nominating a pig for president, and the cops are ready to kill!" We laughed with her, relieved, and Shirley added that she'd just spoken to Sam, and that he was on his way, and bringing a small television set from town so that we could watch the convention.

Sam arrived in a rented car, hugged the children, set up the television in the living room, and glued himself to it. The shuttered doors between the living room and dining room were closed, and the kids were sent off with Grace and Gull

Mai to protect them from the violence on the screen. Sam, Shirley, Mimi and I watched until it became unbearable—the beatings, the tear gas, the blood.

"I have to get back to town!" Mimi said, jumping up, hands clenched. "Art's in the middle of that—I can't do anything from here!"

"He's probably safe in the hotel," I said.

"I'll take you," Sam said to Mimi as he rose, flicking off the television.

"But you just got here!" Shirley protested.

"I know, sorry," Sam said, kissing her forehead. "But if Art needs help, I've got connections. I can do more in town."

"What in the world can you do for Art from New York?"

"I don't know, but I'll bet more than I can do from Sag Harbor."

"Then I'm going too," Shirley said.

"No, hon, stay with the kids—they need you," Sam answered as he picked up the television set and his overnight bag and headed for the rental car.

"*I* need you," Shirley whined quietly. If Sam heard her, he paid no attention.

"Wait," Mimi said. "I've got to get my stuff."

"Say goodbye to the kids," Shirley called from the porch.

"'Bye, babies," Sam said from the car.

At that moment, I ran over to the carriage house, where I had the finished one-act ready for him in a manila envelope. I grabbed it and ran back. I handed it to him as Mimi stuck her bag in the back seat and opened the passenger door.

"I finished it," I said to Sam, with Shirley right beside me.

"Great," Sam said, and tossed it on top of Mimi's bag.

We watched the car back out the driveway, turn right to cross the bridge, and then Shirley and I headed back to the house.

"What did you give him?" Shirley asked.

"Just a story I told him about," I said.

"Can I read it?"

"Sorry, I don't have a copy," I lied.

"I can get it from him later," Shirley said, uninterested. "I'm getting a gin and tonic, want one?"

"Sure." I followed her across the porch, through the dining room, and into the kitchen. She didn't bother with the ice tray, just poured a lot of gin and a minimal amount of tonic into two glasses and carried them back to the porch. She handed me a glass and sank into the porch swing. I sat on the railing where Grace had been the midnight that I'd found her with Sam. I told myself to just sip the gin, and watch my words. It wasn't difficult because Shirley was clearly not in a talkative mood. She leaned her head against the back of the swing and closed her eyes. We listened to the drumming of the late-summer insects, and the children's voices beside the water.

"I wish I knew what was going on," Shirley said, after a long silence between us.

"About what?"

"I don't know—about anything."

"I know what you mean," I said, though I didn't. I was feeling real sympathy for her at that moment. She looked drawn and worn out, and there seemed to be tears beneath her blond lashes. I started to say something innocuous, like life being confusing, that we never really know what's going on, but she was asleep before I could form the words.

That brief interlude on the porch played over and over again in my mind after we returned to the city. I'd mocked Shirley's blindness during the summer, and sympathized with her confusion, but as it turned out, I was the one who was a complete fool. The children and I had left Sag Harbor at the end of August as Shirley and I had agreed. Our jammed station wagon might have passed Sam on the Long Island Expressway as he headed back to the beach. Arthur had arrived safely back in New York, Mimi had stayed in town, and Sam and Shirley planned to return after Labor Day.

I didn't hear from anyone during that first week in the nearly empty garden. I was relieved that there was no sign of the rats, and I cleaned with Maddy, and took the children shopping for school as I waited for Sam to get back. Diana was the first to return, and I tried to peek in Sam's living room after visiting with her, but the drapes were drawn and the upstairs windows dark.

It was Ruthie who arrived during the second week of September like the messenger bringing the news from off stage. She appeared at my garden door, bursting with it, and desperately trying not to laugh.

"Are the kids here?" she asked.

"No, they're outside. Come on in."

"You're not going to believe this," Ruthie said, as she closed the door and led me to the sofa.

"What?"

She lit two cigarettes, and handed me one before answering. "Sam's taken off."

"Really?" My eyes must have lit up because she shook her head as a warning.

"He's taken off with somebody we don't know about, and nobody knows where he is."

"What?" I repeated, my voice much quieter.

"It seems," Ruthie went on, "that he was spilling everything to that goody-goody Grace, and Grace had a moral crisis, and decided she had to tell Shirley."

"What everything?"

"About you, about Mimi—"

"Mimi?"

"Yeah, it seems he's been having a thing with Mimi ever since they moved here."

"Oh, my God," I said, barely getting the words out.

"*And* the one he ran off with. Things got hot and heavy during the summer—that's why he wasn't around much."

"With someone else," I whispered. Pain was beginning to go through my body, but my face must have been blank because Ruthie continued, still trying not to laugh.

"So Sam comes back after leaving Mimi in town with Arthur, and Shirley confronts him, says she knows everything—and throws him out."

"How do you know?"

"Grace told it all to Gull Mai, who, in broken Swedish, told it all to me. And Gull Mai thinks Sam was making a play for Grace, but she's nineteen and a virgin! It seems Sammy didn't have a problem after all." At this point she could no longer control her laughter, and I couldn't control the sob that erupted from my chest. "Oh, I'm sorry, Cal, I'm so sorry," Ruthie said, leaning toward me. "It's all so crazy I forgot you really love him." She stubbed out both our cigarettes, and put her arms around me. I sobbed like a child—choking, sputtering—making a mess of Ruthie's shirt. It was the kind of pain and loss I'd felt when my father died, but it was worse because my father had loved me, and Sam didn't even care.

"No one knows where he is?" I asked when I could put the words together.

"Somewhere in Canada they think."

"And he's not coming back?"

"Doesn't sound like it," Ruthie said gently. She led me upstairs, put me on the bed, propping a pillow, lifting my feet, and said she'd be right back. She returned in a couple of minutes with a handful of Valium and a joint. That was how I spent the next few days—calmed by Valium, and stoned on marijuana. Ruthie kept a close eye on me, and kept replenishing my supply. All I wanted was unconsciousness. In odd, wakeful moments, I became aware that that was what my mother had wanted when she'd overdosed on pills and alcohol. She'd just wanted to stop hurting. It was different in the eyes of the world, and the friends who'd gossiped. My mother had lost her husband to a younger woman, which gave her the right to grieve, while I had only lost a fantasy. But the hurt was similar, and I found that I was furious at turning out like my mother when turning out like my mother was the last thing I'd ever wanted.

Shirley wasn't in any better shape. She'd also taken to her bed. While my children and I were being looked after by Ruthie, Maddy and Diana, Shirley had Mimi, whom she had managed to forgive, and Arthur, who had forgiven Mimi, and her parents, who had flown in from Wisconsin. I heard this from Ruthie, and felt a kinship with Shirley that I couldn't have predicted. When I'd hear Sam's voice in my mind, or remember a loving look from his eyes, I'd be aware that Shirley was hearing the same voice, seeing the same look, and probably sobbing the same sobs.

It's all so stupid, I'd say to myself every once in a while, which I took as a sign that I was getting better. It's what Pricket would say, I'd think. No point in getting dressed and going uptown to see her. I could play her back like a tape recorder. Push play and she'd say, "Did you think that lying, seductive asshole was your daddy and he'd love you forever?" "Yes, goddamnit, that's what I hoped," I'd say. "What's wrong with loving somebody?" "Nothing, as long as they're not lying, seductive assholes," she'd answer. I didn't want to see the Hungarian pill doctor either; I was surviving on Ruthie's stash.

As I felt myself improving—crying less, sleeping less—I remembered that I still had to get a job. It was the only way that I could cover the monthly tuition payment. On a crisp, fall morning that only made me long for the summer that was gone, I called my stepmother, Helen, Ben Cramer in Palm Springs, and my brother, Ted, and asked them if they knew anyone, any old acquaintance, who might be willing to give me a job. I said that I could probably handle a receptionist's job, or do research or filing, or anything like that.

A few days later Ted called, and said that he had talked to Martin Fields, a friend of our father's, who was eighty-five at least, but still ran the remains of his music publishing company. He was looking for someone to run his office because, hard of hearing and in a wheelchair, he could only manage to get there one or two days a month. It sounded perfect. I pulled some fall clothes out of mothballs, got myself together, and went to see sweet, feeble Martin Fields. His office, in a building on 46th Street, consisted of a reception area that contained a desk, a phone and some musty furniture, and a back room that was stuffed with file cabinets.

He greeted me from his wheelchair—mottled, palsied hands reaching for mine—and told me loudly what a precious child I'd been, and how greatly he'd admired my father. His nurse, who had pushed him in, stood behind his chair, and nodded her gray bob in agreement. It was decided quickly that I would be paid a hundred and twenty-five dollars a week to sit in this dreary room for eight hours a day, answer his phone and sort his mail. An accountant would pick up the royalty checks on Fridays and distribute them. That was it; he hoped I'd be happy here.

Next to Mr. Meekel and the IRS nightmare, they were the worst few weeks of my life. It was one dead day after another. I'd get up early, dress, get the children off to school, take the subway to 46th and Broadway, get coffee and a donut at Chock full o' Nuts, open the office, sit at the desk, and go back to sleep. No one visited except the accountant, and no one called except Mr. Fields to see how I was doing. They both apologized for waking me. I'd arranged for Maddy to come five afternoons a week, to be there when the children got home and to give them supper. I'd take the subway home, eat leftovers, manage about an hour with the children, and go to bed.

The weekends weren't much better. Irwin was still taking the children about once a month because that was all that Kathleen could handle. So most weekends they played with friends in the garden, watched as usual by chatting mothers on the benches, but I was afraid to go out there. I might run into Shirley. Shirley was possibly afraid of the same thing because she didn't venture out either. Diana and Ruthie continued to check on me, stopping by and offering advice, but I was only interested in word of Sam. There was nothing else I wanted to hear, nothing else I wanted.

Diana thought that my job, from the sound of it, would be a perfect place to write—empty days in an empty office, but I told her that I had no desire to write. I didn't ever want to write anything again.

"What about your play? What're you going to do with it?"

"What play?"

"The play for Sam," Diana answered deliberately.

"He never read it," I said, tearing up. "He probably left it in the back seat of the rental car."

"Can I read it?" Diana asked. "Maybe Lorraine and I can do something with it."

"I don't have a copy," I lied again.

"Well, if you happen to find one," Diana said. "Because, as I remember, you borrowed carbon paper."

I shrugged, and Diana let it go for the time being.

Ruthie had a better idea. She'd found a new diet doctor on East 17th Street, who dispensed Dexedrine like jellybeans. I found that if I took half a tablet in the morning and half at lunchtime, I could stay awake for most of the day, and pay attention to the children in the evening. But they were suffering. It seemed that a miserable mother at home was better than no mother at home. Danny was running wild in the garden after school, shooting off caps, scaring the old ladies, and getting the younger boys to follow him over fences they weren't supposed to climb. Emma was whining, teasing her brothers, and she and Maryellen were caught dropping water balloons down on MacDougal Street pedestrians.

Then one afternoon Jake fell on a nail and got a gash on his leg that clearly needed stitches. He was outside Laurette Tompkins's house, and finding only Maddy at my house, she took Jake in a cab to St. Vincent's emergency room. They stitched him up, gave him a tetanus shot, and once they were home, Laurette and Jake called me at the office. Jake was quite proud of himself and his stitches and Laurette assured me that he was fine, but I closed the office early and rushed home.

"They gave me a shot, and they sewed me, and I didn't even cry much," Jake said as I held him, feeling grateful for his small body safe in my arms.

"He was very brave," Laurette said.

"I'm sure you were," I said, kissing Jake.

"Can I eat now?" he asked.

"Sure, but go slow, and after supper I want you to lie down." He nodded, and I watched as he took careful steps to the kitchen where Maddy was dishing out macaroni and cheese.

"Thank you so much," I said, turning to Laurette. "That really scared me. Thank God you were home."

"It wasn't that bad a cut," Laurette said.

"No, but it could have been. It could've been something worse, and I wasn't here. I can't thank you enough."

"Anyone would've done the same."

"I have to quit that job," I said, talking over her. "It's a total waste of time, and I don't make much more than I have to pay Maddy. I'd rather be home, and cut way back on Maddy."

"What about working part-time while they're in school?"

"I could do that, I guess. I still have to cover tuition."

"Because," Laurette continued, "we need someone to answer phones and stuff in the Scientology office. Business is booming."

"I can't type," I said quickly.

"No typing required," Laurette answered, smiling.

"I don't think it would work, but thank you," I said, as I ushered her out the garden door. Alone in the living room, half listening to the kids in the kitchen, I was assaulted by images of Sam and Scientology. I saw him at a meeting of the garden ghost-hunters at Hal and Laurette's, and on our bench afterward, looking for little Lucy on the swings. I remembered the night when Laurette told us that, through Scientology, we could learn to contact loved ones we had lost. I'd been intrigued. And I saw a snapshot in my mind of Sam and me looking up at the new Scientology in the Village on 11th Street above Blimpie's, the night that I'd told him that Irwin and I had separated.

The images were painful; I wanted nothing more to do with ghosts and Scientology. On the other hand, Laurette had been a lifesaver, and I'd really liked her for the first time. She'd been caring, and taken good care of my little boy. Maybe I could take the job she offered, and force myself to forget the associations with Sam, the joyous moments in the midnight garden. I thought and dreamt about it all that night, waking up every couple of hours with a different decision. No, I wouldn't be able to stand it because it would remind me too much of my dead hopes for Sam. Sure, I could do it; it sounded perfect, and after a while I'd forget all about Sam.

At the office the next morning I called Mr. Fields, told him that I greatly appreciated his help and his job, but I quit, as of that moment. I then called Laurette, and told her that I'd thought it over, and I'd be happy to try the job at Scientology in the Village. Later that day I met with both Hal and Laurette, and we agreed upon my hours and my salary, and they threw in a bonus of free Scientology courses. They said that I could even enroll my children in the Communication course, which was the first step on the road to becoming Clear.

"What's that?" I asked.

"That's being free of all past traumas," Hal said. "Not just in this life, but in your past lives."

"Really." There was a pause. "When do I start?"

"Tomorrow if you'd like, at nine, or when the kids are off to school, and you can leave around two."

It sounds great, I'd said, and that evening I told the children about my new job. They liked the idea; I'd be home after school, and if I were late they'd be able to walk the few blocks to 11th Street. It was harder telling Maddy; she'd been so loyal, and I kept increasing and decreasing her days. She said that she didn't mind. She liked coming, and she didn't need the extra hours; they just added to her widow's pension.

I started the next morning, dropping the kids off at school and ambling up Sixth Avenue. I avoided even glancing at Blimpie's, and climbed the steps on the side street to the second-floor office. Laurette greeted me warmly, and showed me around. There was the outer office/reception room that looked like an ordinary waiting room, except that there was a large table covered with Scientology pamphlets and books. There were chairs, sofas, end tables, and my desk and phone.

She then showed me the three auditing rooms, small, partitioned spaces, each containing a desk, two straight-backed chairs and an E-meter.

"What are the wires and cans for?" I asked.

"They're attached to the E-meter," Laurette said, holding the two cans and demonstrating. "See this machine here," and she pointed to a gauge with a floating needle. "When you hold the cans and talk to an auditor, the needle will swing when you hit a past trauma—they're called engrams—and then float free when you release it."

"Like a lie detector."

"Kind of. But L. Ron Hubbard invented it, and has written everything on Dianetics and Scientology." We passed into the larger conference room, and she pointed to a portrait that loomed over the long table. "That's L. Ron Hubbard," she said. "He's the founder of the Church of Scientology, and the head of it."

"It's a real church?" I asked, staring at the burly, wispy-haired man in the painting.

"Yes, absolutely."

"I'll be damned. Oh, sorry."

"It's not that kind of church," Laurette laughed. She led me back to the reception area, and suggested that I read up on the basics of Scientology, and above all read Hubbard's book, *Dianetics,* which explains the process of becoming Clear. We were interrupted by a bouncy young woman with a blond ponytail, whom Laurette introduced as Katie Baker. Katie was the only full-time auditor besides Hal and Laurette. They showed me an appointment book in which I was to schedule hourly appointments.

"Kind of like a therapist's office," I said. Laurette and Katie looked at each other and laughed.

"People spend the most absurd amount of money on therapy," Katie said. "This works so much faster."

"How?" I asked, thinking of Pricket.

"You'll see," Laurette said. "Now start reading," and she dropped the *Dianetics* book on my desk. I began to read—it was badly written, though interesting—but I became too curious about what was going on in the office. People arrived for sessions, called to make appointments or to sign up for courses. I chatted with all of them, and was struck by how nice they all were. They were mainly young, all races and nationalities represented, and they all greeted each other with hugs and open smiles. I'd hear crying, even screaming, behind the closed doors of the auditing rooms, but they'd come out wiping their eyes, and smiling with relief.

The children pushed to visit, and I let them come one afternoon after school. Danny immediately fell in love with blond, ponytailed Katie, who let him hold the tin cans, and demonstrated the E-meter. Hal and Laurette were patient with their questions, and told them that they could take the beginning course anytime they wanted. Danny was dying to, Jake wasn't sure, and Emma said she'd do it if I did it too. I said that we'd see, let them visit a couple more times, and then received a furious call from Irwin.

"How dare you expose my children to a sick cult?" he asked.

"What d'you mean?"

"It's a goddamned cult!" he shouted.

"They're great people," I said.

"So were the Fascists."

"Irwin, come on, it's nothing like that. It's a church."

"It's called a church because that makes it a tax write-off."

"So, you just converted to Catholicism. That's a write-off, and the Catholic Church has more money than God."

"The Church is God on earth," he said reverently.

"What has gotten into you?" I asked, but Irwin interrupted.

"Just keep them away from there," he said, and hung up. I was fuming, but decided to ignore him, for the time being at least.

Chapter Fifteen

Once I got past the bad writing, I found the *Dianetics* book fascinating. I read it in the office, and I read it at home long after the children were asleep. Since Sam's unimaginable departure nothing else had held my interest for more than five minutes. Not the paper, with news of the awful war and escalating protests against it, not an intriguing mystery or a novel by a favorite author. Sam's face would loom across the page, and I'd hear his voice instead of the words I was reading. But this was different; this was a whole new way of thinking, of possibly believing.

I'd never believed in anything. The idea of heaven with harp-strumming angels was as ludicrous to me as the idea of hell and eternal fire. I hadn't grown up in a religious family, and although I'd married into a Jewish family, Judaism hadn't resonated either. In school I'd read the Old Testament as "living literature," in other words as good stories, and later approached the New Testament in the same way. Jesus seemed to me to have been a beautiful human being, but aside from hearsay, I found no reason to believe that he was the son of

God. As a teenager I'd cried in bed at night thinking about Jesus. I'd found it so sad that as he suffered on the cross he'd really believed that he was going somewhere. The awful truth, I'd thought, was that he was just going to die, and become part of the soil like the rest of us.

I had no knowledge of Eastern religions so I wasn't aware, as I read *Dianetics,* that Hubbard was lifting most of his theories of karma and reincarnation from Buddhism and Hinduism. All I knew, as I read, was that the idea of past lives, and past-life traumas, seemed a lot more probable than the myths of angels and devils. After finishing the book, and reading the pamphlets, I told Laurette that I wanted to be audited. I wanted to erase the traumas of this life, and then go back to other lives. I wanted to know who I'd been, and where, and if I'd known my parents, Sam, Irwin and my children when we'd lived in other bodies. I was so eager that Laurette had to calm me down and explain that I first had to take the Communication course. Then I could move up the ladder.

"When can I take it?" I asked.

"There's a Wednesday night class, and one on Saturday afternoons."

"That's hard," I said. "I'd have to get a sitter."

"The kids could take it with you. We offered it free, remember?"

"They're pretty young."

"So are mine. They've taken it. It's fun, nothing deep, just teaches better communication."

"Okay, I'll ask them."

"And there's a garden ghosts meeting tonight," Laurette said, as I turned back to my desk.

"I can't make it tonight," I said quickly, as I tried to block out Sam beside me on Laurette's love seat, his thigh against mine, and Sam next to me on our bench, hoping for ghosts at midnight. I had to block him out on the way home every time I passed Blimpie's. I'd hear him let me down gently, saying that he'd never leave his children. Well, you left your children, you bastard, I'd think, and I don't even know who for. Bastard, bastard, I'd say to myself, hating how much love I still felt for him. Sam was the trauma, above all traumas, that I wanted auditing to erase.

The children and I took the Communication course together the following Saturday. It focused on being able to look someone in the eye no matter what they did or said. There were about ten of us, and Hal and Katie ran the class in the conference room with the huge likeness of Hubbard looking down on us. We were divided into pairs, who sat across from each other. One partner was told to make faces, and the other not to react. After a few minutes everyone cracked up. The next exercise was for one partner to verbally insult the other, and the one insulted to be fine about it. It seemed like basic stuff to me, no indoctrination of any kind, and the children had a good time. They kept it up at home, an ongoing game.

"You've got a big wart growing out of your nose," Danny would say to Jake.

"Thank you for telling me that," Jake would answer with a straight face as he'd been taught.

"You've got worms coming out your ears."

"Okay, thank you," Danny answered. They thought that this was hilarious.

"You've got ants in your tushie."

"I do not!" Emma would scream, and the exercise would quickly deteriorate.

We finished the course the next Saturday. As far as I could tell there were no noticeable signs of improved communication, but I was now able to be audited. Laurette was to be my auditor, and my first session was on a weekday morning. Katie took over my desk, and I entered one of the cubicles and picked up the tin cans, trembling with anticipation. We didn't get very far. Laurette asked what I realized were prescribed questions, and I went immediately to Sam's betrayal. I cried and raged, and felt the E-meter's needle float free as I sensed relief, but I couldn't go back any further than the loss of my father. I kept trying to come up with a past life, but nothing appeared.

Danny and Jake seemed to do much better. After the fun of the Communication course they both wanted auditing sessions. They skipped back to past lives as if there were no barriers between now and then. After Danny's first session with Katie he acted out at home his death as an Indian chief, a gentle warrior, who was shot in the heart, and fell off his horse as he rode into battle. Danny rode the back of the living room sofa, clutched his heart, and fell to the rug with appropriate groans.

"I was Buffalo Bill or somebody," he said, as he bounced up off the carpet.

"Buffalo Bill wasn't an Indian," I said. "Maybe Sitting Bull."

"Sitting Bull, that's who," Danny agreed. "And Jake got shot in a car, waving to lots of people like President Kennedy."

"You got shot in a car?" I asked Jake, who was sorting baseball cards.

"Like President Kennedy," Jake said, without looking up. "Bang, in the head, and I was dead."

"Couldn't have been President Kennedy," I said. "You were born already, you were three when he died."

"So?"

"It doesn't work that way. You can't be in two bodies at the same time."

"Maybe it was another president," Danny said. "Who else got shot?"

"Lincoln, but he was in a theater."

"I was in a car," Jake insisted.

"It doesn't matter," I said. "The point is not to feel it anymore, not to hurt anymore."

"I feel great," Danny said.

"Good, let's get ready for bed."

"I wanna turn," Emma announced as we started up the stairs. "I didn't died yet."

"No, and you're not going to," I said as I picked her up and kissed her until she was limp and giggly in my arms.

Emma's session the next week didn't go well. She began to cry soon after it began, and couldn't stop. I was in the reception area, trying hard not to bang on the auditing room door, when Katie stopped the session. Emma ran to my lap, and clung to me as her sobs decreased. We all agreed—Hal, Laurette, Katie and I—that she'd been too young, and I felt terrible; the last thing I wanted was to put her through an unnecessary hurt. The real hurts were hard enough, and I still questioned the reality of the past-life traumas. I'd come close, in an auditing session, to reliving an Elizabethan life, but at the same time I was quite sure that I was making it all up. I could close my eyes, and see a stream, a lawn and a castle, and feel myself there, but I'd always been able to do that, always been able to imagine myself anywhere.

Somehow Irwin found out about the children's auditing sessions, and in October I received a legal document that stated that if I continued to expose the children to Scientology practices our separation agreement would be null and void. In other words, no more so-called alimony. It was a simple choice— "Kids, you're too young for auditing. You can do it later if you still want to." They didn't mind too much. They could still visit Scientology in the Village, and hang around the reception area after school while I answered phones or continued my sessions.

Fall turned into late fall; the leaves blazed, then withered in the garden. The children jumped into piles of crisp leaves, and talked of nothing but Halloween. I couldn't sew, so we bought cheesy *Star Trek* costumes at Woolworth's, which they loved. Carving the pumpkin was another problem. I didn't trust myself to do it without losing a finger, and I didn't trust Danny with a knife either. We invited Irwin, and he came one afternoon after work, and he and the children had a carving party in the kitchen. After the snaggle-toothed pumpkin was lit and placed on the windowsill, the children went upstairs to get in their pajamas.

"I've been thinking about getting a Mexican divorce," Irwin said, as I scooped pumpkin innards into the garbage. "Would that be all right with you?"

"Sure. I guess," I answered, not taking my eyes off the garbage.

"It'd be quick, and I could go by myself."

"Fine. What happens to the separation agreement?" I asked, turning to him, leaning back against the sink.

"Nothing. It becomes a divorce agreement."

"Okay." I smiled at him, and he smiled back, warmth in his magnified eyes. For an instant I thought again of asking him to come back, but I knew that he had no desire to. He left the kitchen quickly, before I could think of anything else to say. I heard him saying good night to the children upstairs, tucking them in, as I finished in the kitchen and turned out the living room lights. I blew out the candle in the jack-o'-lantern with a pang of loneliness, but then remembered those last months of marriage. I'd much rather be free and lonely, I thought, than trapped and lonely.

Annie Messenger was having a Halloween party, Danny told me excitedly the next day. It would be after trick-or-treating, and all the kids and parents were invited. I still hadn't encountered Shirley, and didn't intend to, but I asked Diana to take Emma with Maryellen, and find out whatever she could. Ruthie, always curious, said that she would walk over for a few minutes and report back.

There was a flurry of getting ready on Halloween night, then the children were out the door with empty candy bags, and cans for UNICEF donations that they'd brought from school. I stood at our garden door, handed out treats, and then curled in a corner of the sofa to await news of Sam. Ruthie was the first to arrive.

"Shirley looks okay," Ruthie said, as she settled into the rocker and lit a cigarette. "A bit tipsy, and a bit heavier, but cheerful."

"Did she say anything about Sam?"

"Not a word."

"Shit."

"I tried. 'Have the kids heard from their daddy?' I asked, all innocence. She acted like she didn't hear me."

We both shrugged, smoked, had a glass of wine, and after a few minutes Diana brought Emma home. She handed me her UNICEF can, displayed her bag of candy, and ran upstairs with it.

"Just eat a couple pieces now," I called after her, and gave Diana a questioning look.

"I just found out one thing," Diana said from the doorway.

"What? Come on in."

"I have to get home, but I chatted with Mimi—"

"Mimi, oh, God."

"Mimi said the woman Sam's living with—out west somewhere now—worked in his agent's office. That's why he was spending so much time in town."

"While all the rest of us," I added, "were waiting for him at the beach. How stupid could we all be!"

"All's stupid in love and war," Ruthie muttered as she rose to leave. We were all laughing as I saw them out the door.

The boys came home a short time later, wired on chocolate and fun, and I put all three children in warm tubs to calm them down and to scrub off the remains of makeup. I was ashamed of myself for trying again, for pumping the children, but I did it anyway.

"Do you know if Annie's heard from her father?"

"She's gonna see him for Christmas," Danny said as he stepped out of the bath and took a towel from me.

"Here?"

"No, there—out west somewhere."

"Oregon," Jake interjected, from his end of the tub.

"Oregon? Who told you that?"

"Annie did. That's where she's going."

"Oregon, I'll be damned," I muttered. "Okay, guys, let's get pj's on—it's way past bedtime."

I tucked them in, whispered their secret words, turned out the lights, and stared out at the garden. It was Halloween night, with a moon that was almost full, and I thought of our garden ghosts, and wondered what they'd think of Sam three thousand miles away, with a woman they'd never seen. Or maybe they had seen her; maybe he'd brought her out to the garden when they were in the city together. That really hurt—the idea that he'd been unfaithful to our ghosts.

The days grew darker and shorter. All the dead leaves in the garden had been raked away, and by Thanksgiving I was divorced. Irwin and Kathleen had gone south of the border for a few days, and Irwin had returned with a Mexican divorce. It felt strange, but not that strange; there were no apparent changes. Irwin, in a spurt of goodwill, offered to take the children to Cape May for the holiday. I was delighted. Thanksgiving had never meant much to me; I'd never learned how to cook a turkey, and I wasn't crazy about eating one. I hated sweet potatoes, and didn't like pies, so the holiday had always been about sitting there and watching people eat. I was grateful to be out of it. I turned down invitations from my stepmother, my brother, Ruthie and my former mother-in-law, who probably wanted someone to commiserate with about her son's conversion. I spent Thanksgiving in my bathrobe, lounging and reading, and thankful for a whole day without children, and with nothing that I had to do.

The job continued, and I had a few more auditing sessions before Laurette got word from upstairs that they couldn't give any more free sessions. I was surprised; I knew that their office was just a part of the Church of Scientology, but I didn't know that directives came from above. Laurette explained that L. Ron Hubbard knew everything that was going on in all his churches, and dictated policy. That bothered me; this particular offshoot had seemed so independent, but they were subject to all the rules and regulations of the main church, of which Hubbard was the head.

I didn't miss the auditing sessions. I was still convinced that any past-life memories that came up were purely imaginary. I did feel better, but I attributed that to time and friendship, and the fact that I'd gotten off drugs of any kind. In order to be audited you had to be free of drugs and alcohol. I'd given up vodka, pot and Dexedrine, the latter being the hardest, but I'd found that I could get through the days without an artificial start or two. Because I felt better, and was mourning less, I found all the opposition to Scientology hard to understand. Irwin was convinced that I was part of an evil cult. My stepmother and my brother were terribly worried about me, and expressed their concerns with numerous phone calls. Even Ruthie and Diana, my best friends, were warning me about Scientology—don't get caught up in a cult of any kind, they're dangerous.

I kept brushing them off. We were fine, the kids and I, and then one day at the office I asked Laurette and Katie how I should handle all the warnings I was getting about Scientology. We were on a break, sitting around the coffee table in the reception area. Katie and Laurette looked at each other, and Laurette gave a slight nod before answering.

"Ron has laid down some guidelines— "

"Ron? I didn't know we were on a first-name basis?"

"We call him that between ourselves sometimes. People also call him Commodore. Anyway, Hubbard has written that people who are against Scientology, actively speaking out against it, are suppressives, and that we should disconnect from them."

"*What?*"

"Just not talk to them for a while so we're not influenced by their negative reactions."

"But I'm talking about my family, people I love," I said, clearly appalled.

"I don't speak to my parents anymore," Katie said quietly.

"You don't? What did they do?"

"They didn't do anything, except to say that I'd lost my mind, and I might as well believe in witchcraft."

"But that's just their opinion."

"Opinions can be harmful to us," Laurette said.

"Suppressive," Katie added. I looked from one to the other for a moment, trying to ingest this, trying to put it together with my beliefs in freedom of speech, and freedom of religion.

"I couldn't do that. I couldn't cut anybody off I cared about," I said, rising, returning to my desk.

"You're not Clear yet," Laurette said indulgently. "You'll be able to do it when you are." I simply shook my head, and picked up a book. I needed to think.

I wrestled with the questions of loyalty that had been stirred up until Christmas loomed, that merry deadline. Then I became too busy to wrestle with anything. I bought presents, wrapped them secretly, went with the children while they picked out presents for friends and family, especially their father, bought a tree, decorated it with the kids, hung stockings, filled them at midnight, rose at dawn, and still had to get the car and the pies, and drive to my brother's house for Christmas dinner. I couldn't even have a martini or two because I had to drive home. These were the times that I missed Irwin, and I chastised myself for missing his help. I didn't miss *him*—I missed a chauffeur to drive us, a handyman to get the tree straight and string the lights, a shopper, a wrapper and someone to let me sleep in the mornings.

The children were singing in the garden chorus on Christmas Eve. They'd practiced for a month, and there was no way I could avoid being out there. It was a cold, overcast evening, damp fog blurring the lights of the garden tree and the flames of the candles that the children were holding. They stood in rows at our end of the garden, and as they sang "God Rest Ye Merry Gentlemen" and "The Little Drummer Boy" in clear, sweet voices, I found a spot near the glowing tree where I was partially hidden. I was listening, watching my babies, and blinking back tears, when I became aware that Shirley was heading right for me. I stood there, unable to move, like a deer on a country road. No one was near us; they were all gathered in front of the children. Shirley stopped about a foot away from me, paused for a moment, and then hissed, "I hate you."

Of course you do, I thought, and felt so much love for her

that I wanted to reach out and hold her, smooth her blond curls as I would Emma's after a nightmare. I wanted to tell her how deeply I understood, that I'd loved Sam almost as much as she had, that I'd also been betrayed, but not nearly as betrayed as she had been. I wanted her to know that all that love and betrayal bound us together in a way that others wouldn't understand. But I didn't say any of this. She turned away before I had a chance to speak, or even hold out a hand.

Chapter Sixteen

My qualms about Scientology went out the window when I fell in love again—sort of. It was more of a crush than love. It didn't compare with the feelings that I'd had for Sam, but it allowed those feelings to become quieter. Sam's gaze and smile didn't appear as often, obscuring the realities around me. It began, my crush, in the aftermath of a January snowstorm. Schools were closed, traffic was nonexistent, and stalled cars were covered like white burial mounds. Sixth Avenue was dotted with kids, sleds and skiers. The only city noises were the sounds of snowplows as they created great drifts.

I had taken the children out with their sleds in the morning, then left them with Ruthie at lunchtime while I walked up to Scientology in the Village. I had spoken to Laurette, and we were quite sure that no one would make it in, but I'd decided to stop by anyway. As I turned the corner of 11th Street, tired from sidewalks of partially shoveled snow, I saw a man in uniform approaching from Fifth Avenue. I noticed gold braid on his cap and his navy jacket, but the uniform wasn't familiar. He waved and smiled as if he knew me, and I stopped at the downstairs entrance. He held out his hand as he reached me.

"Hi, I'm Dave Fanning, lieutenant in the Sea Org. You going up?"

"Yes, I work here, Callie Epstein," I said, as I shook his thin fingers. All of him was long and thin I noticed as I walked beside him up the steps. "So you're in Hubbard's navy?" I asked as we reached the top step.

"Yes, ma'am," he said with extravagant courtesy.

"I keep wondering—what does he need a navy for?"

His answer was an indulgent laugh, as if I'd understand one day, as he opened the outer door. Hal and Laurette were the only ones in the office, and they both greeted him with surprised smiles and hugs.

"Hey, man, what're you doing in our part of town? You fly your toboggan down here?"

"Nah, didn't want to scare anybody, thought it was a good day for a walk," Dave answered. He took off his cap, and reddish brown bangs flopped onto his forehead. He pushed them back with a freckled hand, and grinned. On first impression he was adorable, making me think of a thirty-year-old Huck Finn in a snazzy uniform. A closer look revealed that, while he was still adorable, the uniform's cuffs were frayed, and the gold braid unraveling. I wondered if Dave wasn't the type to notice such things, or if Hubbard couldn't manage to pay for decent uniforms for his navy.

"You didn't just feel like a walk," Laurette said. "I know you better than that, Fanning. What can we do for you?"

"As a matter of fact," Dave answered, with another grin,

"I'm giving a lecture at the old Adams Hotel—we rented the ballroom—and I've got here . . ." he said, pulling a flyer out of his worn pocket, ". . . a notice I thought you might be good enough to copy, and stick up all over the Village?"

"Now how did I know?" Laurette asked with a wry smile as she took the flyer. "Sure, we'll divide it up," she said, nodding toward Hal and me. "As soon as the streets are clear, you'll be up on every lamppost."

"You're a sweetheart."

"What's the lecture about?" Hal asked.

"Just the usual dissemination," Dave answered.

"The usual what?" I asked. Dave turned to me as if I didn't speak the language.

"Getting people into Scientology," Dave answered.

"Callie's pretty new here," Hal said at the same time.

"No kidding," Dave said, his endearing smile focused on me.

"But I'm interested," I said quickly.

The three exchanged a look that I couldn't read. After another minute of small talk, Dave suggested that we all go out for coffee. "Doesn't look like you're getting any business today," he added.

"No, we're closing up," Hal said. "But Laurette and I are heading home. Take Callie."

"Miss Callie, would you do me the honor?" Dave asked with a bow. It was a bad imitation of a Southern gentleman, but I became aware that I was blushing. I turned away, heading for the door.

"Glad to," I called back. "See you tomorrow, Laurette, Hal."

Dave followed me down the stairs, and out to the snow-packed sidewalk. "How about Blimpie's?" he asked, looking in their steamed window.

"I hate Blimpie's," I said, walking ahead of him. "There's a drugstore a couple blocks down—good coffee, great milk shakes."

"Love milk shakes," he said, catching up with me. We watched the skiers and the kids on sleds as we headed down Sixth Avenue. "I wish I had brought a toboggan," Dave said. "That looks like a lot of fun."

"I brought my kids out this morning. They loved it."

"You've got kids?" Dave asked, as if he couldn't believe it.

"Three. Two boys and a girl."

"Three? You look like a kid yourself. Who's the lucky husband?"

"I'm divorced," I answered.

"What a jerk of a husband."

"It was my idea," I said, aware of his flattery, and feeling self-conscious. "Here we are," and I pushed open the door of the old-style drugstore, and led the way to a booth. There was a lot of activity up front at the fountain, where children and parents were coming in for hot chocolate before returning to the snow, but the back was quiet. Dave put his cap on the seat beside him and clasped his thin fingers on the table between us.

"I'm still married," he said. "But we're separated."

"Oh, I'm sorry."

"No, it's a good thing. We were too young."

"We were too. Any kids?"

"No, thank the good Lord. I mean I like kids, but we were both Sea Org recruits, off on the ship—no time for kids."

"You were on Hubbard's yacht?" He nodded. "Tell me about it!"

"It's pretty much like any ship. You start out doing grunt work and studying, and work your way up. I got to be a lieutenant and OT."

"OT?"

"You *are* new to this. OT stands for Operating Thetan. It's the highest you can get, a few levels above Clear. It means that I've got powers most people don't have," he said, with a self-deprecating smile. "OTs can leave their bodies, and go most anywhere in the universe." I stared at him blankly. This was more than I was ready for.

"You mean their spirits can leave their bodies, like ghosts, except they're not dead?" He nodded, and I started to laugh. "I think I need a milk shake," I said.

We left the drugstore a half-hour later, full of chocolate malt, and lit cigarettes as we walked down Sixth Avenue. Dave was going to the subway station, and I wanted to stop at a market on the west side of the avenue. Snowplows had been through, and for the first time that day, there were a few cars and trucks moving gingerly on the streets. We were crossing the avenue when a delivery truck skidded and swerved out of control. It was coming right at us. I started to run, slipping in the rutted snow. Dave held out a hand, his palm facing the runaway truck, and it stopped abruptly three feet away from us. Dave waved to the driver, took my arm, and guided us to the other side of the street.

"That was close," I breathed with relief.

"I stopped it," Dave said.

"You stopped the truck?"

"Yeah. I created a force field with my hand. Otherwise, we'd be goners."

"That's something else Operating Thetans can do?" I asked, clearly doubting his sanity.

"Yup," he said, and gave me a semi-salute. We'd reached the subway, and Dave started down the steps. "Come to the lecture," he said over his shoulder. "I'll look for you."

During the next week Katie and I made copies of the flyer, and stuck them up wherever it was legal to do so. I hadn't decided whether or not to go to the lecture. At the office I read more Scientology literature—and I use the word loosely—as I tried to figure out if Dave Fanning's impossible claims were possible, if Scientology could teach its members to be super-human. It sounded like science fiction, and I remembered that Hubbard had started out as a science fiction writer. I read that OT was as high as you could get in Scientology, and that was achieved after many auditing sessions, and several expensive courses. You climbed a ladder up to Power, then Clear, then Operating Thetan. Yes, the books said, an OT could move objects at will, and travel anywhere without a body.

At home, when it was quiet, I'd stare out at the wintry garden and try to overcome my skepticism. Why couldn't I just believe it? Why did I have to make sense of everything? I'd almost believed in the garden ghosts, not completely, but enough to get caught up in the idea. So if spirits of the dead could leave their bodies and go anywhere, why couldn't spirits of the living? There was so much that I didn't understand, I told myself, why not just accept it? I didn't understand what made the lights go on, or sent rockets into space, or created rainbows, so why did I think I had to understand the concepts of Scientology.

I decided to go to the lecture. It was on a Sunday evening. I got a sitter, and walked east through Washington Square. The snow was gone, except for dirty patches, and the city sky was full of stars. I thought that I'd like to be an OT and go to one of them, and then laughed at myself. The Adams Hotel was past NYU and had seen better days. The wallpaper in the lobby looked ancient, as did the desk clerk, and the potted ferns were turning brown.

I followed a few latecomers into the ballroom, where the lecture had already begun. Rows of folding chairs had been set up, and the room was about half full. Dave was making them laugh. I hadn't heard the joke, but the audience was laughing and clapping as I found a seat in the back. He looked great up there in his uniform, in front of the lectern, as he told them what wonderful things Scientology could do for their lives. Things that had been hard would become effortless. They would thrive in business or the arts or whatever they chose. Whoever said artists needed to suffer? Anything that had blocked their progress in the past would disappear with auditing. They would sail through this life and on to the next, which would be even better.

Punch and cookies were served after the lecture, and Dave was surrounded by people asking questions and wanting to sign up for courses. He spotted me as he listened to an elderly woman, and held out a hand. I made my way through the circle around him, and he put an arm around me as I reached him. We stayed this way as he continued to answer questions, and be charming at the same time.

"Can you go for coffee?" he asked as the room emptied out.

"I'd like to."

"Sal, Betsy," he called to the young Sea Org members he'd brought with him. "Can you clear up here? I'm going for coffee with Miss Callie."

"Will you stop with the Miss Callie," I said, laughing, feeling flattered that he'd singled me out. We found a coffee shop near NYU, settled into a booth, and again ordered milk shakes.

"You were great up there," I said. "You kept them interested, and you made them laugh."

"I was a comedian in my past lives," Dave said.

"Don't tell me you were an actor?"

"What's wrong with actors?"

"I just got over one."

"Oh, sorry. But I'm not an actor in this life."

"Tell me about your past lives—how do you know? Because I can't get to any."

"You will. It takes time," he said. "Okay, I was in an Aristophanes comedy that got lost, the commedia dell 'arte, the fool in *Lear* at the Globe, Sir Toby Belch in *Twelfth Night.* I remember all the lines."

"That's amazing."

"Not really. It all comes back—you'll see. You want to come back uptown with me? I can show you our 48th Street digs. It's where I'm stationed while I'm here."

"I can't, I've got a sitter. Another time?"

"Another time. I'll walk you home."

He took my hand as we walked back across the Square, my

first romantic moment since Sam. At my door he kissed my cheek, and hurried down the block.

Dave called the next day, and our relationship turned into a lighthearted romance. I was dating for the first time since I was nineteen. They were cheap dates—the Thalia, the Eighth Street Bookshop—because Dave didn't have much money, and I didn't have any extra, but we had fun. The kids thought he was a bit weird, but they liked him all right. I took them to another lecture that Dave gave in the Village, but they were bored by it, so I went to his other lectures by myself. I enjoyed being the one he was with while I watched others fawn all over him.

He introduced me to everyone in the 48th Street office/church, where again he was the center of attention. About twenty people worked there, and the place was dark, gloomy and crowded with battered desks and file cabinets. Once again I wondered what Hubbard was doing with all the money that was pouring in tax-free. Laurette and Hal's office was much nicer, but then I remembered that Laurette was an heiress.

I was even more struck by Scientology's apparent stinginess when Dave took me to his place for the first time. It was a room, a kitchenette and a bath in a run-down residential hotel. Cockroaches didn't even bother to run when the lights went on, and the dirt in the walls and the carpet was so ingrained it would've taken a blowtorch to get it out. Dave was neat, at least, and the bed was clean when we got into it. This was our first time, about six weeks after we met, and it was a huge disappointment. I kept thinking of Sam, and there was no comparison. Dave didn't seem to like touching, and on top of that he was quite small. Since his body was long and rangy, his smallness surprised me. Ordinarily, it wouldn't matter, but combined with a lack of sensuality, the whole experience left me longing for Sam. I cried all the way home in the cab.

We did sleep together again, infrequently, but it wasn't the focus of our time. Mainly we walked and browsed, went to old movies—he loved westerns—talked about books, the stupidity of the war, and Scientology. Dave did most of the talking about Scientology. He was enamored with his powers. He would go on and on about his trips to other dimensions, and his ability to make things happen. He could have anything he wanted, he'd say, just by the power of his desire. I'd listen to him elaborate on his powers, and hear Pricket in my head, "He's got an iddy-biddy prick—of course, he needs power. It's the oldest motivation in the book." I'd laugh to myself. I loved hearing Pricket in my head; it was so much better than going to see her.

Spring came early, in mid-March, and by April bulbs were coming up in the garden, and the trees were again a pale green. The children and I tossed our parkas and boots in the back of the closet, and delighted in the cool air and the spring rain. The children seemed in pretty good shape—the usual fights, but nothing dramatic—and I was certainly better than I'd been the year before. Irwin and Kathleen got married in April, in a small Catholic ceremony, and that was fine with us. We'd expected it.

The big change came, the one that changed our lives forever—when Irwin dropped his bombshell—he'd quit his job, was moving into Kathleen's house in Cape May, and was cutting our support payments to a third of what they had been.

When I asked the lawyer if there was anything I could do—Did I have any recourse?—he assured me that I didn't. No court would order a man to get a job in order to pay alimony. Child support? Not that either.

I went home stunned and frightened. I knew that I wouldn't be able to get a job that could cover our expenses. My part-time job barely covered tuition. We could move to a cheap apartment, but that wouldn't solve it either. I couldn't talk to the children about it. Their school, their friends there, was the center of their lives. I'd have to take them out of Little Red and put them in an over-crowded public school. I decided to tell them when I had some idea of what I was going to do.

I agonized alone, and with friends and family. I realized as I talked to my brother, my stepmother, Ruthie and Diana, that my bonds with them had lessened since my involvement with Scientology. I still couldn't imagine cutting off anyone I loved, but I'd grown closer to Dave, to Laurette, and to the others I worked with. Ruthie was sympathetic. She understood how wrenching it would be for the kids to leave the garden and their school, but she didn't have any practical suggestions. Diana also empathized, but I could see in her eyes that she was thinking, "There but for the grace of God." She knew that she had made the right decision when she let her lover go and stayed with her husband.

My brother and my stepmother came up with the same idea. I visited them separately, laying out my dilemma, and they both suggested that I move to a suburb where the schools were good, get an inexpensive place and some sort of job in the town. I said that I'd think about it, that it probably was the best solution, but it presented a dreary picture in my mind. I saw myself as a suburban divorcee, getting older, working in a local supermarket or library, pinching pennies and becoming an alcoholic.

When I told Dave, Laurette and Hal what was going on they said immediately that Los Angeles was the answer. Scientology had recently built the Celebrity Center downtown. I could work as an auditor there as soon as I got the training, and the public schools were supposed to be good.

"To top it off," Dave said, "I'm going out there in June. I'm going to be stationed at the Celebrity Center for a while."

"You didn't tell me!"

"I was going to," Dave said quickly. "But this is perfect. I can introduce you to everybody there."

"They're great people," Laurette said. "Hal and I went to get Clear—a little nuts, some of them, but fun."

"A lot of actors, musicians, movie people," Hal added.

"It sounds good—possible," I said. "But I don't know."

I left them, saying again that I'd have to think about it, and walked home through the park, breathing in the spring smells, and feeling sick inside. Los Angeles seemed the best choice, but the thought of picking up and leaving everything that was familiar was frightening. I'd never been adventurous, and I'd be uprooting the children as well. On the other hand, that image of myself as an elderly, divorced, alcoholic checkout person kept popping into my head.

After a few more days of agonizing, I decided that we were going to California. I told the children that evening after supper, being as enthusiastic as I could manage to be. They didn't cry right away. They asked a hundred questions, most of which I couldn't answer. They didn't really understand why we had to go anywhere. They were sure that I could get a better job if I really wanted to. When would they see their dad? What could they take with them? When would they see their friends?

My heart hurt for them as I made arrangements to leave, but at the same time I was getting excited. I'd be in Los Angeles with Dave. I'd rent a little house with an orange tree. I'd work at the Center, and after a while the kids would be happy there. Danny surprised me by getting excited too. He wanted to see the Pacific, and live where there were palm trees. Jake had a harder time. I'd hear him crying in bed at night, and when I went to him, he'd say that he didn't want to go, that he didn't want to leave his friends. Emma didn't grasp the enormity of the change. She wanted to take her dolls, her pillow, and to be with me wherever I was.

I sold my mother's silver and the antiques that my parents had left me, and put our few treasures that were left in storage. I bought our tickets, and told the children that we could each take two suitcases to Los Angeles. We were to leave in June as soon as school was out. Irwin, naturally, was upset, but there wasn't much he could do about it. The children would be with him during vacations, and visit whenever possible. The goodbyes were tearful, except for the Scientologists, who would have flown us on their invisible wings to L.A. if they'd been able to.

During my last day of packing Diana came by, and reminded me that I hadn't yet given her the play I wrote for Sam. She said that she had my short stories, and if she had the play too, she might be able to get me an agent in California.

"I don't think I'm going to be writing," I said as I packed the contents of Emma's dollhouse for storage.

"How about—just in case?" Diana said.

"Oh, all right. I'm pretty sure it's in the desk upstairs." I found the play in a folder marked "Sam." It contained a *Guys and Dolls* program that he'd signed to me, matchbooks, photos of the Sag Harbor summer and the play. "It's a carbon. It's the only copy I have," I said as I handed it to Diana.

"I'll make copies, and send you one as soon as I know where you are."

"Thanks. I'll let you know as soon as we're settled." We hugged, said our fifth or sixth goodbye, and I went back to wrapping the miniature tea set that Irwin and I had given Emma for her last birthday.

We didn't arrive immediately at the ugly little house on Whitsett Avenue. When our plane landed in Los Angeles we took a cab to the Celebrity Center, with Danny exclaiming all the way about the number of palm trees. Dave met us in the doorway of the formidable building, stowed our bags, and introduced us to everyone who was working that day. As I shook hands with the staff, Sea Org members, auditors and artists, I kept thinking that Hubbard had spent a lot more on this place than any other "church" I'd seen. There was a vast room with a stage, several offices and auditing rooms, a Scientology bookstore and life-sized portraits of L. Ron Hubbard everywhere.

I couldn't say the same for the house on Crenshaw, where Dave had arranged for us to stay temporarily. He took us there when we left the Center. It was a dilapidated, three-story house for Sea Org members, and it was filled with the children of members who were off on the yacht or stationed elsewhere. There were a few caretakers, and dormitory rooms filled with cots. We were shown to a large room on the third floor, assigned four beds, told when meals would be served, and that was it. I knew that I'd have to find our little house with an orange tree very quickly.

I hunted for the next few days, leaving the children, bored and unhappy, in the Crenshaw house. Emma cried a lot, Danny told me, and Jake threw up after every meal. I sped up the hunt. I'd been told that the best public schools were in the San Fernando Valley, so I concentrated on that area. I bought a clunker of a car for three hundred dollars, got lost over and over again, got pulled over by a cop, who explained that you weren't supposed to stop, as we did in New York, when entering a freeway, and finally found the house on Whitsett. I had cash, but no credit, so I overwhelmed the landlord with charm and a three-month advance. I rented beds for the children, a sofa bed for me, we repacked our bags, moved in, and began the worst year and a half of our lives.

My involvement with Scientology didn't last much longer. We arrived in June, and by September I was utterly disillusioned. Working part-time at the Celebrity Center, I discovered more about Scientology than I'd wanted to believe. It was basically a dictatorship with edicts coming down from Hubbard. The Sea Org, at his beck and call, began to make me think of the Gestapo. Then I found out about "fair game." It was a Hubbard manifesto that said that anyone who was against Scientology was "fair game," and could be destroyed by any method available. That was frightening, much worse than being labeled "suppressive," and being cut off.

I might have stayed involved longer if Dave hadn't told me that he was going back to his wife. He'd come to dinner at the Whitsett house, and we'd eaten at the kitchen table, also rented, while the children watched television in the boys' room. We'd gone outside after dinner to escape the heat, and were lighting cigarettes on the front steps, when he told me that his wife was returning from the yacht, and that they'd decided to get back together.

"But you said you were separated," I said, sensing a familiar pain begin in my gut.

"We were, but—"

"Did you mean that you were separated by an ocean?" I practically spat at him. "She was on the yacht, and you were in New York? That kind of separation?"

"No. We were taking a break from each other."

"You were lying to me."

"No, we were separated, like I told you."

"And what were you doing with me?"

"I was recruiting," he answered.

"Jesus Christ," I said, my voice low and livid. "That's disgusting." I crushed my cigarette on the step, and in the same tone said, "Go! Get out!" I watched him rise, amble toward his car, and then I ran into the house. Furious, I called a captain in the Sea Org. She was a woman I'd met with Dave, and I'd liked her. I told her about our affair, and what I considered Dave's treachery.

I dropped out of Scientology, never went back to the Celebrity Center, but I heard from someone who dropped out later that I'd been labeled PTS, which means in Scientology lingo, "potential trouble source." You can say that again. And that Dave had been demoted and sent back to the yacht. I held a lovely picture in my mind of Dave swabbing decks beneath the blistering Mediterranean sun.

My writing, which I was convinced I'd given up, saved us twice. The first time was due to Diana. She'd sent my stories and the play to a lesser literary agent in Los Angeles, who had introduced me to the has-been producers, who had kept me going for nearly a year by paying me to learn how to write a screenplay. The second time came out of the blue, the summer after I'd paid the IRS, Irwin had stopped the child support, and I had no idea how I was going to support us. Maybe Emma's prayers were answered. Maybe my father's ghost, who had comforted me during the night by settling into the wicker chair, had whispered in people's ears. Maybe my mother's ghost, which had tried to reach me through the Ouija board, had visited executives in their sleep, and repeated my name like a mantra.

At the peak of hopelessness I got a call from CBS saying that they'd read my work, both the play and the screenplay for Quantis, and would I be interested in writing for daytime television? I allowed as how I would be. They asked me to watch one of their shows, and write a sample script. I'd loved soap operas as a child, so this was fun. They hired me to write two half-hour shows a week, for a salary that sounded like a fortune compared to zero income. I found the work time-consuming, but fairly easy. It was time-consuming because it took me longer to type up a scene than to write it longhand. It was easy because, in the early seventies, something happened on a soap about once a week, and the rest of the time everybody sat around and talked about what had happened. I didn't have to concern myself with the plot because the head writer sent a detailed outline. I just had to write what people said, sitting around their kitchen tables.

As soon as I had the job I went looking for a nicer place to live. It was still stifling in the Valley so my main requirement was air-conditioning. I found a duplex apartment in Studio City that I could afford that seemed luxurious after the Whitsett house. It had three bedrooms, an upstairs and downstairs, wall-to-wall carpeting, and central air-conditioning. After I'd paid the first and last months' rent, signed a lease, and pocketed a key, I took the children to our new home. It had been ninety-five degrees in the Whitsett house, and after looking over the apartment and claiming their rooms, the children stretched out happily on the gold carpet in the empty living room. I lay down beside them, next to a vent. We never wanted to leave. As we breathed in the coolness, and argued about what piece of furniture to buy first, I had no idea that this was just the beginning of a marathon.

I worked steadily as a writer, and occasionally a writer-producer, for the next twenty-three years, first in daytime television, then nighttime dramas and movies. It was a good living, not great, because I was never considered commercial, but I brought up the children without help, put all three through college, and contributed to a couple of graduate degrees. I never saw Irwin again, but the children made peace with him during their high school years. They visited him, and loved him, but learned never to expect too much.

There were intense love affairs along the way, but I never

married again. I hadn't been good at it, still wanted freedom more, and my independent streak only worsened. I gained in confidence, learned how to deal with the world—agents, meetings, deadlines, disappointments, even some successes. I still got lost easily, and I still cringed at any communication from the IRS. But, all in all, I'd say that the naive, scared, incapable young woman that I was back on MacDougal Street and Whitsett Avenue finally grew up.

The house on Alta Vista is just about packed up. Labeled boxes are stacked in every room, and Emma and I are left with paper plates, plastic cups, and the furniture that the movers will take in the morning. Emma had driven down and has helped all weekend. The boys couldn't make it from New York and Vancouver, but sent their love and good wishes. Emma and I laugh about that.

"It's like at the holidays," she says. "They really want to help—they just don't know what to do." We're walking across the lawn after saying goodbye to the plum tree. Sandy is at my heels; he knows we're going somewhere, and he has to make sure he's not forgotten. It's early evening, and the yard is again delicious, filled with the scents of jasmine and lemon blossoms. I'm having more qualms about leaving, but I know that it's too late. I reach for Emma's hand. She takes it and lifts it to her lips, kissing my fingers.

"It's going to be great," she says. "It's beautiful there, and you'll be just an hour from us."

"I know, you're right." We're quiet for a minute before I ask, "You getting excited about the wedding?"

"Kind of. But we've been together for five years, you know."

"A wedding's still exciting."

"Yeah, but it's not till December. I'll start getting excited sometime this summer." We enter the torn-up house, feed Sandy the last of the dog food, eat the takeout we'd ordered earlier, and go into the living room to watch the garden video that Emma has never seen. I've told her about it, and left the box of videos open so that she could see it when she arrived. She sits in the rocker, I push play, and there we are in the MacDougal Gardens at Christmas.

"Oh, my God, look at the boys—they're so cute," Emma exclaims. "And you're so young and, oh, my God, there's Dad and me. I kind of remember, but not really. God, Mom, look at Dad carrying me—I was so adorable!"

"You still are," I say, laughing.

We watch the video a few more times before Emma says, "Mom, I think I want Dad and Kathleen to be at my wedding."

"You do? Then I won't be there," I say, before I give a thought to what I'm saying.

"Don't be silly, Mom. You have to be there."

"Fine. Why should they be there?"

"We're fine with them now. Danny, Jake, me, we're all fine with Dad and Kathleen now. It was so long ago, Mom."

"It doesn't always seem like it."

"Well, it was."

"If they come," I say, my eyes on the silent video, "he's not giving you away."

"Of course he's not!" Emma says. "You're giving me away,

Mom. No one else could." She presses rewind, clicks off the television, and comes to sit beside me on the sofa. "You did it all, Mom. I'm so proud of you."

"You are?"

"You know I am. Not only for what you did for us. You were a pioneer." I laugh, but she ignores me and continues, "You *were*—in the seventies you broke into what was pretty much a man's world, and you made it. So, you were a pioneer." She's grinning at me, her dark eyes lit with love, and I take her into my arms.

"If I was," I say, "then it was unintentional, out of necessity."

"Okay, then you were an unintentional pioneer."

"I'll accept that. And have I told you lately how proud I am of you?" I ask.

"All the time," Emma says.

In the morning the movers put everything from the house into the van, and Emma and I start off in separate cars for Santa Rosa. Emma has tied a red bandanna onto her aerial so that I can follow her all the way, and Sandy sleeps with relief in the back seat—he's coming with us. I'm still thinking about Emma's wedding, and if I can handle Irwin and Kathleen being there. I haven't seen them in twenty-five years. I haven't heard Irwin's voice since he said, all that time ago, "I don't have to send you a penny."

I hear Emma's voice, "It was so long ago, Mom." It was, and I've thought that I'd forgiven them, but clearly I haven't, and it's time. I conjure up the Irwin I loved when the children were babies. Can I forgive him for what came later? I think I can; I want to. And Kathleen hasn't had an easy time. I want to forgive her too. The only person I really have trouble forgiving is me. I see Jake's sweet face when he cried into his pillow at the thought of leaving his friends behind, Danny's lonely face on Whitsett Avenue, the fear in Emma's eyes as she prayed for us on the front steps, and feel sick with remorse. I see Irwin when we were married, before the walk-in. I see his reflection in the bathroom mirror in the MacDougal Street house. He's shaving, and I come in, half asleep with morning hair that sticks straight up, and he looks at me and says, "Someday, someone will tell you how beautiful you are, and you'll believe him, and you'll leave me." "That's so crazy," I answer, laughing, but that's what happened, and that's what I did.

I don't know how I'll ever be able to forgive myself, but it's time to try, I think as I drive to another beginning. I hear Emma's voice again, "Oh, Mom, it was so long ago," and I know she's right, and I have to try. I never found the freedom that I longed for all that time ago, but with unexpected happiness, I realize that I'm heading for it now. I see Emma's red bandanna fluttering ahead of me, and best of all, I know that I don't ever have to be lost again.

Acknowledgments

I want to thank my agent, Barbara Hogenson, for her support and belief in me, my editor, Sydny Miner, for her excellent suggestions, and Gypsy da Silva, for being my favorite copy editor.

Above all, I want to thank my children, my family, and my dear friends for being with me all the way.

Hesper Anderson

9 781416 58633